Advance Prai:
Two Jews Can Still Be a

"An important, path-breaking book, fille
workable strategies that will help every
fought about their levels of Jewish commitment and involvement."

–Rabbi Joseph Telushkin,
author, *The Book of Jewish Values*

"By showing couples how to address with creativity and humor their
differences in ways of being Jewish, Jaffe also points the way toward a
grass-roots creative renewal of Judaism itself."

–Rabbi Arthur Waskow,
author, *Down-to-Earth Judaism* and *Godwrestling–Round 2.*

"Consulting the wisdom of rabbis and therapists, Jaffe anecdotally and
lovingly teaches us how to honor Judaism and each other...I welcome [this
book] for its clarity, ease of expression, and its sympathetic approach to
real-life issues of people of good will."

–Rabbi Leonard Gordon,
Rabbi of the Germantown Jewish Centre, Philadelphia

"Developing 'true peace in the home' is a lifelong goal, and Ms. Jaffe
offers helpful insights to help us both appreciate the separateness and
embrace the commonality in our relationships."

–Lorel Zar-Kessler,
Cantor, Congregation Beth El of the Sudbury River Valley

"Negotiating religious differences in a marriage can be a daunting task.
Azriela Jaffe has listened carefully to the stories of those who have managed to honestly and compassionately find a way to reconcile the often
emotionally laden, everyday decisions of Jewish living."

–Dr. Ron Wolfson,
Vice President, Director, Whizin Center for the Jewish Future,
U. of Judaism, Los Angeles

"Azriela Jaffe has written a user-friendly book for all those struggling to
establish religious harmony in their homes. It should serve as a source of
reassurance and insight to all those undertaking a spiritual journey or
dealing with a loved one who has made that choice."

–Lee M. Hendler,
author, *The Year Mom Got Religion*

"A 'must read' for anyone who has ended up in the throes of religious arguments, ritual clashes, and spiritual debates with their spouse, whether they are Orthodox, Conservative, Reform, or another Jewish orientation. Using self-awareness techniques, checklists, and discussion points, Ms. Jaffe has constructed ways to help couples rediscover Jewishness for themselves and their families, without compromising individual ideals and lifestyles. It is the perfect wedding present."

–Judith S. Lederman,
Orthodox Jew, author, marketing professional, and radio host

"…quietly teaches us about what it means to be Jewish while it is healing us at the same time. Bravo, Azriela, on a book that is a gift and a blessing!"

–Rabbi Alan Ullman,
Founder of the School for Jewish Studies, Newton, Massachusetts

"Drawing upon interviews, expert advice, and personal experience, Azriela has made me realize that it CAN work out and that we are not alone in our confusion and fear."

–Jack P. Paskoff,
Rabbi, Congregation Shaarai Shomayim, Lancaster, PA

"In this one-of-a-kind book, Jaffe synthesizes the experiences of Jewish couples with varying degrees of Jewish observance, sharing their conflicts and culling their wisdom. To that she adds the wisdom of rabbis and therapists, as well as the fruits of her own 'intermarried' experience. Intelligent, accessible, thought-provoking, and practical, this book guides couples through the often painful, often beautiful, process of learning how to respect each other and how to negotiate their Jewish differences."

–Jane Ackerman,
Psychologist, Jew by Choice, Pittsburgh, PA

"In addition to some very practical solutions to problems that may arise, author Azriela Jaffe presents factual background information upon which one can base an informed decision as well as a method of approach to situations that different outlooks and levels of observance will create."

–Shaya Sackett,
Orthodox Rabbi of Congregational Degel Israel

Two Jews
Can Still Be a
Mixed Marriage

AZRIELA JAFFE

WITH A FOREWORD BY
RABBI ALAN ULLMAN

CAREER PRESS
Franklin Lakes, N.J.

Two Jews Can Still Be A Mixed Marriage
Cover design by Cheryl Finbow
Printed in the U.S.A. by Book-mart Press

To order this title, please call toll-free 1-800-CAREER-1 (NJ and Canada: 201-848-0310) to order using VISA or MasterCard, or for further information on books from Career Press.

The Career Press, Inc., 3 Tice Road, PO Box 687, Franklin Lakes, NJ 07417
www.careerpress.com

Library of Congress Cataloging-in-Publication Data

Jaffe, Azriela.
    Two Jews can still be a mixed marriage : reconciling differences over Judaism in your marriage / by Azriela Jaffe.
        p. cm.
    Includes index and bibliographical references.
    ISBN 1-56414-473-9 (paper)
    1. Spouses—Religious life. 2. Marriage—Religious aspects—Judaism. I. Title.

BM725 .J34 2000
296.7'4—dc21   99-040519

This book is dedicated to Rabbi Alan Ullman.

You reopened my eyes, ears, and soul to Judaism and Torah. Without the gift of your teaching, I might never have sought or been open to marrying an observant Jewish man such as my husband, Stephen. And then this book would never have been written...by me, anyway.

You are also the rabbi who married us and witnessed the beginning of our journey.

Your teachings are imprinted on my soul, and my love for you will always be in my heart.

Thank you for being you, and listening to *Hashem* when he told you to become a full-time Torah teacher.

You are a blessing in my life and the lives of many others.

Acknowledgments

AS ALWAYS, my husband, Stephen, deserves special praise for not only accommodating the demands on my schedule to finish this book, but mostly for agreeing to go public with our once-private story. Not every man would be so gracious. I am always grateful to him for his ongoing love and support. It is not an understatement to say that without him, this book never would have been conceived or written!

Thanks to my agent, Sheree Bykofsky, and the staff at Career Press for responding so positively to this idea.

This book is dedicated to Rabbi Alan Ullman, who reopened the doors to Judaism for me an changed my life in unfathomable ways. Life is a mystery-who knows where I would have ended up if I had not landed in his School for Jewish Studies as a young adult looking for inspiration and answers. I doubt I would have married Stephen and gone on to bring three incredible children into the world. Stephen and I are indebted to Alan in no small way. Much appreciation also to his graciously agreeing to take time away from his packed schedule to write the Foreword for this book.

Much gratitude to the following people who read my manuscript in draft form and gave me valuable theological and personal perspective: Stephen Jaffe, Rabbi Alan Ullman, Rabbi Shaya Sackett, Buci Sackett, Rabbi Jack Paskoff, Lee M. Hendler, Judy Lederman, Jane Ackerman, Lindsay Stoms.

A gift from heaven was Lindsay Stoms, a co-op student from Millersville University who worked with me on this book from its inception until the final manuscript. She knows more about Judaism and Jewish marriage than she ever imagined she would. Someone will be very lucky to hire her coming out of college. I wish it could be me.

Many others gave me their valuable time as well in phone interviews that lasted an hour or more each. I searched for Jewish couples and experts all over this country who represented the full spectrum of Jewish religious life. Thank you for lending your perspective to this subject and in many cases, sharing with me your intimate struggles. I have noted each of you in the section "List of Interviewees."

Contents

Contents

Foreword

WE LIVE IN AN AGE of à la carte Judaism. Actually we live in an age of à la carte life in general, which has had an impact on American Jewish life. People do not buy whole packages anymore. Rather, they buy pieces and put them together in the way that makes sense to them. This has led to the "Starbuckization" of American life in general and American Jewish life in particular. By using the metaphor of Starbucks, what do I mean?

Many Americans, including American Jews, want a specific cup of coffee (that is, a specific item) of a particular quality, and they are willing to pay more to get exactly what they want, and precisely the way they want it. Gone are the days when you order just "a cup of coffee." Now, you have to decide if you want mocha cappuccino, Brazilian coffee, or any number of other possibilities. And customers are even choosy about the ambiance of the store that accompanies their cup of coffee! People want their children to get a certain quality of education. If the public schools are not providing it, they will send their children to a private school. Americans no longer expect to work at one job for the rest of their lives, nor do they expect one set of friendships to be their friendships for a lifetime. We are an increasingly mobile society, with more choices than our grandparents ever could have fathomed.

As a rabbi who teaches Torah throughout New England, and the founder of the School for Jewish Studies in Massachusetts, I have heard many Jewish professionals lament the state of our à la carte reality in American Jewish life. Yet these same professionals go to specific specialty shops to buy a particular type of exercise machine they are looking for or the latest computer that has just been released. This is the reality of our modern times. It serves us much better as Jews to address this reality and speak to the opportunities and challenges it is creating, rather than complain about it or wish for a different one.

Two Jews Can Still Be a Mixed Marriage doesn't shy away from this reality, apologize for it, or suggest that we, as Jews, should try to eliminate it. Rather, this is the first Jewish book of its kind that recognizes the plethora of "intermarriage" between two Jews who are each selecting the level of Jewish observance that works for them. No longer continuing the myth that two Jews marrying will want and need the same kind of Judaism in their life, this book offers practical solutions to the reality of modern Jewish marriages. When the husband wants a kosher home, and the wife does not, when she wants to go to the *mikvah* and he is dead set against the idea, when one spouse believes in Jewish day schools and the other wants to raise their children in a pluralistic setting, when one wants to join the Reform synagogue in town and the other wants to join the Conservative, how does a Jewish couple create an intimate, harmonious Jewish marriage that meets their most basic needs for spiritual growth, and at the same time supports their desire to pass along a Jewish heritage to their children?

Jews have been in a state of denial, believing that simply because two people are Jewish they have a world of things in common. But to be Jewish no longer means that we look at the world the same way or desire to continue the tradition as we were raised. We stereotype each other with our denominational labels, such as, "A Reform Jew does this," and "an Orthodox Jew believes that." There is no such person as a Jew who represents the perfect model of what it means to be a Reform, Conservative, Orthodox, Reconstructionist, Spiritual Renewal, and so on. Do we think that there is one kind of Christian in the world? Of course not. So why do we think that Judaism is also so easily labeled and compartmentalized?

As a rabbi running a Jewish school for adults, I see Jews of every denomination, including individuals who don't fit at all into any of our denominational models. I am asked frequently, "What kind of rabbi are you?" as if, by my saying that I was ordained Reform, Conservative, or Orthodox, they would then understand who I am as a rabbi and a Jew, what I believe, and how I practice. I, like most of the Jews who I teach and know, am no longer comfortable with a denominational label, and so I don't use one. I am a Jew.

Azriela Jaffe found herself in a challenging situation when she wrote *Two Jews Can Still Be a Mixed Marriage*. No matter what she said, someone would have a judgment about it. If she recommended a level of observance that went beyond just the minimum, she would be accused of being biased toward observance. If she recommended a practice that was not considered kosher by rabbinic or *halakhic* standards, but was practical for a family who is in a power struggle over a Jewish practice, she would be accused of recommending something not blessed by rabbinic tradition. It took courage for her to write this à la carte book. Parts of it will work for everyone, but no couple will find every solution for what they need or want. All readers must pick and choose what will work for them and their marriage.

Just as Azriela does not pass judgment on any couple's particular choices, I challenge you to not approach this book with a narrow point of view that any one way of dealing with these conflicts is "right" or "wrong." The beauty of this book is that it gives you choices and solutions. It doesn't tell you what to do, but rather shows how you and your spouse can make the decisions that will work for your marriage—choices that are rooted in Jewish text and law, yet creatively consider modern issues.

As Jews, we revere the state of *shalom bayit* (peace in our home) in marriage, but until now we haven't had much help in knowing how to get there. Shalom bayit is not something that happens to us in our marriage just because we married someone we love. We work to achieve shalom bayit, and sometimes that work isn't easy. In my classes, I encounter many students who awaken to a renewed interest in Jewish practice. Unfortunately, as they awaken, shalom bayit is threatened when perhaps a spouse is not entirely supportive or aligned with his or her new Jewish desires. Suddenly, that student's spouse and family are viewed as an obstacle to their spiritual growth rather than as a part of their spiritual growth. The Jewish teaching to create shalom bayit in the home does not excuse Jewish couples who have lots of Jewish issues to work out! Shalom bayit is available for all Jewish couples, regardless of the differences between them; some couples just have to work a little harder at it. The beauty is, sometimes the harder you have to work to overcome your conflicts, the more intimacy and joy there will be in your marriage.

We have a challenge and an opportunity before us—to begin to look at Jewish marriage as it really exists in America and as it will exist for more and more Jews all over the globe. We must find a way to create a holy marriage and a sacred life that can be meaningful as well as joyously shared with our family. We must bring Judaism to life for ourselves and for our children. In our far-too-busy lives, we need to find a way to stay rooted in what anchors our soul.

Two Jews Can Still Be a Mixed Marriage is a delightful and enlightening combination of insights and wisdom drawn from traditional and modern Jewish sources and teachings from other psychological and couples-oriented literature. Azriela has written a book that speaks to Jewish couples and educators with wisdom, warmth, and a sense of *menschlichkeit*. The book helps all who read it begin and continue a long and important conversation on how to create marriages, homes, and families that are rich and exciting in Jewish life; homes that are alive to our past, present, and future.

We are charged with the responsibility and the opportunity to spend every day striving to become better Jews, more loving husbands and wives, and more effective parents. We are also searching for a way to do the work on earth that God designed us to do. Sometimes it is very difficult to be involved in all of these pursuits at the same time because of conflicting needs and demands. Yet, please remember, with the greatest work also comes the greatest joy.

No one ever said that marriage or spiritual growth would be easy. Do you know anyone in the Torah who had it easy? It is in the work that we will find God, intimacy, and joy; so don't curse it, but bless it. Learn all you can from whatever circumstances your marriage currently provides. *Two Jews Can Still Be a Mixed Marriage* will help you navigate the sometimes treacherous, often adventurous, and frequently delightful experience of marriage in the pursuit of creating a Jewish life.

Rabbi Alan Ullman
Founder and director of The School for Jewish Studies, Newton, Massachusetts

Preface

If you are irritated by many things in a relationship, perhaps you are fundamentally self-centered and primarily looking out for your own interests. . . . .

—Scott Stanley, Ph.D, *The Heart of Commitment*

Teshuva

I WAS RAISED in a loving, High Holiday Reform Jewish family on Long Island. As a child, I did not celebrate a bat mitzvah, attend Hebrew school or Jewish summer camp, or develop much of a Jewish identity. I was Jewish because I wasn't Christian and my parents told me I was Jewish. I was Jewish because we celebrated a few Jewish holidays every year. I had no real idea what it meant to be Jewish. If I hadn't been born Jewish, I didn't have any compelling reason to be a Jew.

As a young adult, I traveled far from my Jewish roots. I didn't care much about being a Jew and I certainly didn't aspire to marry a Jew. For lack of a better term, I became "new age" and only culturally Jewish, celebrating Jewish holidays with my family, but not considering my spiritual path to be a Jewish one.

A series of events in my late twenties and early thirties brought me back to embrace being Jewish in a new and observant way. Attending a singles event in the Boston area, I heard a rabbi speak about Adam and Eve, introducing me to Torah for the first time in my life. I was enthralled. I went on to study intensely for several years with Rabbi Alan Ullman, a brilliant and inspired Torah teacher who brought Jewish texts to life for me. Alan lit my soul on fire and showed me that everything I was searching for outside of my faith was already present in Judaism. I had no idea.

I joined the unique and vibrant Reform synagogue Temple Beth El, in Sudbury, Massachusetts, where Rabbi Larry Kushner, Cantor Laurel Zar-Kessler, and an enthusiastic and learned congregation helped me discover that synagogue could be fun. To mark the significance of my return to Judaism (teshuva) on *Shabbot Teshuva*, I learned to read Hebrew and celebrated an adult bat mitzvah at the age of thirty-three. I also changed from my given name Linda, to the Hebrew name Azriela, a powerful way to identify myself as a newly observant and committed Jew.

During this time, to my parents' relief, I started searching for a Jewish husband with whom I could share my Jewish awakening.

Not Too Jewish, Please...

In 1992 I placed a personals ad in the Boston Jewish newspaper, *The Jewish Advocate*. I prayed to God when I placed the personals ad: "Please God, send me a nice Jewish man, someone who embraces his Jewish heritage and has a strong sense of spirituality, who will be a loyal husband and a fine father for our future Jewish children, but please . . . don't make him *too* Jewish." I was enthusiastic about my new commitments to a Jewish life, but I was still a Reform Jew and wary of joining with any Jewish man too rigid or observant for my taste.

God must have thought I needed a lesson in flexibility and compromise, because responding to my personals ad was Stephen. Kosher Stephen, Stephen who has six sets of dishes and cleans the entire house for Passover. Stephen who enjoys an Orthodox service of at least three hours in length. Stephen who takes time off from work to observe religious holidays I've never heard of— my adoring, lovable, very Jewish and very observant *beshert*, Stephen.

Under normal circumstances I might not have answered Stephen's letter, so God sent Stephen to me in the most unusual way. Three months after I had canceled my ad because I hadn't turned up the right prospect, Stephen saw my ad while visiting an aunt who was a subscriber to the newspaper. How did he see my ad when the ad had been canceled? Because the one and only time that Stephen looked at the personals in this paper, my ad had mysteriously reappeared—without my permission or awareness.

When I inquired of the paper how my ad had returned to the classifieds, the woman answered: "I remember you calling me and telling me specifically to rerun your ad on Labor Day weekend." I was stunned. I hadn't called her. Labor Day weekend was the weekend Stephen happened to be visiting his aunt. It was also the first weekend that he was "free" to go looking for a new partner, after the seperation from his former wife became official and he knew without question that his marriage was over.

I believed that this matchmaking was the work of *Hashem* (God), so I took Stephen very seriously, observant Jew or not.

Should I Order the Shrimp?

Our first date was at a Thai restaurant. In the brief getting-to-know-you conversation before selecting our meals for the evening, I learned that he kept kosher. (*Oy vey*, I remember thinking. One strike against him in the "future husband" tally.) I told Stephen that I didn't keep kosher, and immediately I was faced with my first Jewish dilemma in our relationship. Did I order what I really wanted, shrimp, or would that offend him? Did I start giving up who I was already, on our first date?

I explained to Stephen my version of bringing Judaism into my meals. I said the *ha-motzi*, the Jewish blessing, before every meal—even when eating pork chops, shrimp, and cheeseburgers. To me, saying the ha-motzi meant saying thank you to God for the food. Since I didn't keep kosher, and saw no reason to, I said the prayer over nonkosher food. I'm sure that Stephen had a hard time keeping a straight face as I explained my rationale.

I chose a vegetarian dish. Little did I know it would be the first of hundreds of compromises I would make in our life together.

Engaged!

When we announced our engagement to our families, everyone, including Stephen and me, felt tremendous relief that we had found a Jewish mate. It's hard enough these days to find a compatible life-partner. Two Jews marrying one another was an event to be much celebrated. From the beginning of our relationship I felt great joy . . . and angst.

If choosing a Jewish mate should make my life much simpler, why were we having difficulty choosing which rabbi would marry us, or agreeing on the synagogue we would use for the wedding ceremony? Why did the idea of keeping a kosher home feel like such a big deal to me? If I found Stephen's synagogue services to be dreadfully boring and long, and he found my synagogue enjoyable but not traditional or complete enough for his taste, how would we ever pray together? We knew that issues over Judaism would only come up more and more frequently and become more complex after we brought children into the world.

Committed to our union, we began negotiating and looking for ways to make it work instead of reasons why it wouldn't. It wasn't easy, and still isn't, but the belief we both carried in our hearts that we were beshert guided us through each new obstacle.

"You Want Me to Do What!"

During hundreds of negotiations in our life together, there have been many times when I have said . . . *"You want me to do what!"* You want me to keep a kosher home, go to the mikvah, and raise our children in the Orthodox way of life?

And my husband has also spoken: *"You want me to do what!"* Drive on the Sabbath before sundown, accept an abbreviated Passover seder, and allow my children to eat nonkosher food outside of the home?

As Stephen and I have engaged in many heated discussions about what is "right," I have defended my choice to *not* observe certain rituals and ardently argued against the perception that I was any less authentic a Jew for choosing so.

Initially in our marriage, I witnessed Stephen's disdain for nonobservance, a judgment that I experienced as a personal attack and one that hurt me deeply. We have come a long way on this issue, as we have come to understand and accept each other's position. We are now an observant family in many respects, as I have chosen to join Stephen in most of the Jewish practices important to him.

I am continuing to define who I am as a Jew, sorting out what I do simply out of love and respect for my husband, and what I practice or don't because of my own beliefs. No denominational label fits us anymore. We are a Jewish couple, figuring out our individual spiritual and religious paths in the world and how we wish to raise our children. We are perplexed at times about how to do it well and how to accommodate our marked differences in approach to Jewish observance. But we are never confused about one thing. We know that we belong together, for better or worse, and that we will either work out our differences or learn to live with them.

Whoever said that living life as a Jew would be easy? But it is a blessing, nonetheless. And so is our marriage—even on the hard days.

Author's Notes

Respecting Individual Preferences

SOME WOULD SUGGEST that I am crazy for stubbornly insisting on the relevance and suitability of this book for Jews of all denominations and spiritual paths. If not this book, which one? I fully expect that at some point I will offend just about everyone. Orthodox Jews might recoil at our discussion of trading sex for synagogue attendance or the attitude of some Jews that *mitzvot* should be chosen according to personal meaning rather than because they are commanded. Feminists might be unable to see the beauty in the mikvah ritual.

It is my intention to be respectful to all Jews. Nothing that I say should be misconstrued as suggesting that one Jewish path is more right than another. Please approach this book looking for what works for you and your marriage, and leave the rest. I do not expect, or intend, that every strategy offered will appeal to all equally. That would make no sense, since at the core of this book is a recognition of individual differences and couple preferences.

This book does not pretend to have the answer for any couple or individual. Its aim is to help you ask the right questions, to learn from other couples who have resolved similar problems, and to pass along what the teachers in our tradition convey about the subject. *You* are the expert on your marriage.

Beshert

According to the Jewish tradition, everyone has a predestined soul-mate—their beshert. Some rabbis believe that an angel, Achzariel, decides who will marry whom even before they are born, while others believe that souls are divided in two in heaven before birth and that the two halves are placed in a man and a woman.

It is my hope that you are currently in a union with your beshert, and it is also my belief that if you are, you must work out Jewish conflicts if they exist, no matter how painful at times. This book is targeted toward Jewish couples who intend to remain together in a committed relationship. Divorce is not a topic for discussion, even though divorce is an available Jewish option when conflict becomes irreconcilable. Some Jewish couples do divorce as the result of sensitive issues we'll discuss, or for other reasons entirely. For this book, we assume that you are fully committed to your present marriage or partnership.

Many readers may be Jews in a committed relationship who are considering marriage but are worried about the potential impact of Jewish differences. You can apply all of these strategies to your current relationship, substituting the word *spouse* for *fiancé, girlfriend,* or *boyfriend.* We do not, however, address the issue of helping a couple decide whether Jewish differences are too significant to keep from marrying. Married Jewish couples with significant differences can have a happy life together, and Jewish couples with minor differences can be on the verge of divorce. What matters is not the degree of your differences, but your ability to work them out, and your faith that the person you are marrying is the life-partner meant for you—that you are beshert.

Identities Disguised

More than 146 Jewish individuals, couples, experts, and rabbis gave their time and expertise to this book. In many cases, confidentiality was requested. Full names are the actual names and quotes of individuals I interviewed. All other names have been disguised.

Converts and Intermarriage

For this book, if one spouse has converted to Judaism or has committed to a Jewish home and raising Jewish children, the couple is considered a Jewish couple. We do not address conversion issues, such as whether to convert, how to convert, what to do if you don't want to convert, and so on. This book also does not discuss issues relevant to Christian-Jewish intermarriage. This book focuses exclusively on reconciling conflict in a Jewish marriage.

Israeli Jews and Rabbinic Marriages

Israeli-born Americans and Jews living in Israel must address Jewish issues particular to living in Israel. Rabbis and their spouses have complex issues to work out in their marriages, relative to being a rabbinical marriage in public life. (What do you do if you are an observant rabbi, leading an observant congregation, and your wife wants to shop on the Sabbath?) These particular issues are not addressed in this book due to space constraints.

Gay and Lesbian Couples

Although many Jews acknowledge gay and lesbian partnerships as intimate unions, and some synagogues even offer commitment ceremonies, as of now, these partnerships are not recognized in Jewish law as married couples. If you are a gay or lesbian couple, all of the guidance in this book applies to your committed partnership. Please forgive the omission of vignettes that illustrate a gay or lesbian partnership in particular.

The Talmudic sage Rabbi Jose, son of Rabbi Hanina, once told of two miracles. The first was the miracle of the manna. When God provided the Israelites with manna in the desert, said Rabbi Jose, the manna assumed whatever shape and taste they desired: to infants it seemed like mother's milk; to the young it was succulent; and to the old, reviving. On a grander scale, continued Rabbi Jose, was the miracle of God's word. When God revealed Himself to the children of Israel in the desert, each individual standing at the base of Mount Sinai heard God's words as a personal and unique address. A public message to a people was also a private message to each person. All who stood expectantly at the foot of that arid mountain understood the meaning of revelation in accordance with their own striving, their own capacities, their own heart.

—Rabbi David Wolpe, *The Healer of Shattered Hearts*

PART I

Understanding What Shapes Your Jewish Identities

1

Every Jewish Marriage Is an Intermarriage

What does "happily ever after" really mean? It means that you never step out of the relationship and look into the marriage at your wife or your husband like an outsider. You accept that this person is your purpose in life and that it's a sacred responsibility to make him or her happy. If your husband or wife happens to have a problem, and you have to take care of that problem, that's not an interference in your life. That is your life.

—Rabbi Mani Friedman, *Doesn't Anyone Blush Anymore?*

What Is a "Jewish Home"?

WHAT IMAGE does the term "Jewish community" bring to mind for you? Your neighborhood? Your synagogue? Hasidic Jews in Brooklyn? Israelis or Jews around the world? What about Jews not so easily identifiable, perhaps unaffiliated, intermarried, or High Holiday Jews who mask their Judaism most of the year? Would you include atheist Jews whom you'll never see in a synagogue but you might find doling out soup in a homeless shelter on Christmas day? The diversity of the Jewish community, only 13 million strong around the world, and 6 million in the United States, is almost unimaginable. Take a snapshot of any one town, one congregation, or even one Jewish family, and you will see enormous variance in Jewish practice.

When you and your spouse dream of creating a "Jewish home," based upon your upbringing, beliefs, and spiritual desires, you each have a different representation of what that will look like on a daily basis. Even if you and your spouse reach agreement, each of you will evolve and change that understanding over your lifetime. What does it mean in this modern age to "follow the *halakhah*," or "keep kosher," or "observe the Sabbath"? Ask any two rabbis for guidance, and you might get three opinions. Ask any husband and wife to address these questions, and the variety of answers you'll receive may astound you.

If you were to tell us that your new car is "blue," but it wasn't parked right in front of us, we would imagine what the color blue looked like. But blue isn't just blue. There are thousands of variations of the color and each of us would picture in our minds a different shade. Similarly, when someone uses the expression "I'm Jewish," or "I want to raise our children Jewish," we can closely approximate what that person might mean, but each of us will hold a different perception depending on our background and beliefs. Language has its limitations.

We Are All "Intermarried"

When a Jew marries a Christian, everyone expects numerous emotionally charged conflicts and negotiations related to religious observance. No one is surprised if the couple gets into heated debate about how to observe the holidays or if they have trouble creating a wedding ceremony that satisfies both sides of the family. I read in a book on intermarriage the following misleading statement about a Jew who married a Christian: "Had they fallen in love with another Jew they might never have had to reexamine their feelings about Judaism. Those emotions heat up in the crucible of an intermarriage, where they feel their identities are threatened." The author of that piece clearly hadn't spoken to enough Jewish couples or he would have realized that religious conflict is not a stranger to Jewish marriages.

Every marriage, even between two Jews, is an intermarriage between two individuals with different souls and backgrounds.

Whether you marry a Jew of the same denomination, a different denomination, a Jew by choice, or an entirely unaffiliated Jew, you *will* fight for your identity, and your emotions *will* heat up in the crucible of your marriage. Deciding how you will express your Jewish beliefs and practices in the world isn't the same as negotiating what kind of living room furniture to purchase.

For many couples, fights centering on Jewish issues come as a great shock, since the couple began their union with the naive notion that marrying another Jew would mean little religious conflict. Other Jewish couples start out life together knowing they have much to negotiate. They assume that since they share a 4,000-year history with a Jewish civilization, marrying a Jew couldn't be so difficult. It's not as challenging as being married to someone of another faith, right?

Wrong. Jewish conflict in marriage is more prevalent than ever before, and for many couples marrying another Jew is as complex as a Christian-Jewish intermarriage. Societal changes infiltrating the Jewish community have made religious conflict universal to every Jewish marriage. As modern women have shifted from submissive to equal relationships with their husbands, they no longer automatically adopt their husband's Jewish practices. Women are finding their voice and charting their own spiritual path.

When every Jew can choose to be anywhere from nonobservant to ultra-observant and can then choose to marry someone who has the same range of choices, the complexities of combining spiritual paths become apparent. Add to this the trend of marrying outside of one's family circle, as arranged marriages occur infrequently these days, and little in Jewish life is predetermined anymore.

Jewish Reawakening Stirs Up Many Marriages

Although one of the greatest sorrows in Jewish history is the vast number of Jews who are turning away from their heritage and intermarrying, the Jewish renewal movement and synagogues all over the world are also seeing record numbers of Jews hungry for a more spiritually meaningful Jewish life. Jewish adults like myself who ventured far away from Judaism are coming home. Jews who walked away in disgust or boredom are peeking in the windows again. Jews who thought their religious activity would always be limited to the obligatory High Holidays, Passover seder, and Hanukkah, are catapulted into a more active Jewish life when a child becomes a bar mitzvah, a loved one dies, or a midlife crisis triggers a search for deeper spiritual meaning. Agnostic and atheist Jews who take pride in their Jewish heritage but feel no need to be religiously dedicated to God or Torah are finding communities like Secular Humanism that provide the opportunity to celebrate Judaism outside of a synagogue environment.

This societal trend toward Jewish experimentation, learning, and searching is challenging thousands of Jewish marriages. A newly religious Jew is not necessarily married to someone who wishes to join him or her in new observances. A Jew who chooses to abandon observance isn't often married to someone who is ready to give up rituals he or she holds sacred. Creating a shared spiritual and Jewish path when the range of choices is so vast is one of the greatest challenges to Jewish couples today. Conflict in Jewish marriages is not antithetical to being Jewish, however. In fact, differing opinions is in character with being Jewish.

Disagreeing Is So . . . Jewish

The world is fashioned so that different paths serve different people, and each adds something unique to the world. That means that different people worship the same God, but they use a different religious language, just as we can speak the same messages to each other all over the world, but in different spoken languages.

—Rabbi David Wolpe, *The Healer of Shattered Hearts*

Having a different religious perspective from your Jewish spouse is not at all atypical. Our rabbis never suggest that shalom bayit—

the Jewish goal of peace in the home—is available only for a husband and wife who agree on all aspects of theology and practice.

If you were to eavesdrop on any yeshiva or academy of Jewish
learning, you would not find a silent room of students dutifully
accepting everything the rabbi teaches as the absolute truth. You
would hear boisterous questioning and arguing between peers, as
the students debate what the "truth" is. There have always been,
and will always be, multiple truths in Torah. The joy and struggle
of being Jewish is that there are few absolute truths, and the
process of pursuing and shaping truth is what enables us to grow.

Rabbi Arthur Waskow, who spearheaded the spiritual renewal
movement and author of *Godwrestling, Round 2*, says:

> The Amidah prayer begins with the words, "The God of
> Abraham, the God of Isaac, and the God of Jacob" instead
> of the more economical, "The God of Abraham, Isaac, and
> Jacob." The repetition indicates that God appeared differ-
> ently to each of the patriarchs. No single vision of God suf-
> fices for all.

Judaism not only tolerates questions and personal interpretations of Torah, it demands it. The joy of Torah study with a group
of peers lies in eliciting the lessons that can be drawn from an
ambiguous text, through the unique interpretations of each
reader's perspective. How boring Torah study would be if everyone around the table saw and heard the words the same way.
Torah is a living document. Our patriarchs struggled to understand God, and expressed anger, disappointment, doubt, and confusion at some of God's actions, or lack of actions. Our role
models are not men and women of perfect faith and obedience
but rather men and women who struggled to know God. Whereas
other fundamentalist religions may demand absolute faith, Jewish
tradition celebrates questioning and the evolution of faith.

To struggle as a couple with Jewish matters is something to be
celebrated, not something to be saddened by, apologized for, or
eradicated. It is in this struggle that you have the opportunity to
experience greater intimacy between yourselves, and with God.

It is the Jewish couple who is not grappling with these issues that I worry about.

Resolving Conflict in a Jewish Way

Because Jewish practice reflects the core of who you are and the life you wish to design, decisions about what you will and won't do regarding Jewish observance will require extraordinary patience, your best communication skills, and greater tolerance than you feel you can muster at times. It will challenge you to be a better Jew and a more loving spouse.

What does our Jewish tradition tell us we are supposed to do when we are angry with a spouse or when a loved one does not join us in a desire to observe halackah? How do we observe the commandment Jews call *ahavat Yisrael*, the love of one's fellow Jews? This commandment doesn't just refer to loving the Jewish drug addict on the street or rescuing the Ethiopian Jew in need. Perhaps such detached acts of kindness accomplished from afar are easier than loving one's spouse and others who are close.

Jews are taught to respect their intimate partners as unique beings made in the image of God, joining with them to do God's work. How do we become a "holy nation" if our marriages and families are not holy? If each of us is a divine spark of God, we cannot deny the individuality of our partners or expect them to submit to our will. This is the great challenge before us: to not only find a way to reconcile the Jewish differences in our marriages, but to do so in a way that is synchronous with Torah.

If you find yourself in confusing, circular, tense discussions with your mate—discussions that seem unresolvable—you aren't alone. You may wonder at times how you'll ever be able to merge your divergent spiritual paths and still create the intimate marriage you long for. Just as any spiritual journey is fraught with obstacles, detours, and moments of doubt, so is any marriage. When you combine the two, it can lead to periods of despair. Yet, when managed it can also bring you the greatest opportunity for spiritual growth you will ever encounter.

Rabbi Daniel Gordis, in *God Was Not in the Fire*, reminds us:

Judaism understands, deep in its soul, that the most profound of all relationships are relationships of struggle and growth. Our relationships with our parents, with our lovers, with our children, and with our closest friends are not always easy ones. But they are the most nurturing of relationships in our lives because they are the relationships through which we grow. They are the relationships in which we have the capacity to be the most honest, and as a result, they are the relationships that ultimately transform us.

Merging Two Spiritual Journeys

Do you think about yourself as an "I" in the world or as a "we"? Or perhaps both? A spiritual journey is a solitary one, but when you are married, you are traveling that solitary journey with, paradoxically, a companion. How can you be alone and together at the same time? This question is the primary quandary of all marriages. Sometimes what is best for your individual spiritual journey is not what will work in your marriage. Sometimes the challenges of married life are what shape your spiritual journey more than anything else. For example, how do you dance with each other without stepping on each other's toes? What music will appeal to each of you? How do you stay in love?

When I was in the midst of writing this book, my extended family arrived from all over the East Coast for our Thanksgiving celebration. We assembled around the table on Friday evening to light the Sabbath candles and sing the Sabbath eve *kiddush* over the wine. As my husband and I and our girls sang along with my parents and my brothers and their families, I noticed that we all used a slightly different melody for the Sabbath song. Each melody was beautiful in its own right, but our voices didn't harmonize well as we awkwardly tried to get in synch with each other. Still, a feeling of intimacy pervaded the room as we joined together to bring in the Sabbath.

We all have a Jewish song that our *neshama* (Jewish soul) expresses in the world. When you and your mate join together in marriage, you bring your unique melodies to the marriage. Sometimes one of you will defer to the other, giving up the song you were raised with and adapting the melody of your mate. You may harmonize your melodies or alternate tunes each week. You may create your own chant as a couple, different than what each of you brought into the marriage. Sadly, some couples give up singing together at all, believing that their neshamas are too different to reconcile into one shared poem.

Dealing With the Fear in Your Marriage

My fiancé and I relate on just about every level except the Jewish issues we've been avoiding.

—Alexander Kukurudz, Los Angeles, California

Jews were once united in fear against anti-Semitism. Now, although that threat still exists in many parts of the world, most American Jews don't worry about their life or livelihood being threatened because of their Jewish identity. Instead, many Jews are feeling a different kind of fear, one that is showing up in their marriages. This fear is summed up by one observant Orthodox Jew married to another observant Orthodox Jew and in a committed marriage. Lest you assume that such a couple would never have any significant differences, they do. This is what Dan Garfield of Leeds, Massachusetts, has to say about the rough times in their marriage:

I believe that Hashem's hand was present in us coming together. Our commitment to Hashem is such an essential bond in us being together. When we have Jewish differences, it really scares me. It feels like the basis of us coming together is being threatened.

Fear can show up for any number of reasons, but it usually comes down to one basic fear—the fear of abandonment and loss of the marriage. If one of you starts diverging too much from the other in your basic values, beliefs, and practices, the integrity of your marriage may be threatened. Fear of losing your marriage can make you think about these kinds of questions:

- How different can we each become and still sustain an intimate, committed marriage?
- If you get connected to a different group of people than me, will I lose you to an affair?
- If I don't share your interest in certain intellectual ideas and activities, will you find my companionship boring?
- Will you keep me from moving at the pace I need and desire on my spiritual path?
- Will I need to make a choice between seeking God or staying married to you?
- What if there is no way to make both of us happy? What will we do? Get divorced?
- If you become much more observant of Jewish rituals, will I still recognize you? Will I still love you? Will you still love me?

A second fear is that your spouse will demand or ask of you sacrifices and behaviors that you find deplorable, unacceptable, annoying, or at the very least, inconvenient ("You want me to do what!"). Will you have to make a choice between making a spouse happy and abiding by a deep principle that you hold? How can you keep peace with your spouse and still be true to yourself? What are you afraid *will* happen or *won't* happen because of the Jewish differences between you? Rabbi Dan Alexander of Charlottesville, Virginia, tells of a poignant moment he shared with his wife:

A year and a half after our marriage, a Hillel Rabbi asked me, "Have you ever thought of rabbinical school?" "As much as professional wrestling," I said. "Why don't you go talk to the dean of students at the rabbinical college?" he suggested. And, so I did, and I began rabbinical school.

In the beginning, my wife was frightened that I was going off the deep end. I remember one Shabbat we were spending in Jerusalem. I put my *tallit* over my shoulders and I was going to walk that way. She looked at me as if I was a *Hassid*. She was really scared that I was going to become an Orthodox Jew and that we would become incompatible. I wasn't sure what I was becoming.

Marriage is always about merging who you are becoming as individuals with who and what you wish to become as a couple. Perhaps you and your spouse are struggling to define how Judaism will be expressed in your household and are perplexed at how much compromise is required. You may be surprised that marrying another Jew didn't necessarily eradicate religious conflict in your lives together.

You may long for a deeper intimacy with your mate and for a deeper spiritual life. You want to understand what it means to you to be a Jew and to raise a Jewish family. You are striving to create the melody of your lives together, figuring out when and how to be in harmony, and learning to tolerate those moments when your separate voices create cacophony.

If you believe you and your spouse are beshert, and I hope that you do, you believe Hashem knew what He was doing by bringing the two of you together, even if, on some days, you aren't too sure. You each have particular lessons to learn in this lifetime, and your partner is the perfect teacher. If you are open, you will learn and you will grow. You will become a better Jew, and a better human being.

2

Who Are You as a Jew?

HAVE YOU AND YOUR SPOUSE ever taken the time to articulate your beliefs about God, the universe, and the purpose of life? Maybe you've spent more time discussing the wallpaper in the kitchen than the feelings you each have about a supreme being. Although these thoughts may be private and individual, they influence your preferences for Jewish practice and should be shared with your spouse. For example, if one spouse is an atheist or agnostic, and the other believes that God spoke to Klal Yisrael at Mt. Sinai, you will have a significant bridge to cross. However, if you both believe that Moshe received the Torah from God at Mt. Sinai, but you disagree about details of Jewish rituals, you have a different kind of conflict to resolve.

To help you and your spouse broach the subject, here are several questions for each of you to reflect upon and then share with one another.

You can discuss all of the questions at one time in a lengthy conversation, or agree to discuss a few questions at certain times each week. You may even want to discuss these issues over a nice dinner and some wine, or cuddle up in bed. The key is to make it feel intimate, special, and enjoyable, not just more work. Allow your partner to share his or her beliefs and feelings without being judged. If you neglect to follow this rule, the discussion will end quickly and painfully, and you will discourage your spouse from wanting to discuss personal religious feelings again. Remember that these are sensitive topics for discussion.

You can also turn these questions into stimulating family discussions at the Sabbath table or another time that is good for your kids as well. If you haven't ever asked your children to share their thoughts about spirituality, here's an opportunity.

Questions for Discussion

THEOLOGICAL BELIEFS

- Do you believe in any kind of supreme being or entity responsible for creating and influencing the universe? If not, who or what do you believe is responsible for creation?

- Do you believe in a personal God who watches over you and cares about your daily behavior and experiences? If not, what do you believe God cares about and gets involved in?

- What is your perception of God's qualities and characteristics? For example, compassionate, judgmental, forgiving, righteous, and so on. What qualities do not describe God?

- What commitments do you believe God has made toward you?

- What commitments do you believe you must make to God?

- Have you ever doubted the existence or compassion of God?

- What do you believe about fate and free will?

- How central is God and spirituality to your daily life?

- What are your beliefs about heaven and hell and the afterlife?

- How do you define a sin?

- Do you believe that God forgives you for your sins? What do you have to do to earn God's forgiveness?

- Do you ever talk to God? What does prayer mean for you? Why do you pray? Do you think God hears your prayers?

- Do you believe that God had a hand in you meeting and marrying your spouse? Do you believe that he or she is your beshert?

- How has your conception of God changed since young adulthood? Since your marriage? Since having children? Is there any significant life event that changed your beliefs about God?

- How does the Holocaust influence your conception of God?

JEWISH RITUAL, IDENTITY, AND COMMUNITY

- Do you think it matters to God if you observe certain Jewish practices or not?

- Do you believe there is such a thing as a neshama?

- What does it mean to you that the Jews are "the chosen people"?

- Do you believe it's important for Jews to continue as a distinct ethnic and religious group? What obligation, if any, do you feel toward raising Jewish children? How important is it to you that your children identify as Jews and marry Jews?

- How often do you feel a desire to be around other Jews?

- What kind of meaning do Jewish rituals and holiday celebrations have for you? Does a ritual provide you a spiritual experience and a deeper connection to your family or does it tend to be an empty, meaningless experience for you? Do you have a strong need or desire to congregate with other Jews and family on the holidays?

The Limitations of Denominational Labels

If you don't have the conceptual framework or language to communicate how you define yourself and what you want as a Jew, you will have trouble deciding how you wish to be Jewish as a couple. There have always been many different branches of Judaism throughout history. And diversity is only increasing in the Jewish community today. Some of us identify ourselves as Orthodox, Reform, Conservative, Reconstructionist, New Age, Spiritual Renewal, Secular Humanist, "Jewbu," and any number of other labels. Some Jews, including some rabbis I interviewed, refuse to disclose a denomination or put themselves in these perceived boxes.

The denomination box does have its purpose. The categories give us a sense of comfort and a feeling of belonging to a larger community. Knowing what denomination we belong to helps us have dialogues with other Jews about our beliefs and practices.

We like to be in the company of like-minded Jews. We think we know someone better by knowing their denomination.

As a mixed Jewish couple you may also feel frustrated at times that you don't fit into any one denominational box. However, here's the problem, summarized succinctly by Rabbi Shaya Sackett of the Orthodox synagogue, Degel Israel, in Lancaster, Pennsylvania: "Labels do more injustice than justice. It disturbs me when you bring up a Jewish custom or tradition, and someone says— 'I don't have to do that because I'm Reform,' or 'I do that because I'm Orthodox.' Few people are legitimately Orthodox, Conservative, or Reform. Ninety percent of people who consider themselves that denomination have never investigated what that label means."

All of my adult Jewish life, and especially since marrying Stephen, I have wanted an easy way to describe who I am as a Jew. I had hoped that researching this book would help me identify to which group I belong. One evening I came down the stairs of our home, beaming, and gave my husband a big hug. "I just had a life-changing conversation with a rabbi, dear!" He looked up with an expression that seemed to say both, "Cool, tell me what you discovered," and "Oh no, what do you want me to do now?"

In the course of interviewing a Reconstructionist rabbi for this book I learned for the first time about the Reconstructionist Jewish perspective. Until that moment, I had always defined myself as a Reform Jew, because that was how I was raised, and when I lived in Boston, I affiliated with a Reform synagogue. Also, I had always related to the freedom of choice I associated with Reform Judaism. I had labeled my husband a Modern Orthodox or Observant Conservative Jew because of the synagogues he chose to affiliate with and his desire for as much traditional observance as possible.

As I listened to the rabbi describe the basis of Reconstructionism, I heard a description of both Stephen and myself. I got excited as I contemplated a Jewish denomination that could honor both of our needs—my desire for choice and the importance to me of finding personal meaning in Jewish rituals, and my husband's need to be a part of a community that protects and regards tradition. I thought Reconstructionism was our solution.

So, on this day I proclaimed to Stephen: "I think we are Reconstructionist Jews!" He responded, "Really, what's that?" I pulled out my new Reconstructionist brochure and showed him all the descriptions that rang true for both of us. I wanted to believe that the answer for our challenges lay simply in finding a Reconstructionist community we could join.

It wasn't that simple. I continue to hold respect for Reconstructionist Judaism, but after a little further study, I quickly learned that the Reconstructionist label didn't fit us any better than did the others. Some aspects worked, some didn't. After all the research and hundreds of conversations for this book, I still don't know what denomination I am. I am a Jew. My husband is a Jew. That's the only absolute conclusion I have reached.

As limiting as denominational labels are, you will find it helpful to have the language to communicate why you choose to affiliate yourself with a particular denomination. To divert you and your spouse from debating about erroneous stereotypes and misconceptions (Reform Jews don't keep kosher, Reconstructionists don't believe in God), here is a brief synopsis of the theology and common practices of the major Jewish denominations in the United States. You may read one of these descriptions and find it fits like a glove, or you might, like me, find yourself reflected in some ways in each one. Either way, it will help you get a better sense of where you and your spouse belong, according to your beliefs and practices. Even though, as we will discuss later, you don't want to use a denominational affiliation as an excuse or a weapon, it is important to understand the basics that shape your Jewish orientation and that of your spouse.

ORTHODOX JUDAISM

The Misconceptions

The Orthodox consider themselves to be the only true Jews. They feel that the other movements are betrayals of God's laws and violations of the Torah and are, therefore, mistaken and sinful.

Orthodox Jews are bigoted and intolerant of other Jews.

Orthodox Jewry has not adjusted itself to modern times.

Women are second-class citizens in Orthodox Judaism. They are not fully involved in religious life.

More Accurately . . .

The majority of present-day Orthodox Jews are more tolerant and accepting of other Jews than the stereotype, although most Orthodox Jews do worry about intermarriage and the loss of traditional observance and are unhappy with other denominations' permission to disregard traditional obligations.

Orthodox synagogues all over the United States have, while defining synagogue practices and traditions as Orthodox, opened their doors to all Jews regardless of personal observance. For example, although you can't park in the parking lot of our Orthodox synagogue on the Sabbath, a parking lot adjacent to the building is available for congregants who drive to *shul*, recognizing that congregants don't always live within walking distance. Many Orthodox rabbis encourage as much observance as possible in the community at large but accept variations in individual practice, as long as it doesn't desecrate the synagogue.

Although individual lack of observance may be forgiven, Orthodox Jewry as a whole will not let go of some commandments, like keeping kosher, just because it is inconvenient. That would be the antithesis of what it means to be Orthodox.

Contrary to the myth of homogeneity, the Orthodox community is the least united of all the religious groups in American Jewry. There is no central seminary, no single rabbinical association, and no unified platform or creed. Orthodoxy has as many divided opinions and widely diverse customs as any other denomination.

What Distinguishes Orthodoxy?

The basis of Orthodox Judaism is the assumption that Jewish law was given by God to Moses on Mt. Sinai. Its view of Judaism flows from that.

Orthodox Jews submit to the commandments of the mitzvot, the system of Jewish commandments and obligations. They abhor the concept of personal choice as a means for selecting which mitzvot to observe or not observe. From the time an Orthodox Jew awakens, Jewish law (halakhah) governs his or her behavior.

The three cornerstones of Orthodox practice include observance of the complete Sabbath, keeping a kosher home, and observing laws of family purity (mikvah). A Jew not performing all three of these would be considered by many to be not truly Orthodox.

Affixed to the doorposts of every Orthodox Jewish home is a mezuzah. You'll find mezuzahs on the homes of Jews who are not Orthodox, but you'll never find an Orthodox home without one. Most Orthodox males usually cover their heads at all times with a yarmulke and married women cover their hair with a kerchief, hat, or wig as a sign of modesty.

Orthodox men are required to pray three times daily and wear a prayer shawl (tallit) and phylacteries (*tefillin*) each morning. Orthodox Jews are encouraged to study Torah daily. In modern times, many Orthodox men do not meet these obligations because of work or the lack of an available daily *minyan.*

Many Orthodox Jews will pray only in an Orthodox shul, where the men and women are seated separately. Orthodox services are almost entirely in Hebrew, although the more modern synagogues have added some English prayers and an English sermon by the rabbi.

Musical instruments and choirs with female singers are never allowed at Sabbath or holy day services. Women are not ordained as Orthodox rabbis nor are they allowed to read the Torah or lead services in front of male shul members.

CONSERVATIVE JUDAISM

The Misconceptions

Conservative Judaism is simply a compromise between Orthodox and Reform. It's more than Reform, less than Orthodox, but no one is really sure what it is.

More Accurately . . .

Many Jews do compromise on Conservative Judaism as a middle ground, but thousands of Jews are raised in and choose Conservative Judaism precisely because of what it stands for and the characteristics of the synagogue services that appeal to them. Several approaches to Jewish law and observance are distinctly Conservative.

What Distinguishes Conservative Judaism?

Conservatives believe that the ongoing process of change in Judaism should be brought about by evolutionary rather than revolutionary means, so they prefer a slow and gradual rather than sudden approach to change. Changes in halakhah may occur, but only as the result of careful study.

Conservatives accept the concept that God revealed the Torah but don't support the Orthodox position that the Torah is the complete and final word of God. Revelation is an ongoing process by which each generation of Jews discovers more and more of God's word. Teachings are rooted in tradition, but interpretation employs all of the modern disciplines at our disposal.

Conservatives believe that God is concerned with the observance of both ritual and ethical laws, in contrast to Reform Jews who believe that God is most concerned with ethical laws.

Conservative Judaism does respond to the demands of living in the modern world and makes adjustments to halakhah to enable rather than circumscribe observance. For example, it is so important for a Jew to attend synagogue that driving to synagogue is permitted if a Jew lives too far away to walk. The Conservative movement keeps the kosher laws but allows a person to eat dairy meals in a nonkosher restaurant.

Men and women have equal roles in religious life. Women are ordained as rabbis and are not prohibited from practicing any rituals.

REFORM JUDAISM

> An entire generation saw Reform Judaism as an escape from Orthodoxy. They wanted something less. They didn't recognize that Reform is an ideology unto itself, not the absence of an ideology.
>
> —Rabbi Jack Paskoff, Reform Rabbi, Temple Shaarai Shomayim, Lancaster, Pennsylvania

The Misconceptions

It's "anything goes" Judaism, whatever is convenient or what they like best.

Reform Jews don't keep kosher, observe the Sabbath, go to the mikvah, or celebrate the second day of any Jewish holiday.

There are no obligations.

Reform Jews prefer a worship service that resembles a church service.

More Accurately . . .

The Reform movement of the past abandoned many Jewish traditions, but over the past ten years, many Reform Jews are returning to greater observance. As a result, there exists a wide range in Reform Jews' levels and intensities of observance.

Ethical commandments of the Torah, such as "Love your neighbor as yourself," are binding for Reform Jews, so they do recognize the category of obligations.

The Reform movement divides historically into the older, "classical" Reform movement, when synagogue services were designed to resemble church services and any observances that were thought old-fashioned or interfering with assimilation were discarded. After 1937, a new, more traditionally oriented movement, Modern Reform, sought a return to Jewish practices. Classical and Modern Reform are very different. When people are stereotyping Reform, they are usually referring to Classical Reform and not recognizing the significant changes and development of the Reform movement over the past sixty years.

Observant Reform Jews may observe as many mitzvot as Conservative or less-observant Orthodox Jews do, but they do mitzvot out of personal choice rather than because they believe that they are commanded by God. When God is central in the life of a Reform Jew, he or she has made the choice to relate to God that way, rather than responding out of an obligation that arises automatically from being born Jewish.

What Distinguishes Reform Judaism?

Reform Judaism was founded on the belief that change in Jewish life is essential and that Judaism must never become fixed or paralyzed or it becomes irrelevant.

Reform Jews choose and create observances based on individual commitment and knowledge. The Reform movement interprets Jewish tradition to say that the Covenant allows for informed individual choice. The key word is "informed." Reform Jews are encouraged to engage in enough study to make an educated decision about their options, instead of just throwing it all away because of laziness or lack of awareness.

Reform Jews interpret Torah as "teaching" rather than "law." Halakhah and mitzvot are not understood as God's law, but as the creation of human beings, which therefore, can be changed.

Reform Jews do not believe that God gave the entire Torah word for word. They believe that the Bible is a collection of people's thoughts throughout the ages, and that the Talmud and the huge body of Rabbinic literature are human creations and not eternally valid or divinely ordained.

The second days of festivals such as *Rosh Hashanah, Sukkot,* Passover, and *Shavuot* have been dropped, although many Reform synagogues still offer members a way to observe it. Working on the Sabbath is not considered sinful. Most of the dietary laws were eliminated, although a small percentage of Reform Jews choose to keep kosher.

Men and women have equal roles in religious life. Women are not prohibited from practicing any rituals and can be ordained as rabbis.

A cornerstone of the Reform movement is *tikkun olam*, a commitment to fix the world and to work for social justice. Reform Jews place greater emphasis on ethical issues and social action than on ritual observance.

RECONSTRUCTIONISM

The Misconceptions

Reconstructionism is so new that it's not to be taken seriously.

No one, including Reconstructionists, really understands what Reconstructionism is.

Reconstructionists don't believe in God.

MORE ACCURATELY . . .

Time will tell whether Reconstructionism will last over the centuries, but currently it is a small yet thriving movement within the United States.

Reconstructionism *is* hard to define and articulate, but many Jews, once learning what Reconstructionism believes and suggests for Jewish practice, embrace its philosophy and feel that it speaks more directly to them than any other Jewish movement.

Reconstructionists define Judaism as the evolving religious civilization of the Jewish people and the means by which we conduct our search for ultimate meaning in life.

Contrary to myth, God is very much a part of Reconstructionist philosophy. Reconstructionists believe in a God who inhabits this world and especially the human heart. God is the source of meaning, generosity, sensitivity, and concern for the world around us.

WHAT DISTINGUISHES RECONSTRUCTIONISM?

Mordecai Kaplan, the founder of Reconstructionism, published his first book, *Judaism as a Civilization*, which became the central source of Reconstructionism along with the Torah. Kaplan suggested that the Jewish people, not God, should be seen as the center of Jewish life. Reconstructionists believe that some things are within God's power and some are not. They do not believe that God revealed the Torah to Moses at Mt. Sinai, but rather that the Torah is a record of the people's search for God.

Reconstructionists believe that everything must be done to preserve the Jewish people, even if it means discarding old ideas and values while creating new ones. For example, Reconstructionists might observe the Sabbath because observing Sabbath teaches us the importance of rest and helps us survive as one people by uniting us. The people, not the rabbis, have the final say in accepting or dropping mitzvot. A famous Reconstructionist expression is: "The past should have a vote, not a veto." Like Conservative and Reform Jews, a Reconstructionist Jew has strong commitments both to traditional observance and to the search for contemporary meaning.

Men and women have equal roles in religious life. Women are ordained as rabbis and not prohibited from practicing any rituals.

Religious practices of Reconstructionists differ widely from congregation to congregation. The movement has been open to experimenting with new rituals and practices. Often such changes are brought about by majority vote of the members of a congregation.

NEW AGE/JEWISH RENEWAL

The Misconceptions
It's hardly Jewish at all. It's mostly Jews doing lots of weird rituals and claiming that these rituals have Jewish roots. It's "woo-woo" Judaism.

It's mostly for lesbians and feminists.

More Accurately . . .
The form of expression may be quite different than traditional expressions and rituals, but many learned, egalitarian literate Jews are attracted to and involved in the spiritual renewal movement. In fact, the Jewish renewal movement is credited with sparking

thousands of Jewish adults to return to Jewish practice and greater observance. It is also felt by many to be a forum for experiencing Judaism in a joyful way. Contrary to the myth that it is ungrounded, the leaders and active participants in spiritual renewal are often quite well studied in traditional texts and fluent in Hebrew.

What Distinguishes Jewish Renewal?

Jewish Renewal Jews often meet in prayer groups that are egalitarian, politically active, and feministic.

Rabbi Zalman Schachter-Sholomi, considered the founder of the movement, helped integrate the feminism, ecological awareness, progressive politics, and egalitarianism of the chavurah movement with Hasidic mysticism. Jewish renewal has been described as "a network of spiritual seekers and communities that combines traditional study of Torah, mystical Kabbalistic and Hasidic traditions, mediation, singing, prayer, and humanistic and transpersonal psychology."

Rabbi Arthur Waskow, a leader in the Jewish Renewal movement, teaches: "When we look at Torah, we don't say, 'We accept it." We say. 'There's an element of divine command.' And then we factor in what Moses and the Jewish people brought to it. We look beneath the historical referent of the Torah portion and ask, 'What is the emotional process going on underneath the text? The Torah is the record of spiritual seekers. What can we learn from their experience?"

Jewish Renewal Jews believe that individual Jews and the Jewish community must examine the mitzvot one at a time and decide which ones will be binding for each person and the community. They emphasize making the prayer and study experience meaningful, joyful, and individually and communally significant. The spiritual quest of Jewish Renewal Jews is central to their life. The desire to develop a deepening relationship with God and with friends, family, and community attracts many Jews from other denominations, as well as Jews who have left Judaism and are now returning.

SECULAR HUMANISM

The Misconceptions

Secular Jews aren't really Jewish. They can call themselves Jewish, but they have removed everything that is essential to being a Jew.

Since Secular Jews don't believe in God, celebrating most of the Jewish holidays doesn't make sense. They aren't interested in observing most Jewish rituals, either.

More Accurately . . .

Many Secular Jews are very connected to their Jewish heritage, proud to be Jews, and committed to bringing Judaism into their lives in as many ways as possible, as long as it doesn't center around God and a theology they do not ascribe to. This movement is growing in popularity as Jews are finding it to be a place that allows them to still be and act Jewish, even if they are atheist or agnostic. Many of the Jewish holidays are celebrated in a community of like-minded Jews who value the family traditions and wish to pass it along to their children.

What Distinguishes Secular Humanism?

Sherwin Wine is credited with being the founder and leader of the Humanistic Judaism movement, founding the first congregation in 1963 and several international organizations since then.

Of all the denominations described thus far, Secular Humanists are the only Jews who do not believe in a biblical creation and the efficacy of prayer. They believe in evolution, the power of human effort and responsibility, and the natural origin of all experiences.

Secular Jews affirm that Jewish culture is the creation of the Jewish people. Whereas traditional Jewish communities center around prayer and God, alternative Secular Humanist communities center around Jewish culture and ethical concerns. Many members of Secular Jewish communities feel a need for Jewish ritual to express their Judaism and provide a way to connect with other Jews.

Secular Humanism is attracting deeply committed but agnostic Jews who keep open the possibility that God exists, but who do not think about God frequently or center their lives around obeying his commandments. They participate in Jewish holidays in much the same way that Secular Jews living in Israel might—because they are Jewish and wish to be in the company of other Jews celebrating their unique heritage, not necessarily because they are religious.

Now that you have a better sense of who you are as a Jewish individual, it's time to reflect on who you are and want to be as a Jewish couple.

3

Merging Two Spiritual Journeys

Religious troubles often spring not so much from differences in formal religious labels as from differences in each partner's need for some spiritual expression. In many couples, one partner is intensely spiritual and the other is not. One needs a relationship to religion or God, the other does not. Unlike many issues in a marriage, this one can't be reasoned through, negotiated, or compromised on; it's a need, a sensibility, a matter of temperament and training that goes deep. It's an area where it's often difficult for partners to understand each other.

—Judy Petsonk, *The Intermarriage Handbook*

Looking at What Happened Jewishly in Your Childhood

HOW YOU FEEL ABOUT being Jewish, both the positive and the negative, is rooted in your childhood experiences and memories. What you want and don't want in Jewish practice is strongly influenced by your childhood impressions. It is important for you and your spouse to discuss how your Jewish behavior and values were shaped in childhood. Where you diverge from one another can often be traced back to your earliest experiences.

WHO WERE THE INFLUENTIAL TEACHERS?

You cannot answer the questions, "Who am I as a Jew, and what do I believe about God?" without remembering who taught you these beliefs. As a child you are born with a blank slate that is filled in by your family, friends, and teachers. From whom, if anyone, did you learn about Judaism? When and how did you first start defining yourself by a denominational label, or shunning one? Were your mom or dad educated enough to pass along a rich tradition? Were your grandparents or extended family influential to you? What was your Hebrew school experience like? Did you have a favorite Hebrew school teacher? Who had influence on you at summer camp? Did you learn from Jewish peers and friends? Did you develop a pivotal relationship with a rabbi, cantor, or any other Jewish professional?

If your answer to all of these questions is a blank, you may long for Jewish learning in your adulthood and want your children to have a better Jewish education than you received. Or you might be intimated by the prospect of your children becoming more learned than you and resist such actions as Hebrew day school for them, because it will force you to confront the emptiness of your own Jewish background. Here's an example of how dissimilar Jewish experiences in childhood can instigate a conflict that is only resolvable when these unmet childhood needs are addressed:

Carol and Seth are arguing over the length of the Passover seder. Seth feels cheated by the abbreviated seder that Carol insists she wants. At the end of the seder, he feels as if he has been served a bag of cotton candy instead of a sumptuous meal. Carol tried doing the seder Seth's way one year, and at the end of the second hour she was ready for bed and quite grumpy.

They argue every year about what is "right" and how to change the seder so that both can be satisfied. They've never bothered to look at how childhood seder experiences influenced their current feelings.

Carol was raised in an unhappy home with two bickering parents. She remembers the seder as a time of strife, not pleasure. Her father would get tense about getting the entire house clean on time and he'd yell at all the children about the *chometz* he found in their rooms. He complained about cooking and the visiting relatives he didn't like. Her mom and dad would fight incessantly throughout Passover week, and Carol remembers wishing that Passover would just disappear.

Seth was raised in a home without a seder. His family would break out a box of matzoh to have with a special meal, but there was no reading from the *Haggadah*. Seth remembers feeling ashamed when he heard about the seders his friends were experiencing. He never told his friends the truth about his; in fact, he made up elaborate stories about the seders he pretended he enjoyed. As an adult, he was still trying to make up for what he felt he lost; he wanted his childhood dreams to become reality.

When Carol and Seth shared these memories, they were able to feel more compassionate toward each other's desires and more open to a compromise. Also, both learned that no adult seder they could create together would ever compensate for painful childhood memories.

Positive Jewish Memories

You will each naturally strive to replicate the rituals and Jewish experiences of your childhood that brought you the most joy and satisfaction. Conflict arises sometimes when what brought you great delight is not greeted with the same enthusiasm by your spouse. For example, perhaps one of you loved the grandparents and looked forward to spending Jewish holidays with them, while the other of you didn't enjoy the same loving relationship with grandparents. Naturally, family celebrations with the grandparents hold different associations for each of you.

Even childhood differences can sometimes bring you to common ground, however. Perhaps the wife who missed out on positive grandparenting experiences as a child will join with her husband to ensure that their children experience what she missed, or she might even delight in spending time with his extended family, if it provides some of the loving and celebratory feeling she missed in her own home. So if you and your spouse do not both have positive memories, you can bridge the gap by focusing on shared goals for creating positive experiences now in your marriage.

What are your best Jewish memories from childhood? What gave you joy? What did you look forward to as a Jewish child? These are the experiences that you will likely wish to recapture and transmit to your family. For example, Stephen Jaffe of Lancaster, Pennsylvania, recalls:

> My childhood memories of *Pesach* were always joyous. The first seder, we always went to my grandpa and nana's house (my mom's side of the family), and on the second night, we always went to one of the relatives on my dad's side of the family. I loved the food—great appetizers and desserts, the singing—my grandpa was really into it, seeing bunches of my cousins, and hunting for the *affikomen*—we anticipated that for months. Since I was the youngest for several years, I got to say the four questions, which gave me a real thrill.

Other examples of happy childhood memories:

- Reciting your Torah portion at your bar mitzvah day
- Family time together on *Shabbat* afternoons
- Exchanging presents for Hanukkah
- Dressing in costume for the Purim play
- Friday evening Sabbath meal
- Kiddush after Saturday morning services
- Breakfast on *Yom Kippur*
- High school youth group activities
- A trip to Israel
- Falling in love with your first Jewish boyfriend in the eighth grade
- Jewish summer camp

Share these memories with your spouse. Get as detailed as possible. In other words, if Jewish summer camp was a positive memory, what specific memories from camp are your favorites? My husband, Stephen, remembers how much he loved singing Hebrew songs at mealtime every day.

Some of you may have to work very hard to come up with any positive memories. Either you were raised in a home with little observance, or you felt lonely in school as a Jewish child, or growing up Jewish was largely a painful experience for you because you engaged in relatively few meaningful rituals. Such awareness is significant. It means you will likely either resist Jewish observance in adulthood or be hungry for it. It also means that you have few reference points for positive Jewish experiences, so if something is really meaningful for your spouse, you may have a hard time relating to it.

UNHAPPY JEWISH MEMORIES

An observant Jewish woman I interviewed was dismayed by her husband's lack of respect for some Orthodox practices, even though he was raised in a very *frum* household. Then she learned that he had been hit regularly in class by his yeshiva rebbe, which tarnished his perspective of Orthodox Judaism. She was able to feel more compassion for his resistance when she understood its origin.

It may be unfathomable to you why your spouse is so resistant to something that gives you so much joy. Why can't he or she share these happy experiences with you? Worse, why does your mate want to take away what is most meaningful to you by making fun of it, denigrating it, or questioning its usefulness?

Often, the answer to that question lies in the childhood experiences of your mate. These painful memories are hard to shake, and it can take a while before a spouse is convinced that adult Jewish experiences can be different, and superior, to what he or she endured as a child. Sometimes you can be married for a number of years and not ever have these important conversations that give you clues to your spouse's and your own resistance.

What are your most painful Jewish memories from childhood? What made you sad, angry, bored, or lonely? What did you dread as a Jewish child? What did you vow you would do again as an adult, or that you would never do to your children? These are the experiences that you will likely wish to avoid in your current marriage. For example, Janice Morganstein of Baltimore shared an unpleasant childhood association with being Jewish:

> Growing up, everyone in the neighborhood was Jewish and went to the same Orthodox shul in Baltimore. When I was twelve and became a bat mitzvah, I had it out with the rabbi because the boys would have their bar mitzvah ceremony upstairs, and the girls were in the basement. We had to wear white dresses that made me look fat, and he gave them things to say. I said to him, "I don't have a clue what a *midrash* is and what the Exodus is. This has nothing to do with me." That was it for me; I didn't go to shul again for twenty-five years.

Her husband, Dr. Warren Morganstein, recalls:

> I grew up in the inner city of Baltimore. The only place to go to school was the talmudic academy. My parents were Reform and ate crab, while I had to wear *tzitzit* and a *kippah*. It made me crazy. I was so confused. When my parents went to the open house, they asked about "Warren." The rebbe didn't know who my parents were talking about because my parents didn't know my Hebrew name, and the rebbe didn't know me as Warren.

Merging Two Spiritual Journeys

Imagine for the moment that you lived in Boston for a number of years, and during that time your spouse lived in Houston. In your late twenties, both of you traveled to Chicago for job opportunities, where you met at a Jewish singles function. You could take out an atlas and magic marker and trace the physical routes that led you both to that meeting place in Chicago where your journeys merged into one.

Alongside the physical representation of your travels, there is also a metaphysical one, a linear description of the events of your life that led you from point A to point B, in the frame of mind that made your loved one seem attractive to you at that function in Chicago. For example, I gave Rabbi Ullman credit in the "Acknowledgments" for sparking my interest in Judaism enough that I found it desirable to hook up with someone like Stephen. Had I met Stephen without the intervening chapter of studying with a rabbi like Alan, I doubt I would have considered him an attractive life-partner. Although Stephen and I were apart for the first thirty-four years of my life, and forty-one years of his, our spiritual journeys can be viewed as always leading up to our meeting, even if we didn't know it at the time.

Take a few hours to learn about the evolution of your mate's Jewish and spiritual development before you married (see the exercise in the next section). Opening up the discussion of what came before the two of you joined together will help remind you of the infintesimal chance that all of these events would play out exactly as they did, so that the two of you could get together at the moment in history that was destined for you. Remembering the miracle of your meeting is a touchstone in difficult times.

Try This!: Write Your Spiritual Autobiography

1. Take a large piece of paper and draw two horizontal lines, one for each of you. (Alternatively, you can each use your own piece of paper.) Along these lines, starting from the left, jot down any and all of the following significant spiritual or Jewish experiences, and others not mentioned, that occurred before your current marriage:

- Your bris or baby naming
- Hebrew school or Hebrew day school
- Jewish youth group
- Jewish summer camp
- Family events like "the year we went kosher," or "the year we started doing Friday night Sabbath dinner," or "the year we took a trip to Israel"
- Bar or bat mitzvah

- Confirmation
- Dating first Jewish boyfriend or girlfriend
- Jewish college experiences, (Hillel, Jewish fraternity, social action)
- Previous weddings, Jewish or not
- Turning points that prompted you to turn away from Judaism
- Turning points that prompted you to return to Judaism
- Significant non-Jewish spiritual experiences
- Significant life events, such as divorce or death, that influenced your spiritual path
- And so on . . .

Now, get as creative as you like. You may color code your time line (red for excitement, blue for depression) or add relevant symbols, such as a lightbulb when you got turned on or a big black X when you got turned off. Add whatever illustrations will help you bring your journey to life, so that you can discuss it with your spouse.

2. Compare your time lines. Look for the similarities and the differences.

3. Create a third time line, a shared one, since your marriage. Chart on this time line the shared experiences of significance to your spiritual journey. For example:

- First date—decided not to order the shrimp
- First time we went to synagogue together
- Wedding day
- Setting up a kosher kitchen
- Birth of children
- Moving and choosing a synagogue
- Enrolling the children in a Hebrew day school
- The Passover seder we'd all like to forget
- The best Hanukkah ever
- First fight about something Jewish

- First trip to the mikvah
- And so on . . .

You can also color code and decorate your shared time line to illustrate friction, happiness, new awarenesses, difficult times in your marriage, periods of questioning and doubt about God.

4. If you have children old enough to understand the spiritual autobiography exercise, you might create a family time line, or encourage them to draw their own time line of significant Jewish experiences, to include their most positive and negative memories of Judaism while living in your home.

The purpose behind all of these family history exercises is to help you recognize how the meaningful moments in your spiritual and Jewish journey influence the choices that you make today. Discussing individual and shared experiences that stand out as most joyous or painful helps you clarify why you feel as you do about certain Jewish practices or the absence of them.

Assessing Your Jewish Similarities and Differences

You probably picked up this book because you are concerned about the Jewish differences between you and your spouse. When you start focusing on these differences, you will come to believe that your entire relationship is discordant. Before long, it can become that way. To protect the beauty of your marriage, and to stay in love, you must spend more time looking for the Jewish bonds you share than concentrating on the philosophies and practices where you differ. You must have a shared vision of what you want as a couple and a family in your Jewish life together. The more anxious you are about resolving differences, the harder it will become to remember, and appreciate, your shared Jewish values and goals. So take a few moments to do so now with the next exercise.

TRY THIS!: REMEMBER WHAT WE HAVE IN COMMON AS JEWS

Take out a sheet of paper, either by yourself, or with your spouse, and list twenty-five to fifty Jewish things you have in common.

Include on that list the Jewish values you share, as well as Jewish activities you both appreciate or choose not to engage in. Here are a few examples:

- We want to raise our children in a Jewish home.
- We are glad that we are Jews.
- We love listening to Jewish music at synagogue and at home.
- We'd like to visit Israel some day.
- We believe in being ethical in our personal and business activities.
- We enjoy a good sermon.
- We have never experienced anti-semitism.
- We do not want to move to Israel.
- We do not want to practice the laws of family purity.
- We love matzoh ball soup and *Shabbos* chicken.
- We love a Sabbath nap.
- We do not want to donate money to the current Israeli government because they don't consider us Jewish.
- We do our best to honor our parents.
- We do not wish to be cremated or to donate our organs upon death.
- We are concerned about the treatment of Jews around the world and wish to give money toward helping Jewish refugees.
- We do not want to keep the Sabbath until sundown on Saturday.
- And so on . . .

See that? You have more in common Jewishly than you may be giving yourselves credit for.

Now create a vision together of what you both want in your Jewish life together. What did you dream about during your courtship and on your wedding day? When you picture your children and grandchildren describing the Jewish home they were raised in, what do you hope they will say? When you are old and nearing the end of your life, what will you reminisce about and feel good about achieving? What will be your best Jewish memories?

You may choose to express your shared vision through a piece of artwork, a collage, a written statement, or a poem you both find appealing. Or you can set aside just a few hours for this important discussion. Knowing that you have a shared vision that you can return to in the midst of conflict will be a source of comfort time and again.

TRY THIS!: SHIFT THE FOCUS FROM METHOD TO GOAL

Every married couple suffers from what Mira Kirshenbaum, in her 1998 book, calls "difference sickness" at certain points in their marriage. That's when all you can see is your differences, and any reconciliation of those differences seems hopeless. That's why it's helpful for you and your spouse to have a shared vision of your life together, one that you can return to when you are feeling overwhelmed by your differences.

Here's a neat trick psychotherapists use to help troubled couples shift from seeing nothing but the differences between them. Jeff Klunk, a family practice psychologist in Lancaster, Pennsylvania recommends couples "separate the goal from the method." He shares this example: "If the wife's goal is to have her children grow up to become committed Jews, her husband may agree with that goal, but disagree with her methods."

Discuss your shared goals before you choose the method for getting there. For example, Marvin and Denise are fighting about how to provide Hebrew education for their children. Marvin wants to enroll the kids in the yeshiva. Denise wants to enroll them in a public school in a Jewish neighborhood and send them to Hebrew school a few afternoons a week.

In order to progress in their brainstorming and problem solving, they needed to start viewing themselves as teammates working together to reach a shared goal. When they articulated their shared goal, "We want our children to be well-educated Jews with a strong Jewish identity and a feeling of connection to God and the Jewish people throughout the day," they stopped feeling so far apart. Both the yeshiva and the public school in a Jewish neighborhood could achieve these goals.

Marvin and Denise still disagree about the method for best reaching the goal of educating their children, and the negotiation and problem-solving discussion is tricky. But a discussion first of what they have in common will go a long way toward ensuring that they attack the problem together, instead of attacking each other.

Are you a couple with a shared vision, working out a problem that has arisen between you, or are you two individuals living together trying to fix the other person who has become a problem? Go back to your wedding day or early courting years and remember the person you fell in love with and how it felt to be in love.

If you are fighting over something related to raising children, return to a generalized discussion about your dreams rather than get caught in the specifics. For example, you both might agree that:

- We want our children to grow up loving Judaism.

- We want our children to marry Jews.

- We want our children to be well educated about Jewish history and our tradition.

- We want our children to look forward to Jewish holidays.

- We want our children to be *menschen*.

- We want our children to keep the laws of *kashrut*.

- We want our children to grow up to raise Jewish children.

The rest of the work is in the details—which can still be significant. But at least begin those discussions with an appreciation of the common ground you walk on.

> I spoke to a couple who felt that they are so different from one another that they don't have any common goals. I first asked one, then the other, "Would you like to live a happy life?" Both the husband and wife replied, "Yes, very much

so." "Great," I commented, "this is your common goal. Let's see how you both can treat each other in a way that will give each of you a happy life."

—Rabbi Zelig Pliskin, *Marriage*

How We Differ as Jews

Even though you are both Jewish, you may have varying preferences for prayer, disparate theological beliefs, attraction to different kinds of spiritual communities, different family backgrounds, or personality traits that lead you to prefer one kind of spiritual practice over another. Here are some examples:

Sheila likes to pray in mixed company and Tom prefers *davening* in an Orthodox shul with a *mechitzah*.

Sheila prefers that the Passover seder be less than an hour long. Tom enjoys a longer seder.

Sheila believes that God had nothing to do with the Holocaust; it was the outcome of man's free will. Tom questions the existence of God because God let the Holocaust happen.

Try This!: Describe Your Jewish Differences

Write down all of the differences you are concerned about, both big and small. Be thorough and mention the contrasts that worry you the most. You can each write your own list and then compare them, or do this together. Even when you write down your differences you will likely discover that they are fewer than the commonalities you wrote down earlier. The rest of this book will demonstrate how to reconcile and resolve many of the differences you have written on that list.

As you move forward in the book, refer back to these assessment exercises to help focus your discussions on the root issues, not on the superfluous details that you'll likely be fighting about. Return as often as you can to what you share in your vision together, and remember why you fell in love in the first place.

4

Themes of Religious Conflict in Jewish Marriages

> If you want to get exactly what you want every time, then you
> shouldn't be in a relationship. You should be single.
>
> —Dr. Robert Schwebel, *Who's on Top, Who's on Bottom*

When Did Confilct First Arise?

Jewish conflicts can be present from the start of your marriage for reasons like the following:

- We were both committed to an active, observant Jewish life, but we approach Jewish practice differently.

- One of us was committed to an active, observant Jewish life, and the other was more of a cultural Jew and less observant.

- One of us believed in God, and the other was an agnostic or atheist Jew.

or, during the Marriage, conflicts like the following might arise:

- A Jewish-life cycle event brought up conflicts we didn't expect.

Jack and Chava belong to a Reconstructionist synagogue where they are frequent Sabbath worshipers and active members of the community. They experienced little religious conflict in their marriage until the bat mitzvah of their first daughter, Rachel. Rachel wanted a big Saturday night party with a DJ, Chava wanted a fancy sit-down dinner for friends

40

and family after the bat mitzvah service; and Jack wanted to use their money for a trip to Israel instead.

- One of us stopped believing in God, or lost interest in Jewish observance, while the other spouse continued to desire active involvement.

Will was a devoted synagogue member and an observant Jew until he lost his son, Charles, in a tragic drunk driving accident. His wife, Linda, turned to God and her religious community for support, but Will became so angry with God he pulled away from all Jewish observance and refused to believe that the God he believed in could allow such a devastating event to occur.

- One of us became much more interested in an active spiritual life and Jewish observance than the other.

Stan and Sheila have been married for thirty years. When the youngest of their three boys left for college, Sheila signed up for an adult education program at their synagogue. She asked Stan to join her but he expressed no interest. Sheila had no idea of the riches that Torah could offer her. The rabbis who facilitated the classes sparked her desire to learn more. She came home from each class bubbling over with excitement—an entire new world was opening to her.

She is disappointed that Stan shows no interest in what she is learning. She worries that she is drifting away from Stan but doesn't know what to do about it. Stan wonders what happened to the wife he loved and knew for so many years. He just wants to play golf, enjoy his grandkids, and do some traveling in his retirement. He loves Sheila and he knows that she loves him, but what will they talk about five years from now?

Four Approaches to Resolving Jewish Conflicts

Although generalized models cannot capture all the nuances of your particular union, you will likely see yourselves reflected in one of the following models of how couples address conflicts about Judaism in their marriage. What might be a fruitful strategy for a couple reconciling Orthodox and Reform theological orientations will differ from what will appeal to a Reform Jewish couple working out a difference of opinion on how their son should celebrate becoming a bar mitzvah.

None of these approaches is better or more right than the other in general, but one or two of them will be more suitable for your circumstances and preferences. Each approach brings with it challenges and opportunities. Which one resonates the strongest with you?

THE LESS OBSERVANT SPOUSE BECOMES MORE OBSERVANT

Mark and Julie

Julie, a young woman in her thirties was raised as a High Holiday Jew during a time when Reform Jewish girls did not celebrate becoming bat mitzvah with a ceremony or party. She received no Hebrew education. Her parents were "bagels-and-lox" Jews with no religious upbringing, so she left home with a minimal understanding of her heritage and little knowledge of Jewish rituals or culture. She believed in God but wasn't sure whether religious practice mattered at all. She was not terribly concerned about marrying a Jewish man: What mattered was whether she loved him, not whether he was Jewish.

Then Julie met Mark at work. She was immediately attracted to his dark, handsome face, and intrigued by the fact that he was wearing a yarmulke. They started dating and she quickly discovered that he was different than most Jews she knew. He seemed to know so much about Judaism. She admired his depth of passion and his commitments to such disciplines as keeping kosher and observing the Sabbath (although she wished he wouldn't refuse to go out on Saturday nights in the summertime until sunset—that really put a damper on in their social life). When they got engaged, Mark asked for three commitments from her: a kosher home, observing the Sabbath together, and observing the laws of family purity.

Julie is not delighted by the first two requests, seeing these rituals as inconveniences at best. She doesn't believe that God cares if she eats a pork chop, and she'd miss cooking many of her favorite meals at home. But she is willing to grant Mark the kosher home and the Sabbath he feels he needs. The third request, however, is more than she is ready to deal with. She never heard of the mikvah growing up. What does he mean that she's "unclean" every month? They have a fabulous sex life, and she doesn't want to cut the frequency of their sex in half. She hesitates to give Mark the commitment he is looking for, but eventually, when she learns how important it is to him, she agrees to try it.

Mark loves Julie; he can't imagine anyone more perfect for him. They share a love for travel, photography, work, and skiing. And thank goodness, she is Jewish. He wishes that she was more serious about Jewish practice and more learned about Judaism. He always thought he would marry a more Orthodox woman, but apparently Hashem wanted him to marry Julie—it was love at first sight. He appreciates her willingness to stretch so far out of her comfort zone to accommodate his needs. He hopes that over time she will come to desire observant practices for her own reasons, not just because he asked for it.

Julie's and Mark's Greatest Challenges

- Convincing Julie of the benefits of increased observance to her and their marriage.

- Overcoming Julie's negative feelings about the mikvah.

- Reconciling Julie's desire for free will with Mark's desire to live a commanded life.

- Retaining Julie's sense of identity as a Jew rather than becoming entirely subsumed in Mark's journey.

- Teaching Julie the observant rituals she knew nothing about from her upbringing.

- Controlling Mark's disdain for Julie's lack of observance.

Julie's and Mark's Greatest Opportunities

- Increasing Julie's involvement in and connection with her Jewish heritage.
- Improving communication and conflict resolution skills.
- Observing commandments as a thoughtful approach rather than observing them by rote or only because of family upbringing.
- Developing respect for each other's differences.

When this model isn't working well, you might hear:

"My partner must change or we can't be together." Or "Why can't she see that the observant way is the right way?!" Or "Does he have to be so unreasonable and rigid?!"

When this model is working well, you might hear:

"I would never have taken on these observances without being prodded by my husband, but now I'm glad that I did. They have enriched my life." Or "I appreciate how much my wife has changed to support my desire for more observance, and I love her all the more for doing so."

THE MORE OBSERVANT SPOUSE DECREASES OBSERVANCE

Eli and Carol

Eli was raised in an learned Conservative Jewish household, attended a Jewish camp for seven summers, and was very active in Jewish youth groups throughout high school. He was fluent in Hebrew and enjoyed attending synagogue services regularly, where he often volunteered to read Torah. He knew he would marry a Jewish woman, and so he was delighted when he met Carol in college at a fundraising event for a local homeless shelter. He gave her immediate brownie points for being dedicated to service, and admired her strong commitments to social action. She was raised in a Reform Jewish family that was very involved in community volunteerism. Although she was a Reform Jew, and he a Conservative, neither of them thought these differences would be that big a deal since they both had strong Jewish identities and a shared commitment to raising Jewish children.

Carol and Eli married, and Jewish differences were scarcely an issue until their first son was ready to go to Hebrew school. Until then, Eli had davened regularly at a local Orthodox synagogue while Carol stayed home on the Sabbath. Once it was time to educate their son, though, they both wanted to find one synagogue they could agree on and attend together. Finding a synagogue where they could both be happy was a mindboggling task. As soon as Carol set foot in a temple service conducted mostly in Hebrew, she wanted to be anywhere but there. Eli, attending Carol's choice of service, felt almost nauseous when he listened to the organ and choir in the Reform synagogue.

After much bickering, Eli finally gave in. He decided that it would be easier for him to adjust to an English service than it would be for Carol to feel comfortable in the more traditional Hebrew services that satisfied him. He wanted them to be able to go to synagogue together.

They joined the Reform congregation, and for the most part Eli is making it work. He does find it uncomfortable, though, when he and Carol go out for lunch after Sabbath services with a group of other couples, and they all order shrimp and cheeseburgers. He and Carol don't have a kosher home, so he can't really complain about it. Still, it makes him uneasy, especially on the Sabbath. He feels the loneliest on High Holidays, when he finds the nontraditional services in the Reform synagogue disturbingly incomplete for his taste. Some days, he wonders what it would have been like if he had married a woman as observant as he would like to be, but he loves his wife and son, so it's a sacrifice he has become willing to make.

Carol feels guilty sometimes that Eli isn't getting what he wants at synagogue, and she wonders if he will resent her for his having given up some of the practices he would prefer to have. It bothers her that he makes fun of the music in services that she finds so beautiful, and she wishes he could relax a bit more when they socialize with other couples on the Sabbath. She also resents his subtle denigration of her Reform approach to Judaism. She considers herself as serious a Jew as he is, even if she doesn't know Hebrew or enjoy a three-hour-long service on the Sabbath. She hopes that in time he will come to love the Reform community and services as much as she does.

Eli's and Carol's Greatest Challenges

- Locating additional Jewish resources to supplement Eli's needs for greater observance from time to time.
- Finding a way for Eli to have a more satisfying synagogue experience.
- Retaining Eli's sense of identity as an observant Jew, when he has agreed to give up some observances in deference to Carol.
- Not allowing Eli's dissatisfaction with his Jewish path to become the cause of friction in the marriage.
- Opening Carol up to be willing to consider accommodating Eli's desire for greater observance in certain circumstances.

Eli's and Carol's Greatest Opportunities

- Finding shared Jewish experiences, such as social action, that are meaningful to both of them.
- Meeting Eli's desire to find spiritual meaning in the path he has chosen with Carol.
- Joining together to create a Jewish path for their son.
- Improving communication and conflict resolution skills.
- Developing respect for each other's differences.

When this approach isn't working well, you might hear: "I can't stand this music. I might as well be in church!" Or "Don't roll your eyes like that when the organist starts to play!"

When this approach is working well, you might hear: "I would rather sit next to my wife in a temple of her choice, than sit alone in a synagogue of my choosing." Or "I really appreciate my husband giving up the synagogue he would prefer so that we can be together as a family. I know that's a big sacrifice for him."

SPOUSES FOLLOW SEPARATE SPIRITUAL PATHS

Chaim and Rivkah

Chaim was raised in a frum (observant) family in Brooklyn. He appreciated many of the blessings of being raised in a large,

Torah-observant household. He would never have considered marrying anyone who wasn't Jewish. However, in his early twenties, he went through a rebellious period when he abandoned keeping kosher, took off his *tzitzit,* and started attending a chavurah in a rabbi's home for his Sabbath worship instead of a traditional synagogue service. His travels to Israel during a vacation introduced him to Rivkah, an Orthodox American woman living on a kibbutz for three months. They fell in love and when they returned to the States, began a courtship that led to marriage.

Rivkah remains *shomer Shabbos* and walks to the Orthodox synagogue in their neighborhood. Chaim drives to his chavura meetings on some Sabbaths and works on others. They keep a kosher home, but Chaim eats *treyf* outside of the house. Chaim and Rivkah make no attempt to join each other in spiritual worship, even on the High Holidays. They see prayer as an individual experience anyway and don't consider it a problem to be praying without each other's companionship. They respect each other's right to choose a form of practice that is meaningful.

If it was only them in the world, they would have little conflict around Judaism. However, their greatest challenges center on how to handle Rivkah's family, who barely hide their disdain for Chaim's nonobservance of halakhah, and how to raise the children. For example, Rivkah feels strongly that the children should be required to keep kosher inside and outside of the home, while Chaim wants them to be able to eat nonkosher food with their friends, such as hot dogs at a ballgame. In most cases, the one of them with the strongest feelings wins, or they make tradeoffs such as, "I'll let them eat nonkosher food outside of the house if you'll support me in requiring them to attend synagogue every week." At the basis of their relationship is a shared commitment to raising Jewish kids and supporting each other's individual path. Their conflicts are in the details of how to merge those two desires.

Chaim's and Rivkah's Greatest Challenges

- Agreeing on a Jewish path for the children.
- Resolving tension with Rivkah's family.

- Staying spiritually connected when they spend much of their worship and holiday celebration time apart.

- Resolving differences of opinion regarding the children's practice when each has strong feelings and requests.

Chaim's and Rivkah's Greatest Opportunities

- Showing a rich, expansive view of Jewish options to the children, including demonstrating how two people can love and support each other even if they have different religious beliefs.

- Learning from each other's studies and practices.

- Improving communication and conflict resolution skills.

- Developing respect for each other's differences.

When this approach isn't working well, you might hear:

"What you do with your spiritual life is your business, but don't inflict it on my kids!" Or "You are embarrassing me in front of my friends and fellow congregants."

When this approach is working well, you might hear:

"When you support me without judgment, I feel even more loving toward you. Thank you." Or "Our kids are lucky they are being raised by two parents who love being Jewish, even if we do it differently."

SPOUSES CREATE A NEW AND DIFFERENT PATH, TOGETHER

Bob and Sarah

Bob and Sarah met on vacation at a holistic health retreat, where Bob was looking for alternative ways to treat his chronic asthma and Sarah was hoping to find an effective way to shed a few pounds. Neither was particularly active Jewishly, nor looking to marry someone Jewish. But they both agreed that it was one more thing they had in common that they appreciated.

Neither had found his or her Jewish upbringing satisfying, yet both felt a strong obligation to raise their children in a culturally Jewish home, primarily because of the feelings of extended family.

Neither believed in God nor wanted to spend time involved in synagogue worship and traditional holiday celebration. Yet, around Christmas and Easter, they felt pulled to share in Hanukkah and Passover rituals with their extended families. They also shared a strong commitment to social action and community activism.

For several years they experimented with new places of worship, different home rituals, and other forms of spiritual practice, agreeing that they wanted to create a shared spiritual path that was more meaningful than just joining the local Reform synagogue in town. They became active in Habitat for Humanity and became active board members of the community YMCA. They gravitated toward *chavurot*, and were delighted when they discovered a small group of Secular Humanist Jews who were getting together on the Sabbath and major Jewish holidays. In this group they felt at home and members were like family to them.

Although for the most part their spiritual life works just fine for each of them, Bob has some difficulty during Passover and the High Holidays. During these times, especially as he gets older, he sometimes misses more traditional Jewish observance. Every once in a while he wonders what it would be like to go to synagogue or to conduct a seder. When he went through a particularly troubling bout with asthma, he started questioning his atheism. He shocked himself by praying to the God he wasn't even sure existed. He worries that if he develops a strong faith in God, it might separate him from Sarah, since atheism is something they have always had in common.

Bob's and Sarah's Greatest Challenges

- Developing a satisfying Jewish path that honors their Jewish roots as well as their attraction to a humanistic path centered more on social action than theological worship and belief.

- Coping with negative judgments from Jewish family and friends who don't understand their attraction to Secular Humanism.

- Meeting Bob's need for occasional traditional observance of certain Jewish holidays.

- Providing a way for Bob to explore his new thoughts about God, without separating him from Sarah.

Bob's and Sarah's Greatest Opportunities

- Developing a shared path that is more meaningful to each of them than what they each experienced in their upbringing.
- Elevating the experience of spirituality and joy that they receive from Jewish observance.
- Enhancing the intimacy in their marriage as they share a meaningful spiritual path.

When this approach isn't working well you might hear:
"I miss some of the family rituals I was raised with. It feels as if we have gone too far from my roots." Or "I wouldn't have thought you, of all people, believed in all that superstitious stuff."
When this approach is working well, you might hear:
"The Jewish life we have developed together is so much richer and more enjoyable than I ever experienced when I was younger. Together, we've created something really special."

The Role of Jewish Conflict in Your Marriage

> Being fully committed to a relationship means that you have no doubts that this is the right place for you to be. It doesn't mean that you have no challenges within the relationship. Remember, we are talking about beauty—with all its irregularities—not perfection.
>
> —Susan Page, *The Eight Essential Traits of Couples Who Thrive*

SOMETIMES JEWISH CONFLICTS ARE REALLY ABOUT OTHER ISSUES

When a couple is failing to uphold their marriage vows, not treating each other with love and respect, and no longer interested in working together to create a loving and sacred home, they will often blame their "Jewish differences" as the reason for incompatibility. Nothing is ever that simple in a marriage. Working out differences and coming to love each other unconditionally, despite and even because of differences in character, personality, beliefs, and needs, is the life work of every marriage.

Sometimes friction arises from Jewish concerns. Other times the dissension really has little to do with Judaism. Often what appears to be only a Jewish issue is really a mask for a much deeper, unresolved conflict in the marriage. For example, when one partner wants a kosher kitchen and the other does not, you can approach this problem from a theological point of view, but you can also see it as a theater for playing out the power struggle in the marriage. Whether or not the kitchen is kosher says something to each one about who calls the shots, who gets control, and who wins.

Virtually every marriage goes through three stages of development, starkly described by Sharon Wolf, C.S.W., author of *How to Stay Lovers for Life:*

Discovery of your beloved
Disappointment in your beloved
Devaluation of your beloved

Depending on what stage you are experiencing with your beloved, you might approach Jewish differences with good humor, annoyance, anger, or despair. Jewish differences that appealed to you in the romantic discovery stage ("Isn't it admirable that he takes off work for the Jewish holidays?") become annoyance in the disappointment stage ("I didn't realize that most of our vacation time would be spent covering Jewish holidays") and can move to rage in the devaluation stage ("What a hypocrite! He takes off work to go to Passover services, but then he breaks fast early on Yom Kippur).

In the disappointment and devaluation stages, you see only your partner's flaws. He or she is not the person and the Jew you thought you married. Sometimes you want to turn your mate in for a different model. During these stages, you will despair more about Jewish differences because they will be on your mind often.

The key difference Wolf says between the disappointment and devaluation phases is this:

> When you are disillusioned with what your partner does, you still give her the benefit of the doubt. Disappointment always contains hope. Devaluation encompasses a depreciation of your partner's character. Devaluation means you are disillusioned with who he *is* (rather than with what he does). Devaluating your partner is scary because it makes you doubt whether you have chosen the right person.

One observant woman I interviewed described a former marriage to a man who started intentionally treyfing their kosher kitchen as their marriage was falling apart. On the surface, he started refusing to keep kosher for theological reasons. But the real truth was that he was using kashrut as a weapon to hurt the woman who had so enraged him. The kosher kitchen struggle was not really about whether or not to keep kosher, but about whether or not to stay married, and about respecting each other. Another Jewish couple divorced after the husband had a brief extramarital affair and the wife became ultra-Orthodox as a way to cope with her grief and anger. He was intolerant of her increased observance and ended the marriage, claiming that she had become too Orthodox for him. The marriage didn't really end because of her migration to greater observance; it began unraveling before his affair even began.

If you understand the phase of your marriage at the time a Jewish conflict arises, you can evaluate whether the intensity of your feelings are warranted or are perhaps more a reflection of deeper underlying issues in the marriage. That doesn't make the conflict go away, but it does help you keep it in perspective.

If you have moved into the devaluation stage of marriage, professional marriage counseling is often warranted. It's a "chicken and egg" question. Did the depth of your Jewish conflicts cause you to move there, or are you using Jewish conflicts as the battlefield for your marital power struggles? A professional counselor can help you sort that out.

The devaluation stage shakes your commitment to your marriage. Susan Page, couples expert, says in her 1994 best-selling book:

> Living in a relationship where the commitment is tentative or intermittent is like living in a rented house. You don't like the color of the walls, but you don't want to put the time and money into painting them because you may be in another house soon enough. It's just not worth the investment.
>
> When commitment happens, a shift takes place in the energy of both partners and in their whole psychological system. They are no longer driving with their brakes on. They are no longer asking, 'Is this right?' When two people are accepting of each other, it does not mean they can never ask for change. Quite the contrary. A spirit of acceptance in a relationship creates a non-judgmental, safe atmosphere that makes asking for change much easier. All successful negotiations in a relationship start with a spirit of acceptance and goodwill.

Sometimes the spiritual changes in an individual rocks a marriage, but often the reverse is true. The loneliness of an unhappy marriage may prompt seekers to look for more fulfillment in their spiritual lives as compensation for the emptiness in their marriages. Discord in marriage may lead a spouse to cry out to God in anguish or frustration, thus propelling their spiritual journey to a deeper level. For example, Al-Anon is an entire movement of millions of spouses who are encouraged to ask for God's help to handle the trauma of dealing with an alcoholic spouse. There are also Jewish twelve-step support groups to stimulate a Jewish spiritual journey from the process.

JEWISH CONFLICT CAN STRENGTHEN YOUR MARRIAGE

Marriage is hard work. More than 50 percent of us fail at it. We give up, walk out, throw up our hands, move on to another partnership, or stay married, but unhappily so.

Throughout your marriage, conflicts around Judaism will challenge your patience and tolerance for circumstances you find less than desirable. If the struggle is heated enough, you might even find yourself questioning your marital commitment or the wisdom of your choice to marry your current partner. Some of the issues we'll discuss in this book hit deep and stir up a cauldron of negative emotions. Jewish conflict may be a major theme in your marriage, or just something that crops up once in a while. Every marriage has its issues to work out—and for a Jewish couple, some of the difficulties will likely be about Judaism.

The good news is that working out your differences on these issues will improve your communication skills, and when done well, will bring you closer together and enhance the love in your marriage. You can, over time, come to see these conflicts as one of the greatest gifts in your marriage.

5

Seven Principles for Positive Communication

If someone paid you a large sum of money to develop the skill of remaining calm and centered when faced with criticism, anger, and other unresourceful states, you would definitely be motivated to do so. If the amount would make you one of the wealthiest people in the world, you would read anything you could, consult experts, and practice daily until you mastered this skill. Living a joyous life with a happy marriage makes you wealthier than the richest person if that wealthy person is unhappy.

—Rabbi Zelig Pliskin, *Marriage*

THIS CHAPTER PROVIDES YOU with seven principles for preventing, minimizing, and resolving conflict related to differences over Judaism between you and your spouse. Every couple is unique; certain solutions may not suit your circumstances. The principles in this chapter, however, are universal. They will work no matter what your circumstances, because they help you achieve a more loving approach toward one another. Choosing the path of love and respect will not only make you a better Jew, spouse, and parent, it will also help you get what you want.

These principles are demonstrated through the illustration of a couple in conflict, Susan and Brad. Brad defines himself as an observant Conservative Jew and he wants a kosher kitchen. Susan defines herself as a Reform Jew and she does not want to kasher their kitchen. Let's learn from Susan and Brad how to apply the following principles to resolving their conflict.

Principle One: Avoid Hostile Arguments About Denominations and Theology

Rather than spending time arguing the superiority of our own tradition, let us argue its excellence.

—Rabbi David Wolpe, *The Healer of Shattered Hearts*

If you ever hear yourself quarreling with your mate about the perceived rightness or wrongness of a denominational approach to Jewish practice, you have traveled into no-win territory. Instead of brainstorming a creative solution to your differences, you'll quickly get sucked into defending your denomination's theology, and trying to prove to your mate that one particular approach is superior to another.

Here are some examples of inflammatory phrases you should avoid at all costs (where you see one denominational label, substitute any of them):

"Orthodox Jews always . . ."

"Reconstructionist Jews never . . ."

"It's because of Reform Jews that . . ."

"That makes no sense."

"You can't prove that."

"It wasn't God who said that, just a bunch of rabbis."

"If you claim that you are Orthodox, then why do you . . ."

Here's what you may do that gets you into trouble: You want your spouse to start doing something (keeping the Sabbath); stop doing something (praying at a synagogue you don't like); support your position (we should tithe 10 percent of our money because it is commanded); or generally admit that he or she is wrong, and that you are right.

Likening to a lawyer making a case before the jury, you bring out the big guns and attack the denomination itself. Instead of telling your spouse that his or her individual theology or choices for personal practice don't suit you, you try to strengthen your argument by pointing out why his or her entire denominational theology is senseless and wrong. Perhaps, you think, if you argue your case vehemently or wisely enough, your spouse will stop clinging to a foolish point of view and agree to do what you want.

This approach to conflict resolution *never* works. What you create is the opposite of what you intend—your spouse will passionately defend his or her position. Suddenly the two of you are like two lawyers in court arguing the merits or faults of "Conservative Judaism" versus "Reform Judaism," instead of figuring out how to create a meaningful Sabbath together. Besides the fact that this approach won't lead to solutions, it will also leave you feeling hopeless about ever achieving harmony. You'll become focused on the differences, and you'll miss your common ground.

One Sunday afternoon, Stephen and I visited friends who practice a quiet Judaism, attending High Holiday services and sending their oldest child to Hebrew school at the local synagogue, but little other observance throughout the year. We saw no Judaica art or ritual objects displayed on the walls or shelves, whereas in our home objects of Judaica are in every corner of the house.

Until this point, Stephen and I had engaged in many heated discussions about Reform Judaism. I would defend it and Stephen would attack it, expressing his concern about the lack of observancy in most Reform Jewish homes. We got nowhere but frustrated with our debates. Stephen didn't feel his concerns were heard, and I didn't believe that his stereotypes were fair or valid.

In the car on the way back from our friends' home, I said to Stephen: "I understood today your judgment about Reform Judaism. I see what it feels like to visit a home where Judaism is not a pervasive presence. I can see where you'd be concerned about the level of Jewish observance that will still be present in this family in one or two more generations."

Stephen's response surprised me. He said, "I don't have anything against Reform Judaism per se. It's the lack of observance of Jewish rituals and traditions that troubles me. I have more respect for an observant Reform Jew than a High Holiday Jew who calls himself Orthodox."

This conversation was a breakthrough for us after six years of fruitless debate. We stopped using the labels "Reform" and "Orthodox" in our discussions, since doing so emotionally charged the conversation and artificially separated us. When Stephen attacked Reform Judaism, I felt compelled to defend myself and all of Reform Judaism. When I refused to acknowledge Stephen's concerns, he thought that I wasn't troubled, as he was, by the increase in intermarriage and the decline in observance of Jewish tradition. I am! We aren't as far apart as it seemed when we got trapped in labels.

TRY THIS!: ASK FOR WHAT YOU WANT

When a particular practice or ritual associated with one of the denominations disturbs you, steer the conversation to what you want rather than attacking the denomination. Show respect for your spouse's theological beliefs rather than denigrating them.

Here's an example of an ineffective approach that attacks denominational theology:

Brad: I want to kasher our kitchen.

Susan: I'm not going to deal with separate pots and pans just because some rabbis hundreds of years ago said we've got to separate milk and meat. That's ridiculous!

Brad: Reform Jews think anything that is inconvenient is ridiculous.

Susan: That's not true! Reform Jews don't believe in doing something that has no point. You haven't given me a good reason why we should go through all the trouble.

Now Susan and Brad are caught up in an argument about Reform Judaism, rather than resolving their private conflict about whether or not to kasher their kitchen.

Now an example of an effective approach that respects denominational theology:

Brad: I would like us to consider kashering the kitchen. As an observant Jew, I am very uncomfortable living in a home without a kosher kitchen. Since you don't believe that we are commanded to do it, would you be willing to explore how keeping a kosher home could benefit us as a couple and family?

Susan: You're right—I don't believe that the Torah obliges us to keep kosher, but I'm willing to see if there are other reasons to kasher our kitchen that would make sense for us. Like you, I also feel badly that several of our friends and family are unwilling to eat in our home because it isn't kosher.

DON'T TRY TO BE YOUR SPOUSE'S RABBI OR THERAPIST

What accompanies an attitude of denominational superiority is often the dangerous approach of trying to psychoanalyze your spouse's religious issues or offer advice that is better left for his or her rabbi to provide. People choose a religious path to support deep psychological needs. Rabbi Manis Friedman, author of *Doesn't Anyone Ever Blush Anymore?*, warns of the danger of overstepping marital boundaries:

Men and women do not forego the right to private space just because they are married. We all have the right to a place where we can draw our curtain and say, "No further." Anyone who enters this space, even our spouse, is an intruder.

Some people get a real thrill out of tearing people's masks off. A wife, for example, may realize that her husband has a very strong defense mechanism. He doesn't open up and allow her to come in. She can't live with the fact that he won't share his most intimate thoughts, so she says, "That's not healthy; I'll help you tear it down."

He protests: "I don't want to tear it down. I need you to leave it alone." But instead of respecting his boundaries, she tears down his curtain, and she tears down the marriage at the same time.

Explaining to a spouse how "his or her religiosity is just a psychological crutch to manage stress in a chaotic world" is an assault on their belief system and that which orders their life.

Here's another reason not to step out of bounds when you perceive your spouse is spiritually off track. It may be a projection of your own failings and insecurities.

Andrew Heinze, Director of the Swig Judaic Studies Program at the University of San Francisco, recalls tension in his marriage when he was a ba'al teshuva and learning about observance: "When I was less secure of my own observance, I was crankier with my wife when she wasn't doing things right. I didn't have the feeling of inner certainty, so I was more moody, irritable, and sanctimonious about what I was doing. It was a big show on the outside because I was actually afraid of outside judgment.

There may be one God, but there are an infinite number of ways of relating to him. When a truth your spouse holds seems false to you, remember that your truths are not THE truths, they are your truths.

Don't try to be your spouse's spiritual leader. You are not responsible for your spouse's morality. Religious beliefs and behavior serve a vital purpose to help us stay sane; don't be so quick to tear down your spouse's belief systems just to prove a point or to minimize the perceived differences between you. If you don't agree with your spouse's view of the universe, you can still value what your partner's beliefs do for him or her.

Principle Two: Address Your Mate's Concerns and Understand His or Her Perspective

Fight the tendency to invalidate or ignore your spouse's concerns and objections when you make a request of your spouse. When you believe that you hold the *right* point of view, it is very difficult to see the situation from your spouse's perspective. Continuing the example we've been exploring, maybe Brad can't fathom Susan's resistance to giving up pork, or Susan will never really "get" why Brad cares so much about a kosher kitchen. However, developing such empathy and compassion is essential to making compromises and decisions that stem from loving and respecting one another.

When your spouse holds a perspective that differs from yours, and you want to retort, "That's stupid," or "That makes no sense," or "Let me show you why you are wrong," replace that self-centered response with "Tell me more about why you feel that way," or "I don't share that perspective, but I can see why you would feel that way, given what you believe about God and Torah." You can validate your spouse's experience even when you don't share it.

If you are puzzled by your spouse's behavior or resistance to something you are suggesting, it is often because you are looking at his or her behavior through the lens of your theology. Through those glasses that behavior looks nonsensical, but view the choice through your spouse's eyes and then you will understand. Once you understand why your spouse feels a certain way, you can choose to be compassionate or accepting, rather than judgmental.

For example, if Brad wants a kosher home because he believes that God commanded him to do so, Susan will see his rigidity in a more compassionate light if she reframes it: "I appreciate Brad's concern with fulfilling what he believes he is commanded by God to do; I like being married to someone who takes God seriously."

Notice, Susan didn't have to join him in his belief to experience empathy. Contrast that thought with this disdainful one that comes from looking at Brad through Susan's belief system: "I don't know how Brad could believe that God commands us not to mix meat and milk. You won't find that anywhere in the Torah. Why does he believe this *mishegas*? How does "don't boil a kid in its mother's milk" make it wrong to eat a cheeseburger?"

Let's look at how Brad and Susan might respond to Susan's resistance to kashering the kitchen. Susan loves pepperoni pizza and Chinese food, and she doesn't want to give up those comfort foods in her home. In the following two examples, watch what happens when Brad isn't willing to address her concern, and how it becomes resolved when he is.

Susan: If we kasher the kitchen, I still want to be able to eat pepperoni pizza and Chinese food at home on Saturday nights like we usually do.

Brad: Are you so addicted to junk food that you would be unable to give it up for something as important as kashering the kitchen? I thought you had more self-discipline than that!

Susan: Excuse me, when did you become Mr. Rabbi? You are forgetting that I don't happen to think that kashering the kitchen is important at all! I'm not the one who ate an entire container of chocolate ice cream the other night, so who are you to attack me for not being disciplined enough? Take a look in the mirror!

Brad missed the boat by not honoring Susan's objection and agreeing to see if there was a way to address it. Instead, by insulting her, he pushed them further away from a solution. Now Susan feels compelled to insult him in return, and the war begins.

Now the effective approach:

Susan: If we kasher the kitchen, I still want to be able to eat pepperoni pizza and Chinese food at home on Saturday nights like we usually do.

Brad: I know how much you enjoy those foods. If we kasher our kitchen, you can still bring treyf food in and just use paper plates. As long as the pizza doesn't touch anything kosher in the kitchen, we're still kosher. I don't think I'll join you, since I don't want to eat treyf food anymore. But it's okay with me if you do.

Susan: Chances are, if you won't join me, I'll just eat those foods outside of the house. But I appreciate knowing that I have the freedom to eat them in the house if I choose to.

Principle Three: Make Sure That Any Solution Addresses the Real Underlying Issues

Many significant decisions in marriage are made without complete communication regarding the issues at hand. Couples are too busy to schedule adequate time to discuss important concerns in depth. They either rush to solve problems prematurely, which results in unsatisfactory solutions that don't stick, or they stalemate and can't reach agreement at all. The root cause of both of these problems is the same thing: not understanding what each individual really wants and needs.

Often, the source of the problem in communicating begins with your own confusion. You may insist on something you want, but not really know why it's important to you and be unable to articulate anything more to your spouse than, "I've always done it this way," or "This is how my mother always did it!" Or you may express a fear, "I want you to join me in my refusal to allow our daughter to date a non-Jew because I am afraid that dating non-Jews will lead to marrying a Christian," but may be unable to identify the true basis of your fear ("My grandchildren will not be raised Jewish, and then I will have failed in my responsibility to pass along our tradition").

If you aren't clear about your own feelings when you try to influence your spouse's behavior, your arguments will sound flat. Your spouse will easily be able to poke holes in your logic, and the solutions you reach together may not satisfy your concerns. It is essential that both of you be clear about the real problem you are trying to solve.

Let's imagine that Brad's true reason for wanting a kosher kitchen is not really a sense of obligation toward God, but rather a loyalty toward his parents and grandparents who keep kosher and a desire to create a home where his extended family can eat comfortably. If he's not honest with himself or Susan, he'll try to argue the merits of following God's commandment to keep kosher, when really he should be helping Susan understand how important it is to him to make his family feel welcome in their home.

Susan and Brad can debate for days and weeks about whether it makes sense to observe mitzvot because they are commanded or if observing certain commandments should be a voluntary choice. That debate will never resolve the central issue, addressing Brad's concerns about his family. If they decide to kasher their kitchen, the solution won't be a valid one unless it's kosher enough to meet the standards of Brad's family.

This principle is also the secret to unlocking a stalemate. Often you and your mate are stuck, not because there isn't a creative solution that would work, but because you are arguing only at the surface level of the problem.

Mira Kirshenbaum offers this wise counsel in her book:

> You have to be able to get beyond that stage where the two of you simply say Yes! No! Yes! No! Yes! No! Okay, forget it! And that means you have to be able to talk until you identify what your partner's real concerns are and brainstorm ways of meeting those concerns. You have to crawl inside of what they're saying to get at the kernel that's really important. So ask, "What's your real concern here?"

When you and your partner frequently negotiate agreements to conflict that don't stick, take a look at the solutions you arrived at. If they are not solving the real problem, it only makes sense that they won't last over time.

If your agreements aren't working, it's also possible that you are making them in haste, without giving the discussion the time warranted. Many couples only deal with important concerns in their relationship when an event triggers a crisis or demands a resolution. They don't spend enough time regularly discussing points of conflict in a calm manner. Then they despair because it seems as if they are always arguing. You can't respond calmly and with creativity and humor when kids are tugging on your leg, or you are tired and cranky, or you have one foot out the door and less than three minutes to resolve the issue at hand.

Treat your marriage as if you are working partners in charge of running a complex and demanding business. Schedule a business meeting to have an uninterrupted discussion. Save important decisions and emotionally charged concerns for these meetings rather than bringing them up when the urge hits you. It is hard to wait, but if you get a negative reaction from your spouse by confronting the issue at the wrong time, you've only sabotaged yourself.

One final thought on complaints: Research has shown that to have a contented feeling about our marriages, we need to experience five times as many positive interactions as negative ones. Express your gratitude for what your spouse does and for who he or she is, far more often than you express your complaints.

Principle Four: Find Your Own Reasons for Observing Jewish Practice That Your Spouse Favors

Your spouse will try to convince you to observe a Jewish practice for the reasons that make sense to him or her. Those motivations may never be yours.

Find your own meaning in Jewish rituals, even those that initially strike you as odd, unnecessary, or inconvenient. If you don't do this, then whenever you are angry with your spouse you'll want to abdicate the practice. Fights with Stephen that leave me angry sometimes fuel daydreams about cooking beef stroganoff in our kosher pots and chowing down on fried clams in our kitchen. Luckily for Stephen, I have never acted out these fantasies! But there have been many times when I prepared a meal for the family when Stephen and I were out of sorts, and I resented making it kosher style. That's because in the early years, I saw no point to a kosher kitchen and I was doing it strictly for Stephen.

I realized that we would have a kosher kitchen for many years to come, and that I needed to find my own reasons for keeping kosher so that I wouldn't resent the practice every time he and I weren't getting along. My warning to you is this: It took me a few years before I started seeing its merits, and even now, sometimes I still waiver on my conviction. The other night, Sarah was cuddling up with me watching television when she saw a commercial for a fast food cheeseburger. She said, "Mommy, that's not kosher!" Watching her connect for just a moment with her Jewish identity was heartwarming and one of the reasons I have become more open to keeping kosher.

It's fine to start out a new Jewish ritual with your sole reason being that you love your spouse and are willing to do it because it is important to your partner. That is a noble, kind, good place to start. But don't stop there. Remember Susan, our reluctant kosher Jew? Perhaps Susan will come to appreciate keeping kosher because:

"It makes me eat less meat. Kosher meat is so expensive that I tend to make vegetarian meals more often now."

"It gives me an easy way to tell the kids that they can't eat something I don't want them to have. When I tell them it's not kosher, they just say, "Okay, Mom," instead of begging. It cuts out a lot of whining."

"I'm getting brownie points from my mother-in-law."

"I can invite some kosher friends of ours over for dinner."

You won't find any of these reasons for keeping kosher discussed in the Torah or Rabbinic commentaries. But Torah is more concerned with action than motivation. If Susan finds a positive benefit to keeping a kosher kitchen, and her reasons differ from those of her spouse or those by our Sages, that's fine if it helps her accommodate her husband without resentment.

Principle Five: Replace Complaints and Attacks With Requests

Many individuals see themselves as fair, cooperative people trying to deal with unreasonable or mistaken partners. They think of their own complaints as an effort to "right a wrong."
—Dr. Robert Schwebel, Who's on Top, Who's on Bottom

You know you are in trouble when you are trying to work out a conflict and your sentences are peppered with the word "you" instead of "I." For example, imagine that Susan and Brad set up the kosher kitchen with allowance made for Susan to eat treyf food on paper plates. On occasion, she slips up. Here's how she responded to this kind of attack:

Brad: Damn it, Susan. You promised not to treyf our dishes with your Chinese food. You are so thoughtless. I can't stand being the kosher cop around here. When are you going to stop being so careless?

Susan: What's the big deal? So a little bit of pork got onto one of our forks. The dishwasher will wash it away. Why do you have to be so compulsive about all this stuff? You are becoming so rigid; it's hard to live with you.

Nothing is accomplished by Susan and Brad flinging negative judgments at one another. Brad's request for change is completely lost because he didn't express it as such. Look at the difference in Susan's response when Brad replaces complaining with making a specific request for change.

Brad: We agreed that you'd be able to bring treyf food into our home as long as you didn't use any of our utensils. When you accidentally treyf our kitchen, I realize that you don't think it's a big deal, but I'm feeling really frustrated by this. I'd appreciate it if you'd use paper plates and plastic utensils when you eat Chinese food in the house, as you promised. Are you still willing to do that?

Susan: I'm sorry. I realize that keeping the kitchen kosher is important to you. Old habits are hard to break and I keep forgetting about it. Maybe we should put up a reminder sign in the kitchen until I get better at it. We can take the sign down when we have visitors. I'm still committed to keeping the kitchen kosher. I just slip up once in awhile. Please forgive me.

Or Susan could say: "You are right. I have been careless about using the right utensils. Maybe I shouldn't bring treyf into the house until I get used to the kosher rules. Thanks for being patient with me."

When your spouse complains about something you have done or not done, defending yourself will only extend the fight. Try saying "I'm sorry" instead. If your apology feels insincere because you really don't believe you've done anything wrong, you can still say, "I'm sorry that this upsets you so much," or "I'm sorry that what I've done is so distressing to you."

Here's a hint for married men in particular. If you notice that your wife has a very difficult time making a request instead of venting her frustration, you may be experiencing what research shows about women: They need to vent, and they aren't always looking for a solution to their problems. Often, they only want you to listen without interruption or judgment. They will arrive at their own solution after getting the complaint out of their system.

If you are unsure what to do when your wife is complaining and not making any particular requests, ask her: "Do you want me to listen, or would you like me to offer a solution?" If you are venting to your husband and you don't want him to solve the problem, tell him, "I just want you to listen. I'm not looking for you to solve this one." Remember that most men hear a complaint as a call to action.

Principle Six: Pick Your Battles and Identify Your "10s"

You may have ardent feelings about davening in an Orthodox synagogue with a mechitzah, moderate feelings about your spouse and children eating nonkosher food outside of the house, and negotiable feelings about walking to synagogue on Shabbat. Or if you are the less observant one, you may have strong feelings about *not* davening in a synagogue, moderate feelings about fasting on Yom Kippur, and negotiable feelings about whether or not to observe the minor Jewish holidays.

If you approach your spouse as if every request is an absolute need, a "10," when in fact some requests are negotiable preferences, you will elicit more resistance than is necessary. Also, if you make every Jewish decision, major and minor, a forum for working out conflict, the process will grow tiresome and you'll become discouraged. The fighting can escalate or the opposite may occur: you both decide it's not worth the fights anymore, and apathy takes over.

Choose your battles wisely and be selective in your demands. In many Orthodox marriages, keeping kosher, observing the Sabbath, and observing the laws of family purity are requirements discussed before even agreeing to the marriage. My husband required of me a kosher home when we married (a 10 in his book), but if he had demanded that I attend the Orthodox shul, that would have been problematic. Since it is a preference for him that I attend synagogue with him (about a 3), but not a need, he has learned to live without it.

If you are negotiating something with your spouse, ask a simple question: "On a scale of 1 to 10, what number is this one for you?" Sometimes, the one with the strongest feelings will get his or her way, but this strategy only works if he or she doesn't label everything a 10! At other times, if you are both working with 9s and 10s, a compromise is required to satisfy both of you, or perhaps you'll trade off, granting one person's wish on this 10 if the other gets his or her desires met with another 10. For example, Susan and Brad worked out their differences by meeting Brad's 10 (a kosher kitchen) and Susan's 10 (the freedom to eat what she wants at home, as long as it's on nonkosher dishware).

Principle Seven: Treat Your Spouse With Kindness and Respect

My Torah obligation is to love and respect my wife. The Rambam does not state, "You are free from this obligation if your wife is disorganized and procrastinates."

—Rabbi Zelig Pliskin, *Marriage*

As complex as human beings are, some aspects of relating well are really quite simple. Instead of treating our mates with the respect, kindness, and consideration that will inspire them to be more loving, generous, and flexible, most of us do just the opposite. We criticize, belittle, neglect to express appreciation, and then wonder why our spouses are so darn uncooperative. We know better, yet we have such a hard time doing better. Why? Because we react out of frustration and anger rather than take the higher road and treat our spouse as we would an honored guest in our home.

The key to this principle breaks down into four specific recommendations. We'll see how Brad and Susan can put them into action.

SAY "THANK YOU" OFTEN

Brad: I appreciate the effort you are making on my behalf. I know it's a pain for you to have to think about separate dishes and buying only kosher food since you still think that keeping kosher is rather silly.

Susan: I appreciate you going easy on me when I make a mistake in the kitchen. Thanks for not making a big deal about mixed up utensils and accidentally mixing meat and milk together. That makes me feel more relaxed about it.

Often, you'll say thank you in the beginning of a new arrangement, and then once it becomes routine, the gratitude disappears. Keep it coming; no one likes to feel taken for granted.

DON'T EXPECT TOO MUCH, TOO FAST

Success breeds success. If you ask for too much change too quickly from your spouse, it will blow up in your face. He or she will either refuse to do anything at all or will be easily discouraged when he or she is uncomfortable with a new behavior or ritual. Be patient and allow your spouse to join you gradually.

Brad could demand from the beginning that Susan not bring treyf food into their kosher kitchen, even on paper plates. However, if Susan is very resistant, she will likely rebel against the entire notion of a kosher kitchen when she is pushed too far too quickly. Over time, she may choose to bring treyf into the kitchen less frequently, especially if she finds her own meaning in keeping kosher. Allowing Susan to gradually ease into a kosher kitchen increases the likelihood that Susan and Brad won't turn the kosher kitchen into a power struggle.

It is especially difficult for a ba'al teshuva (a Jew who returns to Orthodox practice or becomes observant for the first time) to slow down and make the transition a positive one for his or her spouse. When these individuals wake up in the middle of their lives and repent for a previous lack of observance, it is common for them to do two things that are not conducive to positive marital relations. First, they focus on the negatives ("No more driving to synagogue"; "We can't have sex twelve days out of the month"; "You can't turn on the lights anymore on Shabbat"; etc.), and as new students trying to get it right and make up for lost time they focus on the minutiae of halakhic practice. They want it all, overnight, and they want their spouses to join them, or at the least, not get in their way.

An Orthodox rabbi who preferred anonymity told me: "A ba'al teshuva tends to be less tolerant and more rigid than his rabbi. I give him permission to take baby steps. He must slow down for the people around him, and it's also better for him to take it slower."

Rabbi Shaya Sackett offers this advice to help the ba'al teshuva shift from impatience to acceptance of a spouse who doesn't join him or her in observance: "When you are feeling judgmental toward your less observant spouse, remember for how long you didn't understand the obligations. You will be better able to introduce observance by accepting where your spouse is and teaching by your example than by turning him or her off by being judgmental."

ENGAGE IN LOVING ACTIVITIES THAT NURTURE YOUR RELATIONSHIP

Weathering the storms of daily life is hard on a marriage, even the best of marriages. The pressures of work, kids, paying the bills, health concerns, sleep deprivation, and other distractions disrupt the love in your relationship and makes it more difficult to work out Jewish conflicts. To ease your struggles, strengthen the love and affection in your marriage. When love is flowing, any kind of conflict will be easier to resolve.

Think about the daily and weekly rituals that solidify and nurture your relationship. These activities may be Jewish in nature (making love on Friday nights, studying Torah together), or they may be secular (going for a walk in the morning or going to the movies). When you are going through rough times in your marriage, you will likely neglect these rituals. That's when you need them the most.

Rabbi Stephen Carr Ruben, Rabbi of Kehillat Israel, the largest Reconstructionist synagogue in the country, states: "In any marriage, what each individual wants most of all is that they are the most important thing in their partner's life, that they are a priority, that they are listened to. Prove to me that I'm the one. Help me to feel valued and appreciated by you."

Your spouse may not know how to do that for you unless you tell him or her how. I told my husband not to bother giving me roses on Valentine's Day because it wasn't that meaningful to me, but flowers during the year—just because he loves me—go over much better. If he didn't know that, he might buy me roses on Valentine's Day just because he thinks it's expected.

Have you told your spouse lately how you like to be loved?

REMEMBER YOUR WEDDING VOWS

Do you remember the words you vowed to your spouse on your wedding day? The sacred promises you made when you were most in love are not lost to you—you may retrieve them at any time, and you should. Assuming you meant every word you said then, your declarations of love and commitment are needed more as your marriage progresses than they were on your wedding day.

Stephen and I wrote our own wedding vows, which I share with you here. We have recited this pledge to each other every Sabbath since our wedding six years ago. We have spoken these words when we were in love, when we were so frustrated with each other the words seemed empty, when the vows seemed impossible to achieve, when we were so tired we could hardly remember the words, when the kids interrupted us every minute and a half, and when we needed to say them the most—at critical moments in our married life. We also hired a calligrapher to transform our written vows to a piece of art, and then mounted it on our bedroom wall.

I will respond to you with honesty, integrity, and consciousness, taking full responsibility for my own *mishegas*, and giving you responsibility for yours.

I will, whenever possible, choose love over fear, patience over impatience, compassion over judgment, openness over rigidity, letting go over control, and optimism over doubt.

I will summon the courage and strength I need to manage whatever life brings our way.

I will take care of myself physically, emotionally, and spiritually, so that I have the resources to take care of you and our family.

I will honor our commitment to absolute fidelity.

I will communicate to you directly when I am troubled, distanced, hurt, or angered by anything you have said or done (unless doing so would not be productive).

I will work to resolve any conflicts arising between us without threatening the foundation of our marriage.

I will strive toward tolerance and acceptance of our differences, with the hope of coming to celebrate them.

I will respect you as my teacher, and be willing to learn from you as my partner and friend.

I will join with you to establish a loving home for our children, guided by Jewish values and traditions.

Dust off your wedding vows, memorize them, and develop a ritual of reciting them to one another on a regular basis.

Wedding vows are a roadmap for how to treat one another, even when you don't feel like it. Your wedding vows can remind you of your commitment to one another and your highest intentions for your intimate relationship.

PART II

Working Out Your Differences

6

Synagogue

Commitment involves making the choice to give up some choices.

—Scott Stanley, Ph.D, *The Heart of Commitment*

FOR SOME JEWS, synagogue involvement is an anchor in their lives, as vital to their sense of well-being as eating properly or exercising regularly. They could skip it for a short while, but they would soon feel out of balance and unhealthy. For those who attend regularly, it is often not just the prayer experience that invites them every week but the belonging to a community of regular synagogue-goers who become like family. When regular congregants don't show up for a period of time, the community misses them.

"High Holiday Jews" are given this label because they attend synagogue twice a year, on Rosh Hashana and Yom Kippur. Occasionally you'll find them attending the life-cycle event of a friend or family member. For them, synagogue attendance is a necessary obligation at the holiest times of the year, or a place to go only to participate in a family celebration.

In a mixed Jewish marriage, a partner who has lapsed in synagogue observance commonly increases attendance after marrying a more active partner. Jon Levine, a Reform Jew from Chicago, describes himself as a "dormant Jew" before marrying his wife, Leslie. He was attracted to her dedication to raising children with knowledge and understanding of the tradition. He says, "It would be easier to be two-days-a-year Jews, but that's not good for the kids. Leslie keeps me from being selfish about it."

Then there are plenty of Jews who see no reason to join a synagogue at all. Some are childless and not in need of a place to prepare their children for bar mitzvah. Some prefer to pray in less traditional settings, like a chavurah. Some are agnostic or atheist Jews who do not wish to pray to God at all. Some are turned off by the cost of joining a synagogue. Also, some Jews do not feel a strong need to affiliate with a Jewish community. They may return to the synagogue of their parents for High Holiday services, out of respect for their parents, but feel no need to be a part of a Jewish community where they live.

All of these choices are legitimate ones. The difficulty arises when the choice you would make as an individual conflicts with the preference of your spouse. Then, some family decisions must be made regarding which synagogue to join, if any. Let's look at how to work out your differences if one or both of you wants to be active in synagogue life to some extent.

Determining What You Want in a Synagogue

Choosing the right synagogue is a little like buying a family car but with a more limited range of possibilities. Most communities only have a few models to choose from, in a few denominational colors. You purchase a vehicle that you believe will suit your family's needs more than another purchase. If it's a station wagon, Dad might not get the sporty car he wishes. If it's a small car with good gas mileage, the family might not be moving lumber in it. You can't buy one car to please every member; you have to compromise.

Likewise, it's possible that no synagogue will ever please every family member all of the time. Some synagogues excel in children's education and youth groups, others in community outreach. Some have stimulating worship services with an inspirational rabbi. Others have a great adult education program and a scholarly rabbi who puts congregants to sleep during sermons.

Then factor in denominational differences: the presence of a mechitzah, the length of services, how much is in Hebrew, whether they have regular Torah study or regular Saturday morning services, the *siddur* that is used, and so on.

Consider the personality and decorum of the synagogue. Is it a welcoming place? Do they require formal dress or are jeans and sweaters acceptable? Who is singing the music in services: a choir, a cantor, or the congregation? Are bar mitzvah celebrations lavish affairs or simple kiddush lunches? Will your child be "tripled" with two other children for his or her bar or bat mitzvah ceremony because the synagogue is overflowing with children? If so, is that a problem for you or do you see that as an advantage? Cantor Renee Coleson speaks to prospective new members every day:

> We have six hundred kids in our Hebrew school. One prospective member commented: "It's so impersonal to have triple bar mitzvah ceremonies." I said to her: "But those kids continue forever in this synagogue. Every kid, all six hundred of them, is known by me and the rabbi, triples or not. We are the warmest congregation I've ever encountered."

Do you like the rabbi and cantor? Are there alternative minyans to worship with outside of the general service? Is it a learned community, a wealthy one, one committed to social action, one that welcomes lesbian and gay individuals and couples? What percentage are intermarried, and how is a non-Jewish spouse or a Jew by choice treated?

Are there chavurot—groups of families and individuals who socialize outside of synagogue? Do you see plenty of young families with children running around throughout the service or mostly adults and older congregants who are perturbed if their concentration is interrupted by children's cries? Are young children welcomed in general services, only in "tot" services, or expected to be left home with baby-sitters? Do you ever see teenagers older than thirteen? Depending on the ages of your children, or absence of them, you may prefer an atmosphere with lots of toddler and youth involvement or quieter one.

What are the *oneg* and *kiddush* following the services like: a simple spread of bread and wine, or a mouthwatering catered affair that will entice a family member or two to come to services just for the food? Are congregants expected to contribute to the oneg?

Consider the cost of membership. Are dues negotiable? Do they have a building fund or other expenses in addition to membership dues? Is financial aid available?

When you and your spouse select a synagogue, consider all of these factors rather than simply choosing "the right denomination." Each spouse will have a unique scorecard based on his or her particular standards.

For example, my husband davened at a Conservative synagogue all of his life, and he could easily daven at the Conservative synagogue in Lancaster, which he does on occasion. But he chooses to daven every week at the Orthodox synagogue because he likes to take our toddlers with him. They love to sit on his lap or, when they get bored in services, eat snacks and play with other children in a classroom supervised by a babysitter. The Conservative synagogue does not allow food in the sanctuary nor does it provide babysitting during Sabbath services. Stephen also prefers to pray with the Orthodox siddur rather than the one used in Conservative services.

Another reason Stephen chose the Orthodox shul has little to do with denomination, and a lot to do with the rabbi and rebitzen, Shaya and Buci Sackett. Since we moved to town, they have treated us like family, inviting us to their home for Passover seders, Sabbath meals, and celebrations in the Sukkah, and coming to our home armed with chicken soup and kosher chicken after I gave birth or when I had the flu and was unable to care for my family. In the first year of our arrival in Lancaster, Buci called me on a regular basis, just to see how we were managing. She and the rabbi express no judgment about my lack of observance in certain regards. Although the Orthodox shul is not one I would normally be associated with, it has been a very welcoming place for our mixed Jewish family.

If you live in a town with more than one synagogue, visit all of the synagogues, attend one or two Shabbat services, and meet the rabbi, his or her spouse, and some of the congregants before making your decision. If you are Orthodox and require a mechitzah to pray, and there is only one Orthodox synagogue in town, you won't have a choice. But in some locations with several synagogues, even the Orthodox synagogues vary in style and custom. Don't assume that you know what a particular synagogue will be like without seeing for yourself.

You Can't Agree on the Same Synagogue

Sometimes you get lucky: You and your spouse are raised in the same denomination and when you are synagogue shopping, there isn't really any discussion about which synagogue to join. You are Conservative or Reform or whatever, and so you will both join the synagogue of that denomination that is close by. Other times, you are going to join the synagogue that has been in one of your families for many generations, even though it might not be perfect for both of you. Again, it doesn't occur to you to make any other choice.

Others of you have a greater challenge to deal with, one that my husband and I have confronted. You may not be able to agree on one synagogue, and so, if you live in an area that gives you Jewish choices, you may become a dual synagogue family.

BELONGING TO MORE THAN ONE SYNAGOGUE OR CHAVURAH

Stephen and I are full members of the Orthodox synagogue, but we support the Reform and Conservative synagogues with partial dues. It is difficult financially to manage full membership in more than one synagogue, but you can pledge enough money to be considered affiliated members in more than one synagogue. Or if you have the means, you can be full members in two different synagogues. For some families the best way to reconcile different preferences for synagogue worship is to worship separately. As an observant Jewish couple noted:

My wife prefers to daven behind a mechitzah, and I prefer a more egalitarian observant community. Since we met she has belonged to an Orthodox shul, and I daven with an observant, egalitarian minyan. On Shabbat, we invite members of our different communities back to the apartment for lunch; this gives us an opportunity to come together.

Other Jewish families join a synagogue to please one member, but also become active in a synagogue-affiliated or nonaffiliated chavurah.

A chavurah is a gathering of Jewish individuals and families who pray and study together and celebrate holidays as a group. Some chavurot are organized within the synagogue, and many stand alone, unaffiliated with any synagogue and attractive to those who find synagogue worship unappealing or unavailable. Chavurot members meet in each other's homes or in central public meeting places. Many have a theme: "families with young children" or "older couples with no kids," for example; others are mixed. Some involve Jewish leaders and educators and others are entirely lay led. Some use a traditional siddur and others write and assemble their own liturgy. Each has its own style, just as synagogues do.

For mixed Jewish couples, chavurot offer an opportunity to either supplement existing synagogue involvement or assemble with a group of other serious and dedicated Jews who also aren't attracted to synagogue worship. It is a wonderful way to establish long-term friendships and extended family and Jewish community. In some areas of the country, chavurot have been in existence for years and members have been through life-cycle events from bris to bar mitzvah to wedding and funeral. You can learn about chavurot opportunities in your area through your synagogue or through the national Chavurah Committee in Philadelphia, Pennsylvania (see recommended resources).

CHOOSING TO RELOCATE

We are not surprised when a family relocates for a new job opportunity, but if someone says, "We don't like our Jewish community so we are moving to be part of another Jewish community we like better," some people view that decision as a bit strange, unless they are part of an observant community where these choices are commonplace. Many Jews are accustomed to thinking of synagogue as something to join once moving into a community, rather than intentionally moving into a synagogue community or following a rabbi who appeals to them.

Thanks to the Jewish renewal movement, a handful of rabbis who have left pulpit jobs to become full-time Torah teachers, and a few dynamite synagogues popping up that are worth moving for, this trend is changing. If you don't like your Jewish choices in town, it might make sense to move. This issue arises particularly in families where one spouse becomes committed to greater observance for him- or herself and the children, and is not satisfied with the schools or synagogues in the area. Stephen and I, both committed to Jewish day school for our three children, have to deal with the fact that the Jewish day school in Lancaster does not continue beyond the fourth grade. We are seriously contemplating relocation over the next five years to a community with private Jewish education for the children as they grow up.

Fortunately, Stephen and I are on the same page with this issue. However, if one spouse doesn't share the desire or willingness to move, this conflict can create enormous turmoil for a family.

Janice has been "campaigning," as her husband, Dr. Warren Morganstein, calls it, to move out of their current non-Orthodox community in Baltimore, Maryland, to one that would allow her to walk to shul and keep kosher more easily outside of the home. Since this would result in commuting longer and leaving a neighborhood he enjoys, Warren has little incentive to move. Janice is a smart marketer. She knows that some aspects of their current Jewish community aren't satisfying to Warren, so the door is open a crack. She speaks to him about facets of the Orthodox community that he can appreciate rather than trying to convince him to become observant Orthodox. For example: When a woman in the community was struck with a terminal disease, the entire community pitched in to care for her five kids and take her to the hospital for treatments. In contrast, Janice reminds him that when their daughter cut her chin and had to see a surgeon, Janice was unable to find another mother to take their son home from school.

In some situations, choice of location is essential to allow a spouse to continue his or her level of practice. Rabbi Ian Silverman, from Congregation Beth El in Lancaster, Pennsylvania, has prepared his wife, Beth, for the fact that they will have to move when the temple's planned relocation to a bigger building across town is completed. As a Conservative rabbi, Ian could give up his commitment to walk to shul, but Ian states:

Not driving on Sabbath is a line drawn in the sand for me. It's from the kishkas. I don't care about the weather; I'll only drive if I am deathly sick. I've driven once in the past four and a half years. It is a spiritual practice for me: I am saying to Hashem that he is more important to me than my convenience.

CHOOSING TO LIVE WITH LIMITED CHOICES

We call ourselves a "Reformadox" synagogue. We are the only temple in town, with thirteen paying families and twenty singles. We have a cantor once a month and no rabbi. Our members are Orthodox, Conservative, and Reform. There are only three or four people in the synagogue who can read the Torah. We had to allow women to make a minyan because we can never get ten men. Since we're such a small group, everyone gossips about everyone. We always wonder how we are surviving.

—Anne Goergen, Temple B'nai Israel, Allegheny, New York

One of you may be less than thrilled with the synagogue choices available to you, but since your mate is perfectly happy with it, you will simply learn to live with it, and maybe even make the best of it. Perhaps your husband is the fifth generation of a family to belong to a particular synagogue and, until his parents pass away, you wouldn't dream of joining a different synagogue or moving away.

Robin and Steve Silverman from Grand Forks, North Dakota, belong to what Robin affectionately refers to as "the little shul on the prairie." The one hundred members on the books include a lot of out-of-towners. They are lucky to get fifty people to High Holiday services. Steve was raised in this synagogue, and his family, who owns a family business in town, is a pillar of the community. Robin reflects: "Steve's parents would have disowned me if I had gone to another synagogue." The only choice Robin gave herself was how involved in the synagogue she would become. She decided to become as active as possible, eventually becoming synagogue president.

Sometimes the one of you who is less than thrilled with the available synagogue choice in town will come to see its advantages over time. In small-town synagogues, members wear many hats, learn more (because they are forced to), and become like a big family. If you don't show up to make a minyan, you are missed. The downside is that one shul cannot possibly be all things to all people. Observant congregants will kvetch if the service becomes too abbreviated, and the less observant will complain if the service gets too long, and so on. Someone is always unhappy. But is that any different from a larger synagogue or from being in any family?

Members of a small synagogue learn that all Jews benefit from understanding. They don't expect the synagogue to meet all of their Jewish needs. If they are more observant than the synagogue, they study at Jewish retreats, take adult education courses, read books, connect with other Jews on the Internet, and join Jewish community organizations outside of the synagogue. If they are less educated than the chosen synagogue, they work to beef up their spotty education.

A Jewish man I interviewed comes from an assimilated midwestern Jewish family who belonged to an enormous Reform synagogue with a church-like organ and choir. He was extremely uncomfortable in the Conservative synagogue he joined with his wife:

> I couldn't participate; I felt inadequate; people could tell that I didn't know what I was doing. I didn't want to go, but my wife felt strongly about having her family with her. I shared her desire to belong to a Jewish community and she explained to me that for us to be accepted among the "regulars" in this synagogue, we would need to attend Sabbath services as a family.

This man handled the difficulty by studying on his own until he became educated enough to feel like an equal member of the community.

When One of You Goes to Synagogue and the Other Does Not

You don't have to do everything together. I don't feel the need to go with my wife, Phyllis, for a mammogram, but I support her in doing it.

—Peter Sheras, *Dream Sharing*

There are active, serious Jews who never attend synagogue worship at all—even on the High Holidays. They may not live close enough to a synagogue that is suitable or perhaps their spouse davens at a synagogue that is unsatisfactory to them and they don't want to go alone to another shul. Or they may still be active in supporting Jewish practices in the family, but synagogue worship is not their thing. Dr. Michael Stern, a Brookfield, Connecticut, resident states:

> My wife provided logistical support driving our children to Hebrew school, but when I went to synagogue with our kids, she stayed home. She was raised in a secular home with no religious education. I am sad that she can't enjoy something so meaningful to me, but I don't judge her for it.

Before I met Stephen, I attended synagogue every Shabbat, at Congregation Beth El in Sudbury, Massachusetts. This unusual Reform synagogue, headed by Rabbi Larry Kushner and Cantor Laurel Zar-Kessler, is unlike any other I have ever experienced, and it spoiled me. The congregation is participatory, spiritual, musical, learned, and for me, the perfect mix of observant, new age, and fun. I seldom skipped the stimulating Shabbos morning Torah study, followed by a service that was half song, which we chanted with great enthusiasm while sitting in circular formation looking at each other rather than at the back of each other's heads. It was a great loss for me when we moved to Lancaster and I could no longer attend this unusual synagogue. In Lancaster, my husband attends the Orthodox synagogue every week, and I generally stay home.

Here are some recommendations if you regularly attend synagogue without your spouse.

Don't criticize your spouse for electing not to go. You may be disappointed if your spouse doesn't want to go to High Holiday services with you, but leave righteous indignation out of the conversation. Remember, what works for you may not be satisfying for your spouse; you are not your mate's rabbi or spiritual director.

Make it an enjoyable experience for yourself. Without the distraction of an unhappy spouse, you can fully enjoy the worship and communal experience. When you fulfill yourself in the manner you need, you bring that joy and serenity back to your family and your work.

Ira and Ruth Rifkin of Annapolis, Maryland, are a two-synagogue family. They daven together two Shabbos's a month and separately the other two. Their young son joined an Orthodox synagogue after attending an Orthodox Hebrew day school. They join him at his Shabbos services once a month. Ira davens regularly at a Conservative shul and Ruth joins him there once a month. Ruth prefers davening at home, where she meditates and studies Torah. They come together for chicken soup at lunch time and then spend the rest of the day together. They have a sense of a shared Jewish path as a family, even when davening alone.

An observant Jewish man I spoke with is married to a woman who is devoted to ceramics. She spends her time enjoying her craft while he is in synagogue, and he believes that their marriage benefits from each being enriched by their own individual pleasures.

Some synagogues attach no stigma to worshiping without your family. Rabbi Darryl Crystal of the Reform North Shore Synagogue in Syosset, New York, reports: "We have couples who pay for a single membership because their spouses aren't interested. Lots of folks come alone to services and sit around with friends having coffee and cake for an hour afterward. It's the equivalent of their night out, like playing cards."

Act like a "we" even if your spouse and family aren't with you. Glenn and Marlene Usdin live in Lancaster, Pennsylvania, where Marlene is an active member of the Reform synagogue, and Glenn is more of a High Holiday attender. Marlene sometimes resents Glenn's absence from synagogue, so one day she decided to "send" him a message. She made a contribution to the temple in her name only. Glenn was livid when he saw it in print. He raged: "I'm the one that generated the money. Where is my name? From this day forward, any contributions will be made in the name of Mr. and Mrs. Usdin!"

If you are angry that your mate and family aren't with you, share your feelings with close friends but not the community at large. Complaining to other synagogue worshipers about your family's absence makes it awkward for them when and if they do show up.

Speak about your family so that the community comes to know your loved ones through conversation. You never know when you might achieve the breakthrough you'd hoped for—a family member joins you at temple. It will make your family feel much more welcome if other members of the community greet them warmly, with some knowledge of their existence and recent life events. "Hey, I heard you just got a new job. How is it going?" is a good icebreaker to bring your spouse into conversation with others he or she doesn't know well.

Connect your spouse to your synagogue community however you can. If you are frequently spending time praying at synagogue without your spouse, he or she may not develop the same connection to the community as you will. Look for ways to bring your spouse into the community outside of synagogue services, such as community social events or Saturday afternoon lunch dates with other couples from temple.

Pray at home. Synagogue is not the only place where you and your family can pray together. You may start the day by saying the morning blessings together or singing Modeh ani. You can tuck the children into bed at night with a bedtime shema. You can pray before and after meals with blessings over your food or recite a blessing when you see a rainbow. You don't need to go to synagogue with your spouse to be able to pray together.

When One of You Goes to Synagogue Reluctantly

> Synagogue gave me the same grinding stomachache I used to get as a kid when my mother dragged me to symphony concerts because they were "good" for me. Synagogue was a potential dose of spiritual castor oil.
>
> —Lee Meyerhoff Hendler, *The Year Mom Got Religion*

The case of a family going to synagogue together, all delighted to be there, is a rare event indeed. If you decide to join your spouse at synagogue, even though it's not your place of choice or your favorite way to spend time, here are some recommendations:

Don't denigrate your spouse's love of synagogue. So you can't fathom what your spouse sees in this dreadfully boring experience. Keep your disdain to yourself and put a smile on your face while you are there. It hurts your spouse to have to defend his or her love for shul and prayer. Worrying about your discomfort disrupts your spouse's prayer experience.

Dennis Fischman of Sommerville, Massachusetts, struck a deal with his wife, Rona, when he regularly attended synagogue on Sabbath and she didn't want to be there. He would stop trying to convince her to change her point of view on God and Judaism if she would stop "running down the things that are important to him."

Go simply because it's important to the person you love. You can try to find your own spiritual meaning in synagogue, or you can go just because someone you love wants you to be there to share his or her joy. Rabbi Alan Ullman tells this story: "Our nine year old, Noah, fell in love with hockey. I now watch hockey games, rollerblade, and play hockey. I see what he likes about it. Noah's love of hockey is holy—it's an expression of who he is in the deepest sense—so I honor it with my participation."

> **Ask not what my marriage can do for me, but what can I do for my marriage?**
>
> —Hillel Zeitlan, psychotherapist, Baltimore, Maryland

Find a motivation other than prayer to go to synagogue. If synagogue doesn't create the ideal worship atmosphere for you, stop asking it to. Go for other reasons: to be with your family; to become a part of a Jewish community (the Hebrew word for synagogue, *bet ha-knesset* does not mean house of *worship* but rather house of *assembly*); to hear a good sermon; to introduce the experience to your children at a young age; and so on. If you release synagogue from an expectation that might never be met for you (for example, to give you a powerful spiritual experience), and view it as a place where Jews gather for a few hours, you'll be a lot happier there. Rabbi David Wolpe writes in his book, *Teaching Your Children About God:*

> An old Jewish joke tells of two men walking together to synagogue when they were approached by a third man. He looked at one of the worshipers and said, "Why are you going to synagogue? You don't believe in God! I understand why your friend Schwartz here is going—he is a religious man. But you? Why would you waste your time?" To which the man answered, "Schwartz goes to synagogue to talk to God. I go to synagogue to talk to Schwartz!"

Take separate cars. So your mate loves being in synagogue from the time the doors open until the lights are turned off, while for you even an hour is too long. Separate cars gives you the freedom to come late or leave early, so that synagogue becomes more bearable for you. Some spouses come only for the sermon and kiddush or for Torah study before services, but then leave before services begin. Some families are caring for young children with the attention span of a gnat, so one spouse is the designated davener and the other has primary responsibility to watch the children. This gentleman shared:

> I only want to go to synagogue to hear the rabbi's talk, but my wife wants to go early and stay for the whole thing. I recently formed a study group with a few men who feel the same way I do. We study Torah together during the service, then go listen to the rabbi, and then go home.

Be willing to be bored some of the time. Some Jews thoroughly enjoy themselves in synagogue and find group prayer, connecting with the congregation, and the personal prayers in the service to be uplifting and spiritually energizing. Many Jews feel that the structure of the synagogue service and seating prevents them from having a spiritual experience. If that is true for you, then attend for the other reasons mentioned, or consider this:

Whoever said synagogue is supposed to be entertaining anyway? Liturgical prayer is a spiritual practice; all spiritual practices have boredom. Mt. Sinai moments might happen for regular synagogue-goers from time to time, but even those who show up every week have their moments of fidgeting when they wish they were somewhere else. They show up every week anyway and are available for the high points when they do occur. Most of us don't quiet down long enough to experience a spiritual moment if it were to happen.

As a society, we have lost the willingness to go to synagogue to pray as an altruistic or obligatory act—because we are commanded to do so, because our community needs us, because God wants us to pray, because it is the right thing to do as a Jew. We are addicted to pleasure and meaningfulness in all of our activities.

Actually, Jewish tradition urges us to pray not for our own comfort but for growth and for the well-being of others. A spiritual experience may *not* necessarily come from reciting prescribed prayers in a mechanical, lifeless way; it *may* come from battling the overwhelming urge to run out of synagogue after the first twenty minutes, or from confronting how difficult it is to sit still and do nothing productive or entertaining for one or two hours a week.

If you find the existing siddur too male, anthropomorphic, or formulaic for you, and you want to avert boredom in the service, try what Mark Kramer of Philadelphia did when he accompanied his wife, Jackie, to Orthodox services on the High Holidays. Mark got the rabbi's permission to read a Jewish book, *When Bad Things Happen To Good People,* by Rabbi Harold Kushner, during the service. The rabbi assured him that the most important thing was that he was studying and learning.

Learn the service and get to know some congregants. Occasional synagogue-goers get into a vicious cycle: They go so rarely that they don't know the service, and then because they can't engage in the service in a meaningful way, weeks or months pass before they want to return. Because most of the congregants remain strangers to them, they don't feel connected to the community either. Read a book that explains the service, take a short class, or learn some basic Hebrew to become more familiar with the service to give it greater meaning for you. You can also insert personal prayers in such places as the Amidah, the central part of the liturgy. Even if you don't attend regularly, go often enough so that you become friendly with some of the congregants and you aren't walking into a room full of strangers each time.

Convincing Your Spouse to Go to Synagogue With You

My wife, Shari, isn't the kind of woman you work on. You present something to her and she decides if she'll participate.

> You don't say to her, "This is the right way and you should
> do it," you say, "This is meaningful to me, and I can show
> you how this can be meaningful to you."
>
> —Shep Rosenman, Los Angeles, California

For some individuals, sharing the synagogue worship experience
with their spouse is vital to the intimacy of marriage and devotion
to Jewish practice. Their hearts ache when the spouse won't go.
You can preach all you want to these Jews about a spiritual journey being a solitary one, but for these same individuals, a profound loneliness pervades their soul when they go to synagogue
alone. Synagogue worship is viewed by many outside of Orthodox
circles as a couple and family experience. Whereas Orthodox
communities physically separate men and women in the worship
service, in other denominations it is more unusual for men and
women to attend synagogue alone.

Here are some recommendations as to how you might convince
your spouse to join you in synagogue.

Attract with honey. Make yourself more loveable, kind, generous, and sweet, and make sure your spouse correlates that meta-
morphosis with your involvement in synagogue. Your spouse will
be intrigued by what is making such a positive difference in your
life.

Conversely, if your involvement in synagogue *doesn't* make you
a more attractive person, and your spouse is already reluctant to
join you, your synagogue marketing campaign will flop.

Barter something meaningful for synagogue attendance. One
woman I spoke with has an oral agreement with her husband.
He'll go with her to synagogue on Friday nights if they make love
when they get home. Another man offered to help his wife clean
the house on Sundays if she would come to synagogue with him
on Saturdays. Still another man, who despises shopping, agreed to
go shopping with his wife on Saturday afternoons if she goes to
synagogue with him beforehand.

Daniel Karapkin, an Orthodox rabbi in Allentown, Pennsylvania, expresses concern about bartering synagogue:

It is unhealthy when religious choices are framed as part of a reward and punishment program. It places Jewish observance in the marketplace. These different options—shopping or shul—should not be equivalent. Instead, the partner should say: "I am going shopping with you, not because shopping is equivalent to synagogue, but because you wish to go shopping, and I love you, so I support your choice."

It may appear blasphemous to trade synagogue for sex, shopping, or a cleaner house, but the only reason some Jews are willing to go to synagogue is to please their spouse and to receive something in return. What if a trade for sex is not explicitly spoken, but a husband notices that whenever he goes to synagogue with his wife, she's grateful and affectionate, which usually results in lovemaking? Wouldn't that be a good reason to accompany her?

Although bartering can be effective, Rabbi Jonathan Girard, family therapist and Reform rabbi in Easton, Pennsylvania, offers this caution:

> Never say, for example, "You aren't going to get sex unless you come to temple with me." That crosses the line of appropriate and effective behavior. You may wish to barter synagogue attendance, but don't use blackmail.

Find the right motivation for your spouse. Don't lecture your spouse about the importance of synagogue observance if he or she doesn't believe it matters—you are wasting your time. Instead, find the motivation that is meaningful to him or her, as this woman, did:

> When my son was ten, it was time for him to start Hebrew school. My husband refused to join a synagogue. He thought that it was too costly. I hired my son the most expensive tutor I could find and I gave my husband the bill. He quickly realized that it would save him a lot of money to cooperate, and so we joined the synagogue.

In this case, the husband was motivated by his desire to minimize expense. He would never have responded to her philosophical arguments about the vital importance of synagogue involvement. She knew how to motivate him to the action she desired by demonstrating to him that her desire to join synagogue would be less costly than the alternative.

In another case, the husband knew that his wife was strongly committed to social action causes. Although she had little need or desire to pray in synagogue, she supported the community work that synagogue committees were involved in. He didn't try to convince her to come to synagogue to pray. He spoke to her about how she could achieve many of her social action goals by becoming active in the synagogue's social action programs.

Don't make it all or nothing. Instead of pushing your spouse to join you regularly, encourage him or her to attend synagogue with you on selective occasions that are the most meaningful to you or when the service is most likely to be enjoyable for your mate. For example, one couple only attends synagogue together one night a year—to listen to the *kol nidre* service, because both enjoy the music. Another couple attends together on *yahrzeit* anniversaries for their parents and grandparents.

Your spouse may fear, "If I encourage your involvement, I'll be left out if I don't join you. But I'm not sure I want to join you." Back off from trying to convince your spouse to join you and allow it to happen slowly on his or her own terms. If you aren't patient, your spouse will likely put the brakes on and do less than he or she might have been willing to do without the pressure.

Start small—in time your spouse may start to attend more often.

Ask someone else to invite your spouse to synagogue. Sometimes your request to attend synagogue will not be well received because you are in a power struggle with your spouse: He or she stubbornly refuses to go, in defiance of you. In the worst cases, a spouse *can't* attend because it would appear as if he or she was "losing" the battle over observance issues. Often, if the rabbi or another congregant encourages your spouse to come, he or she will be more receptive. Perhaps there is a simple job in the synagogue that needs to be done that will make your spouse feel needed and welcomed. Or maybe just a personal invitation by the rabbi or rebbetzin will prompt your spouse to join you.

Don't guilt your spouse into coming. Avoid statements such as: "It would kill your father if he saw you refusing to go to temple," or "Because of you, I don't go to synagogue anymore." Take responsibility for your own observance. Never blame your spouse for not observing a Jewish practice. That's a cop-out. The only place where that accusation legitimately belongs is if a woman chooses not to go to mikvah, and her observant husband is therefore unable to observe the laws of family purity the way they are written. No other Jewish practices require your spouse's participation.

Marlene Usdin of Lancaster, Pennsylvania, noticed that the more she pushed her husband, Glenn, the more he rebelled by not going. She changed her strategy. Now she hands him an invitation to an event and says, "I'm going. If you'd like to attend, tell me and I'll RSVP for you." He goes more often now that she's not trying to push him into attending.

Sometimes, no matter what you do, you will be unable to persuade your spouse to join you in synagogue. Respect your spouse's prerogative to make his or her own choice. Your spouse has a legitimate right to not attend synagogue, even if it is something meaningful to you.

Address your loneliness in other ways. Get to know members of the community. Find a friend to talk to, keep a journal, or talk to your spouse about the experience when you come home. Study regularly with a Jewish peer who also has an inactive spouse. When your spouse can't or won't participate with you, reach out to other friends and family to help you feel less lonely in synagogue.

Convincing Your Spouse to Allow You to Go to Synagogue

"What do you mean, *allow* me to go to synagogue? I'm an adult, and no one gives me permission to go to synagogue!" This may be true in theory, but it's not that simple when you are part of a family.

Synagogue takes time. It makes you unavailable to drive the kids to soccer practice or to spend leisure time with your family. They may want you to participate in all the secular activities that were once a regular part of your routine before you got serious about prayer. Although you may feel righteous about doing things that are holier than family activities, watch out! That kind of attitude will alienate your spouse and children. Two Jewish women on different sides of the fence share their perspective:

Lee M. Hendler, who became a committed synagogue attender later in her marriage, remembers:

> When I started to go to services, the boys had to babysit for the girls on Saturday mornings. Then when I started to attend the Shabbat afternoon study group, it meant that my husband Nelson had to do more chauffeuring. For 19 years, he had been a free agent when it came to domestic responsibilities. Now I was changing the rules.
>
> When I extended the Shabbat afternoon study group commitment to staying for *mincha* (afternoon) and *ma'ariv* (evening) services, Nelson got downright irritated. "Isn't that enough davening for one day? When is enough enough, Lee?"

A woman who is married to a recent *ba'al teshuvah* is indignant:

> We used to go regularly to the theater on Friday nights. Now my husband will only go to shul on Friday nights. He and others say, 'You can go to theater any night, it doesn't have to be Friday nights.' The message is: 'What I am doing with my Friday nights is holier than what you want to do with yours.' I resent that accusation. I enjoyed going to the theater on Friday nights with my husband and I don't think there was anything wrong or unholy about it.

Here are some recommendations to ease tensions when you are trying to convince a spouse to support your synagogue involvement:

Respect your spouse's limits and don't overdo it. Carl Choper, the Reconstructionist rabbi for Temple Beth Shalom, in Mechanicsburg, Pennsylvania, describes a common problem for synagogues that are run by volunteers:

> There is a lot of work involved in running the synagogue—even our Hebrew school teachers are volunteers. Inevitably, there comes a time when an involved spouse says, 'I can't be there because I have to do something that my partner is interested in to save our marriage.' So, on a Sunday morning, when we are having an educational event, that family might be at a football game.

Pick and choose carefully what you commit to and ask your spouse what the limit is before he or she starts resenting your involvement. Hire a babysitter instead of depending on your spouse. If you have been working many hours on a synagogue project, take a break to reconnect with your family before committing to something new.

Show your spouse how your involvement serves you as a couple, and not just making you unavailable.

> I was president of the temple for two years and on the board for 14 years. My wife resented the amount of time it took and saw it as just meetings. Then I spoke to her about the religious connotations for me of this kind of service and how it was important for my spiritual and personal growth. When she saw what it was doing for me, and therefore for us as a couple, she became more supportive.
>
> —Dr. Peter Sheras, Charlottesville, Virginia

Does your synagogue involvement make you a better person, spouse, and parent? If not, your spouse has good reason to resent your absence.

Find a suitable way for your spouse to get involved. If your spouse is intimidated or turned off by worship or adult study, find other ways for him or her to become part of a Jewish community. A husband may not know a word of Hebrew, but his accounting skills would be an enormous asset to the finance committee. A wife may be an atheist, but she can still have fun helping with social action or community holiday celebrations.

Don't present synagogue as only a place of worship or Jewish learning; relate to it instead as a Jewish community to which you both would like to belong. If your spouse is made to feel like a member of the community, he or she will be less resistant toward your involvement.

Should You Force Your Children to Attend Synagogue?

You may have to work out not only tensions when one of you wants to go to synagogue and the other does not but also differences of opinion about what to do with the children.

Couples I interviewed are divided on whether or not children should be forced to attend synagogue if they don't want to. One gentleman was concerned about "inflicting Judaism" on his children. He didn't want to force his kids to suffer in synagogue as he had to as a child. He preferred to encourage his children to attend and let them pick and choose activities that would be fun, so that their Jewish experiences would all be positive. His wife felt much differently. As an observant Jew, she felt it was her obligation to provide their children with a Hebrew education. She viewed it the same as insisting that they go to math class, whether they are in the mood or not.

Another gentleman brought his two daughters to alternate Shabbat services until they left for college, telling them the following:

> I am asking you to do something with me for three hours every other week. I expect you to do it because I'm your father and I have asked. I believe the tradition will give you a peaceful, contented, uplifting way to live. It is my gift to you as your father.

He is delighted that his grown daughters are now choosing, on their own, to attend worship services at college.

Many couples cut deals with their teenagers regarding synagogue attendance that are not much different than the deals they make to get them to do other chores around the house or to study hard and get good grades in school. They give them something they want—say, a ride to the mall—in exchange for their going to services a certain number of times a month. The most effective strategy is to enroll them in active Jewish youth groups and summer camps that propel them to want to participate in order to have an enjoyable experience with friends. Of course, there are also teenagers who genuinely enjoy going to services.

Managing a recalcitrant teenager is more difficult when one spouse is not interested in going to synagogue. If one parent stays home, it becomes very difficult for the other spouse to insist that the children go. The parents must decide what their position will be and both must support it. Don't allow the kids to play one parent off the other. Never undermine one parent's position in front of the children. If one of you has made a legitimate decision to stay home, but the other wants the children to attend, you can say, "When you are an adult you can make the decision for yourself whether to stay home like "Daddy" does. For now, we both want you to have the experience of going to synagogue." To make this work, the one who is staying home must encourage the children to attend and support the parent who is pushing the children to go.

The easiest solution is to introduce children to synagogue when they are very young, so that they grow to love attending. Many synagogues have *Tot Shabbot* programs on Friday nights and Saturday mornings, and some congregations offer children's services on High Holidays.

Rabbi James Gibson of Temple Sinai in Pittsburgh, Pennsylvania says: "The parents may pretend they are going to Tot Shabbot for the child, but they really enjoy it. They don't feel competent with the siddur. It helps them master the songs and feel more comfortable in the service."

Synagogue isn't the only place for Jewish community, prayer, and study. Now we move on to how to reconcile differences in opinion regarding adult Jewish study, Jewish day school, and summer camp.

7

Adult Study, Day School, and Jewish Summer Camp

Formal prayer is one way to God, but hardly the only way. More important than the specific framework of prayer is that we pray. One can pray at any place, and at any time, if the prayer arises from the heart.

—Rabbi David Wolpe, *Teaching Your Children About God*

Adult Jewish Study Can Change Your Life— And Your Marriage

THE TALMUD STATES that Jewish study is more important than action, because study leads to proper action. Many Jews stop studying at the age of 13, and then some life event propels them into adult study of Judaica. Others, such as Jews by choice or Jews returning to the faith, begin study as adults.

Rabbi Alan Ullman, recognizing the need in the Jewish community for adult learning, quit his pulpit job to start the School for Jewish Studies in Worcester, Massachusetts, in 1988. I was his first student. I met Alan when he gave a talk about Adam and Eve to a Jewish singles group, just as he was about to open the school. I didn't even know what the Torah was and had never celebrated becoming a bat mitzvah or received any Jewish education. I wasn't just hungry for Jewish learning; I was famished.

I studied Torah with Rabbi Ullman for several hours a week, for several years. I credit those studies with directing me toward an observant Jewish life. Once he opened the door for me, my curiosity was insatiable, and I have been an active, serious Jew ever since. I strongly encourage adult Jewish learning for all Jews, regardless of their background. You cannot fathom the depth and richness of our tradition until you have studied with a rabbi or teacher who helps you glimpse the gift of Torah through a new lens. Even secular and cultural Jews who have no strong need for spiritual studies can benefit from learning about our tradition— and about themselves.

When an individual's soul is awakened and the spouse's does not awaken at the same time and in the same way, the original "rules" of the marriage need to be renegotiated. "You want me to do what! Kasher the kitchen and go to mikvah?" The deeper one spouse moves into study and Jewish exploration, the more threatened and angry the other spouse may become if the experience is not shared. One gentleman shared his resentment with his wife:

> It seems like you are more in love with your rabbi than with me. You spend more time sharing your intimate thoughts with him than me. It feels like you are having an affair with him, even though I know you aren't having sex.

If your husband is jealous of your cherished relationship with a rabbi or any other Jewish educator, don't attack him for being a crazy fool—he will interpret your emotional response as evidence that he is on to something. Instead, introduce your husband to your rabbi or teacher and help one get to know the other. Second, take measures to increase the affection in your marriage. If your relationship with the rabbi develops at the same time you are pulling away from your husband, he will naturally correlate the two events. Third, do your best to convince your spouse to join you for a class. (This dynamic, still rare between male students and female rabbis, is increasingly common when a Jewish woman spends hours a week studying with a charismatic male rabbi.)

When you become more learned than your spouse on Jewish texts and come home from class bubbling over about what you've learned, your spouse may feel intimidated and left out.

Amy Gorin of Wellesley, Massachusetts, started studying intensively with two rabbis. Her husband, Norman, felt her being swept away from him. When she enrolled in an intensive two-year adult learning program, Norman joined her. At first she felt that he was encroaching on her space, but she was soon glad he was there. Norman relates:

> Amy was connecting with other people in a way she couldn't connect with me. I was afraid that she would go down a path of Orthodox behavior and practice that I couldn't live with. Marriage is based on shared values. What would we do? She would say to me, 'You are critical but you don't understand what you are criticizing.' Intellectual, controlling rationalist that I am, I said, 'You're right—I need to increase my knowledge.' Now we actually have arguments that are Talmudic!

Judy Meltzer is the director of the Stulman Center for Adult Learning at Chizuk Amuno congregation in Baltimore. Chizuk is highly regarded for having perhaps the most comprehensive adult Jewish learning program of any synagogue in the United States.

When Judy sees one spouse in a couple moving much faster than the other spouse and tensions rising, she advises: "Be patient and try to contain some of your exuberance. Maybe your spouse is enamored with sports cars, but do you want to hear about it all the time? Bring him or her to one session of your class to hear firsthand what you are learning. Read a Jewish book together. Dispense your medicine one pill at a time instead of trying to give out ten pills at once."

Recognize the truth in your spouse's concerns. If Jewish learning has consumed you and caused you to be obsessed with learning more, at the expense of spending time with your spouse and children, you may be becoming more learned, but you are not becoming a better Jew. Commitments to marriage and family are central in any serious Jew's life. When you start seeing your family as an obstacle to your growth, instead of a part of it, you are using them as an excuse for your abdicating your spiritual growth.

On a positive note, your spouse may start studying only because you requested it but then finds his or her own benefits from the process. Betsy Katz is the North American director of the Florence Melton School, a two–year school offered in locations around the country in which adults can gain a foundation in Jewish studies. They encourage couples to take the program together by offering a couples discount. Betsy notes, "When you are dealing with couples and family, it is very important that they experience it together. When one takes the lead, the other may follow, and then the path is smoother and more pleasurable for both."

Studying Torah and other Jewish texts with your spouse can be an extremely intimate experience that greatly enhances the depth and commitment of your marriage. You will learn not only about Judaism, but also about your spouse. In the pace of modern life, how often do we take a few hours a week to engage in discussion with our spouse about what is meaningful to us?

Jewish Day School and Summer Camp

THE PROS AND CONS

Of all the experiences you can give a child, Jewish summer camp and Jewish day school is reported by rabbis, Jewish educators, and parents to have the strongest influence on the development of a child's positive Jewish identity. Children experience Judaism as fun and come to integrate Judaism as a central theme in their lives rather than as something they do a few times a year. Commitments to these activities take a lot of money and agreement between the parents, which isn't always easy to achieve. In areas where public schools are weak, and private school is considered a necessity, the money obstacle is less significant. When the choice is between a private Jewish school and a strong, well-respected public school, money is a big deal.

The argument against Jewish camps and day schools goes something like this: "I don't want my kids to receive a narrow education that won't allow them to be active participants in a pluralistic society. Being in Jewish schools or Jewish camps won't give them a realistic idea of what it is like to live in mainstream America. They'll be brainwashed to become more observant than I think is necessary in modern times."

Other parents are often intimidated by the prospect of children becoming more learned about Judaism than they are. No parent wants to feel dumb around their child. Sometimes parents increase their own learning; other times they restrict their children's learning.

Rabbi David Wolpe of Los Angeles, California, a strong advocate of Jewish day schools, tells concerned parents the following:

> Graduates of Jewish day schools are doctors, lawyers, business men, sports columnists, and music critics. They know who they are. Without roots, you don't get branches. Don't worry—America will intrude through music and malls. Jewish day school gives the child the ability to make an educated, informed decision.

Parents who had positive Jewish school experiences often advocate strongly for the same for their children. Parents who had negative experiences want to steer their children away from having "the same miserable experience I did." Parents who had an enjoyable public school experience and believe they achieved a strong Jewish identity through other means often fight passionately against Jewish day school education for their children.

When the Answer Is Pro, Which School or Camp?

For some families, the argument isn't pro or con for Jewish day school or summer camp, but rather, which one? Perhaps Dad wants to send the girls to an all-girl Orthodox high school, but Mom prefers a progressive Orthodox mixed school. Some communities have Reform, Conservative, Orthodox, and Hasidic day school options (day school, yeshiva, or *cheder*), some with better Hebrew education and others with better secular education. Some meet eleven months out of the year and hold classes on Sundays. Jewish summer camps all differ on levels of observance as well.

Judy Lederman and her husband are both yeshiva graduates. However, he gave up on most things Jewish and she's been the sole person pushing *frumkeit* in their marriage. Her children are experiencing great conflict in public school as they are torn between two worlds:

> Jason goes from being a black-hat yeshiva-type kid with his Orthodox Jewish friends to being anti-Jewish with his public school ones. My middle child was totally embarrassed in public school when he threw up on his shirt one day and the school nurse "caught him" wearing tzitzit under his shirt. He refuses to wear a kippah in the car because he is too embarrassed to be seen with it. This breaks my heart.
>
> The latest incident happened on Purim. We went to hear the Megillah reading in Monsey and all the kids were in costume. As we crossed over to our side of the bridge, they peeled off their costumes, afraid that their public school friends might glimpse them.

So, how do you and your spouse decide which school or camp, will work for your family? Here are some guidelines:

Determine your budget for Jewish commitments. Being serious about Judaism costs money—lots of it. Synagogue membership, bar mitzvah celebrations, adult study programs, Jewish summer camp, yeshiva, kosher food, *tzedakah* (charity), and so much more, are major line items in the family budget. Some religions may consider money to be the root of all evil, but poverty is not esteemed in Jewish life. Jews are encouraged to tithe (donate) ten percent of their earnings to charity.

Do you and your spouse view Jewish expenses as essential or discretionary? If both of you are fighting constantly about money for Jewish activities, you probably differ on your answer to this question.

You may wish you could send your kids to Jewish summer camp and Jewish day school, but may not be able to afford to do both. You may make a choice to spend your money on summer camp and forego synagogue membership. You might skip summer camp and Jewish day school and choose a synagogue with an active Hebrew school.

Accommodate each other's decision-making styles. If one of you pushes off decisions until the last minute after doing a lot of research, and the other prefers to come to a conclusion quickly by using intuition, you'll have a hard time making important financial decisions together. Move too quickly and the more conservative, detailed one will feel pushed into a decision prematurely and then will not be fully on board. Go too slowly and the intuitive one will resent the other for dragging the process down with what feels like unnecessary caution.

Construct a process that honors such differences in decision-making style, moving slower than one would like, and faster than the other prefers. Agree on a deadline you both can live with. For example, if the deadline for Jewish summer camp enrollment is April 1st, it may drive one spouse batty if she is worried about getting her child accepted, and her husband is still dragging his feet on March 30th because he needs to do more research. If they agree that a check and an enrollment form will be mailed before April 1st, she can relax and allow him his research process.

Communicate about what values motivate you. If you don't know why you want to spend money on something, you'll have a hard time convincing your spouse. If one of you is a proponent of Jewish day schools and the other is not, it is insufficient to insist that Jewish learning is important when you are looking at writing a check for ten grand to a Jewish day school. You need to be clear about *why* it is important, and how a Jewish day school, in your opinion, supports that value.

If one spouse refuses to consider Jewish day school, request Jewish summer camp as a compromise, or vice versa. If both Jewish day school and Jewish camp are too much, here's a way to compromise. Agree to baseball camp, as long as the child attends Jewish day school during the year; or Jewish summer camp if the child will attend public school.

Check out all the Jewish day school and summer camp options. Suspend your denominational stereotypes—you may be surprised that even though you consider yourself Reform Jews, the Conservative summer camp seems like the best choice. Or, even though you are active in an Orthodox community, as a compromise for a resistant child, you might select a Conservative day school. Visit the schools and speak with parents, teachers, and rabbis before enrolling your child. Give your child a vote!

Experiment! You don't have to commit to Jewish day school for your child's entire school career. Try it for one school year and see if it is a positive experience for your child. Or agree to do it for the earlier period of the child's life (like ages five to ten) with the plan to switch to public school after that. If you can't agree this year, agree to reconsider the choices the following year. This principle can be applied to just about any Jewish practice. Try it—you might like it. And if you don't, you can always change your mind. Little is set in stone.

8

The Major Jewish Holidays

So much is the love for a wife assumed in Jewish society that
the Bible explicitly commands us to love God, to love our
neighbor, to love the stranger, but never once does it explicitly demand of man that he love his wife. That is because to
love God we must relate to the supernatural; to love our
neighbor requires the sometimes impossible feat of associat-
ing with a disagreeable person, and to love a stranger we
must overcome ubiquitous xenophobia. But the love of a
wife, as the love of one's homeland, is taken for granted as
natural and needing no explicit command.

—Rabbi Maurice Lamm, *The Jewish Way in Love and Marriage*

How Not to Negotiate a Jewish Holiday

HOLIDAY OBSERVANCES take on the unique personality of your
family, with an infinite number of variations on how to observe
them. Jews outside of Orthodoxy often assume that Orthodox
Jews experience little friction around holiday observance. This
isn't true. Orthodox Jews don't debate about *whether* to observe
the holiday, but they engage in plenty of heated discussion about
how to observe. Holiday negotiations and compromises take place
in every Jewish home.

While I was writing this book, Stephen and I engaged in a
"negotiation" pertaining to Purim. The flyer arrived in the mail
from the Reform synagogue advertising a gala event for Purim

this year. Members of the synagogue had put together a comical *Purimshpiel*. Pizza and *hamantashen* cost a dollar, and the event would be over before the kids' bedtime.

My family had settled into a routine around the Jewish holidays. My husband Stephen observed all of the Jewish holidays in the Orthodox synagogue, usually taking our toddlers with him. The babies had grown up in this synagogue, attending almost every Shabbos, so they were very comfortable there. It was the perfect setup for Stephen and the girls. The only problem was me. I always stayed home with Elijah, our youngest baby, not observing Jewish holidays. The Purim celebration at the Reform synagogue prompted me to ask for a change in our holiday routine.

Perhaps you have been involved in a similar negotiation. If so, then you know that doing any of the following doesn't work:

ATTACKING DENOMINATIONS

In bold type the flyer stated: "No *Megillah* Reading. You've read the book anyway." This was my idea of heaven, but offensive to my observant husband who is mortified by the notion of eliminating such a central part of the holiday celebration. If Stephen had started the discussion like he has in the past with, "I can't believe they would have a Purim celebration without a *Megillah* reading. This is just the kind of thing that makes me feel hopeless about Reform Judaism," I would have launched into my defense of Reform Judaism, and we would have quickly escalated into a no-win battle.

CRYING "IT'S NOT FAIR!"

We never go to the Reform synagogue as a family. We don't alternate, (i.e., go to the Orthodox synagogue half the time and the Reform the other half). Stephen won't attend the Reform synagogue for any Jewish holidays because of the parts they skip and I find the Orthodox service just as unappealing. We didn't launch into the following tired argument that gets us nowhere, but if we had, this is how it would have turned out:

Azriela: It's not fair that we never do anything the Reform way.

Stephen: (he can show me how my scorekeeping is wrong) We don't have a Passover seder the way I'd prefer, and we don't keep Shabbos the way I'd like either. It's not true that we're always Orthodox.

Or,

Stephen: (defending why structuring our holiday observance so that he gets his way makes sense) I can't condone attending a synagogue that skips the required Megillah reading. That's not the way we should be educating our children.

INSULTING EACH OTHER

We could stoop to insults and pushing each other's hot buttons:

Azriela: We have an opportunity for an enjoyable family experience, but you are ruining it. You are so rigid and selfish!

Stephen: If it were entirely up to you, the children wouldn't learn anything meaningful about being a Jew. How can you claim you are a serious Jew when you don't take the holidays seriously?

This approach guarantees that we won't achieve harmony!

Researching for this book has taught me a few things. Hopefully, we will refrain from any fruitless arguments, such as those above. Here are the strategies we used to reach agreement on Purim and explanations for how you can use them to negotiate your holiday choices as well.

Five Strategies to Minimize Holiday Conflicts

1. Come up with several options for each holiday. List all your alternatives and articulate the pros and cons of each choice, without making a decision. Get all your options out on the table before you start trying to agree on a solution. Here are some examples of what Stephen and I came up with for Purim this year:

- I go with the girls to the Reform synagogue, and Stephen goes to the Orthodox one with our son, Elijah. We miss being together, but we each go where we'd be most comfortable and the children all have a positive experience.

- We all go to Reform on Monday night of Purim, and Stephen goes to Orthodox on Tuesday morning to hear the Megillah reading. That way, he has fulfilled his obligation to hear the Megillah reading and we've spent a part of the holiday together.

- We go as a family to the Megillah reading at the Orthodox shul. It's just not as much fun for me and the girls will miss out on the Purimshpiel, but they do enjoy going to their familiar shul.

- This year we choose one way and plan to do it the other way next year.

- Stephen gets his way for Purim, and I get my way for Passover, or vice versa.

- We flip a coin, and whoever wins gets to choose how the family celebrates the holiday.

- We stay home and do nothing at all.

- We go as a family to the Conservative synagogue instead.

- We all attend both celebrations in the evening, splitting our time between synagogues.

In order to select the most suitable option from the list of alternatives, we followed the rest of these principles:

2. *Be willing to give up something you want, at least for this year.* Not all holiday conflicts are solvable without one person being disappointed. That's what marriage is all about—compromise.

For Stephen and I to reach a compromise, both of us had to be willing to let go of our vision of the ideal which wasn't going to happen. If we clung to that fantasy (maybe Stephen will stop caring about whether or not he hears the Megillah reading, or maybe Azriela will suddenly have the urge to hear it), we'd only end up disappointed. Rather, given our mixed marriage, we have become accustomed to one or both of us not getting exactly what he or she wants in order to achieve what we want more than any-thing—marital harmony. But, we have also employed the follow-ing strategy, which is the only way strategy two works.

3. Compare how important something is to each of you. On a scale of one to 10, Stephen rates hearing the Megillah reading on Purim at least a 9. I would actually prefer not to hear it. If I insisted on Stephen's going to the Reform service with me and therefore not hearing the Megillah reading on Purim night, I should have a reason that rates at least a 9. I preferred his being at the Purimshpiel, but his absence wasn't as big a deal for me as it would have been for him to miss the reading. So we decided that I would take the girls to the Reform synagogue and Stephen would take our son to the Orthodox shul. I missed Stephen being with us, but not enough to insist that he abandon his religious practices for us. If being together for Purim as a whole family rated a 10 for me, we would have arrived at a different solution. Compromise works best when neither has to give up something really dear.

4. Ask for something positive, rather than complaining about something negative. I asked Stephen to consider making Purim a family event and presented him the benefits of doing so. I also spoke my request in the first-person positive, rather than merely complaining: "I'd like us to spend Purim together as a family, and I'd like to find a way to give the girls the Purim experience at the Reform synogogue." I also didn't demand that Stephen change his practice, only that he be willing to look at alternatives. He was much more open to discussion with this approach.

5. Look for creative alternatives. As I was putting the girls into their car seats after enjoying the Purimshpiel with them, it sud-denly occurred to me: "It's only seven o'clock. They are just get-ting started over at Degel. I can bring them over, they can join Stephen in listening to the Megillah reading, and enjoy the ice cream party afterward." The girls joined their Dad, delighted in twirling their noisemakers at the mention of the name Haman and, of course, they loved the ice cream party too. I relieved Stephen of Elijah, who was feisty and ready to go home early.

Stephen and I didn't spend time together on this holiday, which was frustrating for me, but at least the girls got the full benefit of both synagogues and they enjoyed themselves immensely. In order to reach this solution, we had to break away from black-and-white thinking and look for a creative way to have both celebrations. Sometimes it's right in front of you, but you are so locked into narrow-minded thinking so you don't even see it.

Passover/Pesach

Most Jews celebrate Passover to some extent. Even many non-observant Jews gather together for a Passover seder with family and friends. Passover brings with it a myriad of family issues. Let's look at some of most common of these issues.

THE LENGTH OF THE SEDER

Seders (including the meal) may take from one hour to more than four hours and end in the wee hours of the morning depending upon family customs. Stephen's idea of heaven—two seders that end past midnight—is extremely difficult for me. I was raised in a family that had one seder, breezed through the Haggadah in 45 minutes or so, and got right to the meal. The importance of the holiday was the family gathering, not the telling of the story. Couples like us will likely never resolve this difference completely. Here are some possible solutions:

- Since there are two sedarim, each of you plans one seder the way you like it.

- Hold a shortened version of the seder at home on one night, and then the more observant spouse attends a full seder on the second night in another observant home.

- Make the seder two hours, instead of one, three, or longer.

- Alternate years. One of you is in charge this year and leads the seder you enjoy; the other gets to do the same next year.

- Go to extended family for seder and follow their customs.

- Make the longer seder more meaningful for the less observant spouse by introducing engaging adult discussions, creative skits, props, outside readings, inviting Jewish and non-Jewish friends, and so on.

- Prepare for the seder ahead of time with adult study so that the less observant spouse understands the significance of the tradition, making the reading from the Haggadah more meaningful.

- The more observant partner can return to the seder after the meal, while the less observant person does not. Or, the less observant partner can come in and out of the seder, tending to kids, the kitchen, or whatever.

Another way to compromise on the seder is to choose a Haggadah that will be satisfying to both of you, or use more than one. In 1999, Stephen and I hosted a seder for the first time in several years. We purchased new Haggadot that are kid-friendly, beautifully illustrated, and filled with provocative adult questions. If you are reconciling Jewish differences, shop around for an alternative Haggadah that appeals to both of you, instead of automatically using the ones given to you by your family. More editions of Haggadot exist than any other Jewish book in history.

LEADER'S AND PARTICIPANTS' ROLES

When the male father figure or the grandfather leads the seder and attendees merely read a paragraph or two from the Haggadah when it becomes their turn, it can make for a very long and boring seder for participants who aren't intrigued by the stories told in the Haggadah. To get everyone involved, do some planning ahead of time and assign guests a role in the seder. For example, a few people could make a short skit out of one of the Haggadah stories, a woman might bring a midrash on the role of women in the escape from Egypt, or even something like the following:

For the person who resists religious observance, find something that doesn't involve the religious part of the celebration. One guy who comes to our seder every year is a wine expert who would normally cower in the corner and not say a word. We asked him to choose four different wines for the seder. He got so excited when he explained the history of the wines he selected.

—Dr. Ron Wolfson, Director of the Wizen Center for the Jewish Future

Another alternative is to have the wife lead the seder. Stan Selib and Claire Boskin of Newtonville, Massachusetts got together later in life, after long first marriages for each of them. Stan says: "I always led the seder as the father, but when Claire and I got together, I discovered that she had been leading the seder at her home for years. Her seders are a gathering of her community of friends and family. She does a wonderful job teaching the story of Passover and leading fascinating discussions. I have been happy to have her lead the seder ever since we started living together."

Children are an integral part of the seder, for it is here that we tell the story of the liberation of the Jews from slavery in Egypt and transmit that history to our children. Kids participate by asking the four questions, searching for the affikomen, dipping fingers into wine and opening doors for Elijah. When children are so young that they won't sit at the table, an adult or teenager should be designated for babysitting. Don't have unreasonable expectations of very young children who aren't capable of sitting quietly at the seder table for two or more hours. Here are some ways to make the experience fun for children, and therefore, for you:

- Read children's Passover stories before Pesach.
- Help them make a little play to present at the seder.
- Use a child-friendly Haggadah.
- Award prizes for the best questions or right answers to Passover trivia questions.
- Use fun props during the seder, like ping-pong balls for the plague of hail. Give each child a brown paper bag filled with props.

- Make a tent and have the seder under it. Come dressed as Jews in Egypt. Add a new question to the four questions. Come with a knapsack full of things you would bring out of Egypt if you were there. Create a treasure hunt for the affikomen with clues.
- Have the kids hide the affikomen and the parents find it.

There are so many ways to make the seder a fun experience and still be respectful of the tradition. Don't get trapped in automatically doing it the way your family did, especially if you didn't enjoy it!

WHETHER TO BREAK WITH FAMILY-OF-ORIGIN CUSTOMS

The time may come when it is important to create your own seder instead of going to your parents or in-laws.

One observant couple I interviewed, who were both raised in Reform households, told me: "We just couldn't stand the 'get-to-the-meal-fast' seder anymore. We announced to both sides of the family that from now on, we would be holding our own seder, and they were welcome to join us. We haven't had a seder together since then. That's okay. Doing the seder the way we wanted it was more important to us than the family get-together. We invite serious Jews from our community instead."

Breaking away from family tradition can be extremely painful for all involved. It is especially difficult if only one of you wants to, while the other is still attached. Consider doing so in small steps, or doing your own seder one year, but then joining your extended family's the following year. Since the seder is often during the week and it is impossible to assemble my extended family together for the seder, we often see my family during Passover week but don't share the seder together. This allows my husband to have the kind of seder he desires and for my parents and brothers and I to enjoy getting together for the holiday and bringing all of the young cousins together. In my family, the religious part of the Passover seder was always secondary to just being together as a family.

What Food to Serve at the Seder Table

Sephardic and Ashkenazic Jews serve different kinds of food at the seder table. Rabbi Rifat Sonsino, a Sephardic Jew, remembers teaching his wife how to make haroseth the way he was accustomed to. You don't have to be from different cultural backgrounds to run into food differences—over 100 different ways to make haroseth exist, depending on family custom.

Be respectful of your spouse and include some dishes reminiscent of his or her background as well as yours at the seder table. Or serve entirely different meals at each of the two seders. Or buy a Jewish cookbook and make new seder dishes that neither of you has experienced before. Ask your in-laws how to make the dishes familiar to your spouse. If the matzoh ball soup that pleases your husband is too salty for your taste, it's a small sacrifice.

Sephardic Jews may also eat rice and corn during Passover, while Ashkenazic Jews do not. Typically, a mixed couple will go by the husband's custom or defer to the Ashkenazic's desire to avoid rice and corn.

Whether to Be Observant During the Entire Week of Passover

Growing up at home, we ate matzoh at the seder for one night, and that was the extent of our Passover observance. We were munching on bagels the next morning.

Stephen requested of me that we clean out our house of all *hametz*, use special dishes for Passover, and observe all of the Passover laws for the entire week. Because I do all of the cooking and because Stephen works long hours outside of the house and I work from home, I also ended up doing most of the Passover preparation, cleaning, and cooking.

Every year since we've married, one of our biggest fights has been during Passover, usually because my buried resentment comes spewing out toward the end of the week. Every Passover, I vow that this year I won't resist the process and be such a baby about it. I am ashamed of how addicted I am to eating what I want, when I want it, and how resentful I become about the extra work for the week. Every year it gets a bit easier.

Here are some strategies I recommend for making observance of kashrut during the entire week of Passover more palatable to a spouse who would rather not do it.

- Find an assortment of Passover recipes from cookbooks and stock up on plenty of diverse "Kosher for Passover" food that pleases your family. It's a wonderful opportunity to break from the routine of the same old meals you normally serve during the year. Be sure you purchase appealing foods for your children so that they don't kvetch the entire week.

- Get the children involved in the cleanup. They will especially enjoy the search for hametz. Some parents hide a piece of bread for the children to find. Judy Lederman's kids hide 10 pieces of bread throughout the house for the parents to find—be creative! You can also be grateful for a thorough spring cleaning.

- Agree to keep a "Kosher for Passover" home, but family members can eat what they want outside of the home. If you can't stand one more matzoh for breakfast, go to the bagel store but eat out of the house.

- Take responsibility! The more-observant spouse should do most of the work involved setting up the kitchen, unless the less-observant spouse wants to do the work to keep his or her spouse out of the kitchen.

- Welcome this opportunity for personal growth. You can use this week to confront weaknesses in your character that you would like to improve. Passover is a time to examine what you and your family are enslaved to and to make the commitment to free yourself from certain addictions in the coming year. The word seder means "order" and Passover is all about discipline. As you are scrubbing your kitchen, imagine cleansing your soul and beginning the Jewish year fresh with renewed determination to improve your character, releasing yourself from enslavement to your own personal Egypt.

- Eat out a few nights of the week. Your observant spouse can elect not to join you, or bring his or her own food. Or get together with friends and share Passover meals so you aren't cooking every meal at home.

- Thank the less-observant spouse throughout the week for accommodating. Just because it comes naturally to one doesn't mean it's easy for the other.

- Compromise with such agreements as "no bread" or "no bagels for breakfast," so that family members experience a distinction between this week and all others.

- Try to do something different each year to observe the holiday. Buy yourself a new Passover pot or kitchen utensil. This year, we treated ourselves to a new set of knives just for Passover— it made the whole week's cooking so much easier than making do with our one koshered knife.

Every year is an experiment. Ask your spouse what worked and didn't work about last year and be willing to make changes. A meaningful seder and Passover holiday doesn't just happen— you have to create it. Whatever your issues, put more effort into making it a positive experience.

Rosh Hashanah and Yom Kippur

Whereas Passover often brings positive family memories with it, many Jews remember the High Holidays as a few dreadful days a year when they were dragged to synagogue in their least comfortable clothing to sit through a boring, impossibly long service. They didn't know what the purpose of the services was, and participating did little to make them better human beings. The only good part was skipping school. High Holiday Jews who find it difficult to participate fully in the High Holidays abound, unless they responded to their childhood vacuum by studying as adults.

SYNAGOGUE: TO GO OR NOT TO GO

Many of the solutions outlined in chapter 5 regarding working out your differences in synagogue apply here, such as taking separate cars and belonging to more than one synagogue, among others. My husband spends from morning until sundown at the Orthodox synagogue for High Holidays. I wouldn't dream of asking him to compromise on the holiest days of the year. I make myself available for babysitting and clear the way for him to fully engage in the holiday, Orthodox style. I devote some time during those days to reading Jewish texts at home. In years past, I spent time writing a new ethical will on Yom Kippur, which gave me the opportunity to do some introspective work in my own style.

If you don't want to go to synagogue, don't feel you must just because your spouse and Jewish friends are going and you feel guilty if you stay home. If you choose to go, but find it difficult to engage in the service, bring your own reading material or attend for only half of the service close to the sermon. Find a chavurah that is observing the holidays in a more relaxed, informal way in someone's home. Arrange to study outside of synagogue with another Jew who feels the same way as you do about going to synagogue.

If you are the more observant one, focus on your individual spiritual journey and don't push your spouse to join you. If the children are accustomed to attending Sabbath services with you, bring them along for part of it. If they haven't been going to services all year, don't expect young children to suddenly adapt to being in synagogue with perfect manners. It's not fair to get angry with them if they haven't been "synagogue trained."

If you want to share some part of the High Holidays with your spouse, but he or she is dead set against spending it in synagogue, you might consider something like what Stan Selib and his partner, Claire Boskin, do on Yom Kippur:

> We spend the day at the beach, dressed in white, in introspection and intimate conversation. We meditate and look at times in the year when we missed the mark. We ask forgiveness and express gratitude to God and each other. We talk about our hopes for each other and the coming year.

As a family, you can do the ritual of *Tashlich*, where you symbolically throw your sins away in a body of running water. The children enjoy throwing breadcrumbs into the water, and it's a non-threatening ritual for the whole family. The High Holidays are preceded by Elul, a month of intense self-evaluation. During Elul, Jews try to make amends with others, apologizing and asking for other people's forgiveness before they ask God to forgive them for their sins. The High Holiday period is a marvelous time to apologize to your mate, children, and extended family for any harm you have caused them in the past year, and to ask for their forgiveness. The spiritual lessons of the High Holidays do not have to be experienced in synagogue.

YOM KIPPUR: TO FAST OR NOT TO FAST

I vividly remember a painful experience in my early 30s when I tried to fast on Yom Kippur for the first time in my life. I attended a chavurah service in someone's home where everyone was fasting. I was starving and miserable. I couldn't figure out what was spiritual about fasting; it only distracted me from prayer and meditation. At about 2 p.m., I gave up. I headed for the nearest convenience store where I bought a stale chicken salad sandwich, a bag of potato chips, a cupcake, and a diet soda. I stuffed everything into my mouth, hardly tasting anything, with tears streaming down my face as I hid out in my car like a fugitive, too ashamed to return to the chavurah.

I was angry at myself for not fulfilling my commitment to fast; I was furious at Judaism for asking me to fast; and I felt very ashamed and alone. That was my first and last attempt to fast on Yom Kippur. Having given birth to three children in the past four years, I have been absolved from any expectation of fasting because of pregnancy and nursing. This year is the first year in a long time I don't have a valid excuse not to fast, other than . . . I don't want to. Every year, I revisit the issue. My husband Stephen would have to be on the brink of death to eat on Yom Kippur.

I am not alone in my painful relationship with Yom Kippur fasting. I spoke to a Jewish woman who sneaks food into the synagogue's bathroom stall on Yom Kippur. She gets glaring looks from her husband when she returns to her seat with a breadcrumb or two on her chin as evidence.

If you are fasting and your spouse is not, remember not to play rabbi. Keep any judgment to yourself. Either your spouse doesn't see the point of fasting, so your lectures will fall on deaf ears. Or your spouse already feels guilty about it, so he or she doesn't need you to rub salt into the wound.

If one of you is committed to fasting and the other is not, here are some ways to reduce tension:

- The one who is committed to fasting can spend the entire day in synagogue, while the one who is not can eat at home.

- The one who has a hard time fasting for an entire day might try fasting just for the morning, eating plenty but abstaining from a favorite food. That way the discipline of sacrifice is experienced to some degree.

- The nonfasting spouse can still attend the break-the-fast community meal so that you don't separate yourself from your family and community.

Hanukkah

> In the first year of our marriage, I got ready to prepare for Christmas in our home. Growing up, even though we were Jewish, we had a Christmas tree and exchanged Christmas gifts. Our parents raised us as Americans and we celebrated Easter and Christmas with the rest of the neighborhood. My husband, Sam, was horrified and struck Christmas from our home.
>
> —Doris Engelman, Los Angeles, California

COMPETING WITH CHRISTMAS

My heart broke the first time Sarah announced, "Mommy, I don't want to be Jewish anymore because Christians get to have Santa Claus and we don't." Holiday traditions, like making latkes and playing a game of dreidel, don't have quite the same magic for some young children as all the glitz of Christmas.

Jews have differing opinions about how to handle Hanukkah. Some try to compete with Christmas and turn Hanukkah into a shopping bonanza. Others feel strongly that doing so sends the wrong message and prefer to hold back on an abundance of presents. Some elect to limit their children's participation in Christmas activities with their friends and school, even lecturing them not to comment on the beauty of Christmas lights. Others are concerned with integrating their children into mainstream America, hesitating to deprive them of the experiences their friends are enjoying.

Try to make Hanukkah as special as possible. Include extended family get-togethers and lots of good food. Don't forget though—your best strategy regarding Christmas is to help your children develop a positive relationship to Judaism throughout the rest of the year.

ESTABLISHING A HANUKKAH BUDGET

If you differ on how materialistic Hanukkah should be, compromise on the magnitude of the gifts and the number to give. Set a budget for gift-giving to your children and extended family. Decide ahead of time how you will handle presents, instead of leaving it to each of you to decide spontaneously while you are out shopping. Many families give at least one present each night during Hanukkah. To help limit the cost of these presents, you might include those from extended family.

PARTICIPATING IN CHRISTMAS CELEBRATIONS

Discuss privately what the ground rules should be in your home for the children's participation in Christian activities and where you will draw the line. Use the "On a scale of one to 10" rule again. If one of you is lukewarm about the kids sitting on Santa's lap at day care, but the other feels, it's a 10, defer to the person with strong feelings and perhaps keep the children home from day care on that day. Most Jews by choice come from Christian homes and may still celebrate Christmas with extended family. Discuss what, if anything, makes the Jewish spouse concerned.

For example, going to Grandma's for Christmas dinner may be okay, but even though you don't keep kosher, the idea of eating ham is repulsive. Perhaps you could ask Grandma to provide an alternative dish for your family, or you could bring one.

For some families, holiday celebrations are a source of great joy. For others, it is a time of strife that exasperates differences. No matter where you are right now, don't despair. Each year you can make strides toward making holiday observance more of what you wish for.

9

Sabbath Observance

The great teachers of the Jewish people taught that religion should be practiced softly and should not become a cause of contention. No man or woman should dogmatically instill fear into the household. He or she should mold kindly though firmly, with love and not threats. The love of God should inspire and strengthen the love of one's lifelong partner.

—Rabbi Maurice Lamm, *The Jewish Way in Love and Marriage*

What Does Sabbath Observance Look Like?

THE JEWISH RITUAL of observing the Sabbath from Friday sundown until Saturday sundown is an anchor in Jewish family and spiritual life. Sabbath observance is centered in the home, although going to synagogue is often a part of it. If you are in a mixed Jewish marriage, how you each wish to celebrate or ignore the Sabbath can bring you closer together or, sadly, drive you apart. The Sabbath experience is richest when shared with family, but can be done alone if necessary.

Once again, lest you think that this issue is only relevant for couples who are not observant, even Orthodox families with a solid commitment to observing the Sabbath from sundown to sundown have to work out different preferences of how to observe it. Rabbi Shaya Sackett shares this example of a couple he counseled:

This couple was 100 percent committed to keeping Shabbos. In the woman's family, they always had elaborate meals and sat at the table half the day singing songs and discussing Torah. In the man's family, they had a quick meal and took a Shabbos nap. Neither way is wrong or right—each could defend their position. He might say, 'It's a day of rest, so I'm resting.' She might say, 'Shabbos is a day for recharging and spiritual growth.' They are both right.

The Sabbath gives Jews a valid excuse to stop working and to reconnect with God, family, and their soul in a restorative way. The restrictions of the Sabbath provide the opportunity for moving into a spiritual space and time. It is not only a day of rest but also a day of distinction, made holy by the contrast between the activities— and nonactivities—of the Sabbath period and the rest of the week.

Observant Jews begin Shabbat by lighting candles, followed by kiddish, ritual handwashing, ha-motzi over challah, and a festive meal, served on designated meat or milk Sabbath dishes and a white tablecloth. Some families include the ritual of blessing the wife and children. They will likely attend synagogue services on Friday evening and Saturday morning. In an Orthodox home, prohibited activities such as writing, cooking, turning on the lights, and riding in cars are not performed. After synagogue on Saturday morning, a Sabbath afternoon meal is served, often followed by singing, studying, a nap, or socializing with friends.

Shabbat ends after darkness falls on Saturday night with the short ceremony of *Havdalah*, when some Jews light a braided candle, say a prayer over wine, sniff the aroma from a box of fragrant spices, and sing songs that mark the end of Shabbat.

The Sabbath is a time for consciously letting go of worries, plans, and ambitions. Sounds fabulous, doesn't it? Some people are willing to pay thousands of dollars to vacation in the Caribbean for the same experience—no work, phones, driving, sumptuous meals, lovemaking, and no-guilt naps. So why isn't Sabbath observance an institution in most Jewish homes?

Sabbath Observance: Constraint or Opportunity?

In this society of satellite paging systems, cellular phones, and online shopping, it's not that easy to come to an abrupt halt for

24 hours—especially one day every week. We are addicted to productivity and we think we are too busy to stop shopping or working for a whole day. We don't want to be told we can't do something. We aren't used to sitting still and we get bored. We don't want to deprive our children or ourselves from socializing on Friday nights or from participating in athletic activities and other community activities on Friday nights and Saturdays.

Many Jews view Sabbath observance as a constraint rather than as an opportunity. Some Jews who weren't raised with the Sabbath don't know how to observe it or how to convince their family members to change the established routine.

In some households, the Sabbath is the centerpiece of the week. In others, it barely makes an appearance. In this section of the chapter, I'll help you and your family determine what role you wish the Sabbath to play in your family life.

What Were the Sabbaths of Your Childhood Like?

What you desire now as an adult is largely related to what you experienced as a child regarding the Sabbath. What were the Sabbath rituals, if any, in your home when you were growing up? Did you look forward to the Sabbath every week, dread its restrictions, or not even know that it existed? Rabbi David Wolpe recounts in his book, *Teaching Your Children About God:*

> Dr. Alvin Mars once told me that when he and his wife, Marilyn, first got married, they dreamed of Sabbath dinners when the family would sit around and talk and enjoy one another. The atmosphere would be warm and loving and the conversation filled with interest and laughter. Then they had kids.
> What happened? The children made noise. They were bored. They wanted to leave. Adolescents rarely name sitting around a family dinner table as their first choice of activity. However, said Alvin, now that his children are grown, what do they say? "Gee, Dad, remember those great Sabbath dinners we used to have together? Weren't they the best?"

Try this! Share with your spouse what you enjoyed, resented, and missed about the Sabbath of your childhood. The same question can be asked about other Jewish holidays.

Potential Conflicts on the Sabbath and Possible Solutions

"I want to start observing the Sabbath but my family doesn't." A common phenomenon that rocks Jewish marriages is illustrated by Judy, a woman in her 40s who became observant when she started studying with an inspirational rabbi. She took a class about the Sabbath and came home all fired up, determined to convert her family into Sabbath-observant Jews. She made three unfortunate mistakes. One, unable to contain her enthusiasm, she failed to understand that her family wasn't dissatisfied with the current household routine, and they had little desire or incentive to change the status quo.

Second, she approached it by giving them a laundry list of all of the activities they could no longer do. Viewing the Sabbath like a jail sentence, they naturally rebelled.

She returned to the class, pouting to her rabbi that she couldn't be a Sabbath-observant Jew because her family refused to go along with it. That was mistake number three.

It is much harder to observe the Sabbath when your family isn't doing so, but you can still do so if you are determined. Start small if you are brand new to Sabbath observance or married to someone who resists the idea. The idea is to separate the Sabbath in some way from the regular work week. Hundreds of ways exist to delight your family without engendering strong resistance.

Here are some ideas for *gradually* bringing the Sabbath into your home and family life.

Friday night:

- Give the kids their weekly allowance before they come to the dinner table. Ask them to put a percentage in the tzedakah box for a charity of their choice (or give them additional money beyond their allowance that they can place in the box).

- Before Shabbat begins, take a shower or bath, and if appropriate, shave.
- Say the Hebrew blessing for your children before dinner. If you don't know the Hebrew, bless them in your own words.
- Make your dinner special with fresh flowers, a white tablecloth, and your best china. Or make a special dessert so that the kids will look forward to Friday night.
- Serve challah and wine with dinner.
- Light one Sabbath candle for each family member, or let your daughter(s) light one candle each.
- At dinner, share something you were grateful for in the past week.
- Turn off the television, computer, and all other electronic devices, and don't answer the phone.
- Read Jewish stories with your children.
- Attend Friday night services as a family once a month.
- Attend religious lectures or discussions as a family or couple.
- Study the parsha of the week with commentaries alone or with your spouse before bed on Friday evening.
- Make love with your spouse. It's a mitzvah on the Sabbath!

Saturday:

> So you are going to a football game on Shabbat. Say kiddish over the lunch that you take with you. Take Shabbat with you.
>
> —Rabbi Carl Choper, Reconstructionist rabbi, Mechanicsberg, Pennsylvania

- Walk with your kids to shul when the weather is nice.
- Talk to the children in the car or on the way home from soccer practice or karate lessons about the parsha of the week.
- Go to a Saturday morning service, then invite friends to your home for afternoon lunch and discussions.

- Take a Sabbath afternoon nap.
- Don't do the work, including shopping, that you normally do during the week, or do it for only part of the day.
- Go for a walk by yourself or with your family. Focus on spiritual thoughts or nature, instead of work-related problems.
- Gather your family together for Havdalah.
- Put aside your work-related magazines and read a Jewish book instead.
- Watch a Jewish video in the late afternoon.
- If you have to drive somewhere, listen to Jewish music in the car.
- Do Jewish arts and crafts projects.
- Get together with Jewish friends and neighbors.
- Attend a Shabbaton (a Sabbath weekend at a retreat center or hotel), which provides a marvelous getaway for the whole family.

For some spouses, the experience of having your mate suddenly start observing the Sabbath marks a shift in a new frightening direction. It might feel like this: "Up until now, what you did with your spiritual life didn't affect me all that much, but now you want me to change too."

If your spouse or older children are feeling this way, don't ask too much of them until they get accustomed to your observance. It's normal for them to feel threatened if you have immersed yourself in Jewish study and pulled away from the family activities you used to participate in. Reinforce your relationship with them by spending more time in secular activities. Step back into their world so that you can gently guide them to join you in yours.

"We're observing the Sabbath but only because I am the Sabbath policeman." So, you have convinced your reluctant family to join you on some level of Sabbath observance, whether it's lighting candles, sharing Friday night meals, or other activities. I spoke to Jews who were initially grateful that their families had

agreed to some Sabbath observance but later became frustrated that all things Jewish were orchestrated and continued because of their efforts. The feeling is, "If I didn't insist on this, or keep pushing, it would all stop." This gentleman expressed his frustration:

One Friday night, I had to take one of our kids to indoor soccer. I hadn't lit the Friday night candles, but left the candles on the table. When I came back, the candles still hadn't been lit. Do I have to be the one who always has to be in charge of this?

To reduce friction on this issue, develop realistic expectations if your family is going along with your wishes, but hasn't yet found their own motivations for observing the Sabbath. Don't expect them to take over the role you normally play in observance, unless you explicitly ask them to. If the gentleman above had asked his wife to light the candles in his absence, his frustration would be valid. To expect that she will somehow intuit that he wishes for this is unreasonable.

Keep in mind that you may have a level of Jewish knowledge that exceeds that of your family, so they naturally defer to you as the family "rabbi" out of respect for your learning or fear of doing something wrong. Teach them how and why to do certain aspects of the rituals involved. Involve them in household related chores, and if you want someone to take on more than that, (such as lighting the candles before sundown if you are not there), then spell it out and get their agreement.

"You can't tell me what to do." In some Jewish households, conflicts over Sabbath observance originate from a deeper power struggle in the relationship. During the writing of this chapter, I received a phone call from a distraught, observant Jewish woman who had heard about this book. She was in a quandary about whether to marry a culturally Jewish but nonobservant man. She expressed to me her fears, and I could hear immediately why she and her fiancé were stalemated. Her conversation to me focused on the Sabbath restrictions that she insisted he must agree to once

they had children. Not surprisingly, he was unwilling to make that commitment to her.

This woman made a common mistake—She focused all of their conversations on the activities that she *didn't* want him to do. That set up an inevitable power struggle. Even if he might be convinced to observe the Sabbath for positive reasons, he was polarized into the role of fighting for his independence.

Another woman told me of an opposite story "I had a greater interest in Judaism before my husband went through eight years of reading nothing but Jewish books. I've become less Jewish in response to his becoming too Jewish."

The quickest solution to this problem is to lighten up on discussion about restrictions and focus more attention on the *benefits* to the resistant spouse. Here are two cautions: Firstly, make sure you emphasize things that your partner would deem positive, not just what you value. For example, if your spouse is attached to watching television on Friday nights and you want the television off, don't try to convince him that he's better off without TV. Instead, help him see the rewards to him of you becoming more relaxed, along with the two of you getting closer together on Friday nights . . . without the distraction of the television. Secondly, hold back on delivering a forceful sales pitch on the Sabbath. The stronger you push, the more your spouse might push back. Go gently on this one.

"I believe that God commanded us to observe the Sabbath, but my spouse doesn't agree." Orthodox observance rests on the principle that you observe certain Jewish practices whether you feel like it or not because God commanded them. My husband observes the Sabbath because he relishes the break to recharge, but mostly because he believes God commanded us to observe the Sabbath and he wishes to pass along this tradition to our children. I am committed to observing the Sabbath as well, although not as completely as Stephen does and not because I believe God commanded it.

We join together in our commitment because of what the Sabbath does for us as a family. No matter how little time we spend together during the week, I know we'll be together on Friday nights. I love preparing a special meal and serving it on our best china. I delight in my young children's Sabbath prayers and songs and the way they wake up on Saturday mornings excited about going to synagogue. The Sabbath is an institution in our household, as firm a commitment as our wedding vows and there is something very comforting to all of us to have such a predictable anchor in a very unpredictable world.

If you and your spouse hold different theological viewpoints about the Sabbath, it's best not to argue about it. Instead, look for common ground that allows each to have his or her own opinion of the reasons to observe, or not observe, the Sabbath. If your spouse doesn't believe that God commanded Sabbath observance, he or she surely won't be amenable to your commanding Sabbath observance either. Rather, you must find a way to entice your partner to join you because of the positive vision you are able to create. Otherwise, you must observe as you can on your own without insisting that your family join you.

"The Sabbath is supposed to be a time for peace, but it makes me tense and irritable." In many households, the wife comes home from work on Friday with the intimidating prospect of getting a Sabbath dinner pulled together before sundown. Let's say this family extends their Sabbath observance into Saturday. Perhaps during Saturday morning, she's watching young children while her husband is in synagogue. Then, as they often do, she gets ready to serve guests from synagogue for Sabbath lunch. Rabbi Pliskin, who is Orthodox, shares his personal experience in his book, *Marriage*:

> I love to have guests for Shabbos. The more people, the better. I consider the *chesed* a high priority. My wife also likes to do *chesed*, but she is the one who does most of the work when we have guests.
> When someone calls me up to ask if he or she can come to our house for Shabbos, my tendency is to say, "Of course, we are happy to have you as our guest. Let me check with my wife to make certain it is okay with her."

My wife complained that this wasn't fair to her. When she feels too tired for company, she wants to be able to refuse without me making her sound like the mean one.

Anger and quarrels about preparing for the Sabbath are incongruous with the spirit of Shabbat, and yet a likely outcome of two overworked parents. Here are some suggestions for managing this stress:

- Don't put the complete burden for Friday night preparations on one spouse. If one of you gets home too late on Friday afternoon to assist, help get the kitchen and house cleaned up on Thursday night, or make Shabbat dessert ahead of time.

- Change your normal working hours on Friday if possible.

- Ask your spouse how he or she feels about Friday evening or Saturday afternoon guests, how many times a month it is enjoyable, and when it becomes a burden.

- Involve your kids in Sabbath preparation.

- If you can afford it, hire a cleaning service to help you clean the house before sundown on Friday. If your children are very young, get a babysitter on Friday afternoons so that you can devote your energy to the preparation.

If keeping the Sabbath makes you a kinder, gentler person, your family will pay attention and be more interested in participating. If doing so makes you tyrannical and short-tempered, they may resent the Sabbath.

Studies show that when television is taken away for a period of time in a household, at first the loss stirs up great anxiety and anger. Over time, as creative activities and family connection fill the gap that the television once occupied, the loss is felt less keenly. Continue the experiment long enough and the absence of television becomes appreciated. So it is with the Sabbath. Over time, your family may become as attached to the Sabbath as they presently are to other activities. But you must be patient.

"My spouse doesn't observe the Sabbath on Saturdays and I do, so we're in entirely different moods." Dennis Fischman is an observant Jew from Sommerville, Massachusetts, who often participates as a *gabbai* in his synagogue. Though he and his wife, Rona, spend Friday nights together at home, he goes to synagogue on Saturday while Rona works from home. Dennis used to come home from temple wanting to share his shul experience with Rona, but she was still in work mode. He's learned to wait until Rona has put the workday behind her.

Some professions demand Saturday work. Some professionals feel the need to work on Saturdays and choose to limit their Sabbath observance to Friday night. Some Jews are committed to Friday night Sabbath, but prefer the freedom to shop, drive, or do whatever they are used to doing on Saturdays.

Here are some suggestions if you and your spouse differ in the length and extent of your Sabbath observance:

- If you would prefer your spouse to take more of a break on Saturdays, and he or she chooses not to, be careful about how you express your disappointment.
  Not effective: "The reason you caught that cold is because you work too hard. If you didn't work on Saturdays, you wouldn't get sick."
  More effective: "You've been working very hard lately. No wonder you've caught a cold. Why don't you give yourself a much deserved break this coming Saturday and not work for the day?"

- If you don't spend Saturday during the day together, reunite for Havdalah and spend Saturday evening together.

- If your spouse has to work on Saturday, but you want to support him or her in getting more of a day of rest than normal, make the day easier so he or she at least gets a taste of the Sabbath. Make breakfast, do the dishes, watch the kids, or whatever else might lighten the load for your spouse.

- Take responsibility for your own Sabbath experience on Saturdays. If your husband, for example, wants to watch the ballgame on television, and you want silence, ask him to watch it in one room, or use headphones, but don't complain that if he doesn't agree to turn off the television, you can't observe the Sabbath.

It is certainly easier to observe the Sabbath on Saturdays if your family joins you, but you can still observe it without their participation. One woman told me that she decided to start observing the Sabbath on Saturdays as well as Friday nights, but she didn't announce it to her family because that would have brought about resistance. She simply stopped doing certain activities she used to do but allowed the family to continue with their routine. However, she also occasionally gives up her Saturday observance if it's creating too much hardship for her family. She has this perspective: "My relationship with God won't be compromised if I drive my daughter to the mall, but it may be compromised if I disrupt my relationship with my daughter."

Be as consistent in your behavior as possible. If you ask your family to turn off the phone and television and forgo trips to the mall, and then you sneak into your office to check your e-mail right after Sabbath dinner, you are likely to get rebellion from the troops!

"My commitment to the Sabbath inhibits my family's social life." It isn't easy when one member of the family is committed to keeping the full Sabbath and others in the family don't join him or her. What do you do when your commitment to Sabbath observance is bringing the opposite of shalom bayit into your household? Even Orthodox rabbis I spoke to advised making some compromises if necessary.

One observant woman I spoke with makes exceptions on Saturday evenings in the summertime, agreeing to go out with her husband before sundown so that their social life with other couples isn't curtailed. Another observant woman struggled with wanting to keep the Sabbath on Saturdays but didn't feel right about missing all of her children's soccer games. Then a Rabbi told her that Shabbos is about taking care of oneself and one's loved ones. From that point on, she started attending their games.

A Reconstructionist Jew encourages his teenage children to invite friends over for Friday night dinner and afterward allows them to turn on the television. He figures, better that than my kids not wanting to be home on Friday nights.

These compromises reflect the complexity of observing the Sabbath in modern times. Compromises can be made to keep the peace with the spirit of Shabbat still intact.

Negotiating With Kids About Sabbath Observance

If I'm going to raise a shomer Shabbos child, I want him to be in a community where he's not different than everyone else, where the norm is shomer Shabbos.

—Hillel Zeitlan, Orthodox Jew, Baltimore, Maryland

We live in Charlottesville, Virginia. The kids have lots of friends who are not Jewish. It's important to us that the kids don't feel that being Jewish is a burden. We allow them to be involved in school and athletic activities on Friday and Saturday night. We say, "I wish the event was not Friday night, but I don't want you to miss it, so you can go."

—Rabbi Dan Alexander, Charlottesville, Virginia

A great source of stress for Jewish families who are not living in Orthodox neighborhoods where everyone observes the Sabbath, is how to keep Sabbath observance from feeling like a jail sentence to rebellious children who do not wish to be excluded from activities that most of their friends are engaged in.

The question inevitably arises for most Jewish families: "When will we allow them to break the rules? What will our household rules for Sabbath observance be?" The answer to this question becomes trickier if you and your spouse differ on how stringent you believe Sabbath observance must be, especially if one of you believes that no exceptions should be made and the other wants more leeway.

Start with this rule: Decide together what your rules will be and present a united position to your children. Don't create a situation where one of you becomes the "bad guy" for not allowing a child his or her precious freedom. Figure out where you can compromise so that it's not black or white, but rather, the day still has some distinction and sacredness to it, even if secular activities intrude. You might break the rules for an occasional birthday party, but no soccer every Saturday. Or maybe a certain sport, like karate, is good for your child's well-being, so you'll say, "We'll allow karate lessons on Saturdays." You may allow your teenagers more freedom, as long as it doesn't interfere with your Sabbath observance. For example: "You can go out on Friday night after our family dinner, as long as someone else drives you and brings you home."

Ken and Lauren Firestone of Lancaster, Pennsylvania, came up with a creative system for handling their teenagers' desire to participate in secular activities on Friday and Saturday nights:

> The kids are in public school and we want them to fit in with their friends. We made a deal. They can go to one party a month on Shabbot. Since we have three children, three out of the four Sabbaths a month could be broken up by parties, so we coordinate the weekends if possible. On Friday nights, they can go to a Jewish home for sleepovers, or invite their friends to our home, as long as the friends are cool with our Shabbos scene (some of them really like it!). We look over the schedule for school dances, homecoming, and football, and they can pick three nights out of seven to attend. We don't allow the phone on Shabbos, but they can use the computer to e-mail their friends. These are compromises we've learned to live with because we live in a non-Jewish area and don't want our children hating Shabbot.

Outside of the most observant Jewish families, it is natural for Sabbath observance to ebb and flow according to the demands of secular life. Don't despair if you must give in a bit in order to defuse your children's rebellion against the Sabbath. You wish it to be a source of joy for your family, not pain. You will likely discover that, as much as a child might test the limits, he or she also comes to look forward to the recharging time that the Sabbath provides. Even the most rebellious teenager sometimes appreciates a valid excuse to beg off from social activities to be at home with family—even if he or she won't admit it.

Going back to the earliest story of Adam and Eve, as human beings, we all have a natural reaction to being told not to do something. Sometimes the spirit is there and other times we are going through the motions waiting until the sun sets. Sometimes we will view Sabbath rest as a gift and at other times it will feel like an unnecessary inconvenience.

Whatever choice you make regarding Sabbath observance, do so with this in mind: The opportunity exists to distinguish Friday night sundown through Saturday night sundown to some extent, whatever extent you choose. Whether it's a day of rest, a reminder to slow down and express gratitude toward God or loved ones, a good excuse for connecting with other Jews, or an opportunity to strengthen and celebrate your Jewish identity, the Sabbath is a gift—one of your greatest tools for achieving shalom bayit in your home, if you don't allow to become a divisive issue.

10

Jewish Life-Cycle Events

Don't allow God to be the wedge in your marriage.
—Rabbi Reuven P. Bulka, Ottawa, Canada

WHATEVER JEWISH DIFFERENCES may exist between you and your spouse, life-cycle events will exaggerate them. Even many nonobservant Jews connect to their Jewish heritage, family, and God at these high and low points in their lives. Weddings, *britot*, bar mitzvahs, and funerals awaken feelings about Judaism some Jews didn't even know they had and stir up family dynamics that often turn entirely reasonable people into stubborn mules.

Every Jewish life-cycle event includes a baseline of minimally required Jewish prayers and rituals; the rest is optional, depending on family customs, your preferences as a couple, the rabbi or officiator that you chose, the *mohel* you select (for a bris), and the synagogue or location you choose for the event. For example, when we had a bris for our son, Elijah, the *mohel* asked us if we wanted to prepare an explanation for the meaning and choice of his Hebrew name and its significance in our family. It wasn't required but was offered as an option.

A Jewish wedding ceremony, as another example, has three essential elements: the betrothal, which is the declaration by the couple that they are consecrated to each other; the marriage contract, which is signed by two witnesses and read aloud; and the exchange of an item of value (traditionally a ring), which accompanied by the following blessing, seals the contract: "Behold, you are consecrated unto me with this ring, according to the law of

140

Moses and Israel." Customarily, most Jewish weddings also include a *chuppah*, the sharing of wine, the breaking of a glass, and seven blessings which are recited by friends and family or by the rabbi. Learn from your rabbi or a Jewish text the purpose of these rituals, so that you aren't including them merely because they're customary but rather because you understand what they can bring to you as a couple.

Besides including what is common in almost all Jewish weddings, learn what is customary for the particular rabbi and synagogue that you choose. The rabbi may be flexible, but he or she will likely give you a standard ceremony, unless you request otherwise. Discuss with your spouse and rabbi the myriad of optional prayers and creative rituals that you can choose to include or exclude.

Also discuss customary rituals that you find offensive or ones you would like to modify. For example, perhaps you will choose that both the husband and wife strike the glass at the end of the ceremony, if you have a problem with it only being the man's responsibility.

Speak with your rabbi, read Jewish wedding books, and attend other Jewish life-cycle events to learn of new rituals and other variations in terms of practice and entertainment you can include in the ceremony. If you want to create something entirely unique, ask your rabbi for permission to include it and for guidance on how to make it appropriate for the ceremony. Consider what will make the rabbi and other guests comfortable or uncomfortable. For example, one woman elected not to serve shrimp at her wedding, even though she did not choose a kosher caterer, because she knew it would make the rabbi and her parents uneasy.

If you and your spouse differ in preferences, return to this question: What is essential? What is customary? Be careful of asking your spouse to give up an age-old family tradition that he or she cherishes or for a change to custom that makes your spouse feel embarrassed or uncomfortable. Putting your unique stamp to the celebration is a fine idea—just make sure that you accommodate each other's needs.

Consider the pros and cons of each option. For example, when we celebrated Elijah's bris, we had to decide whether to have it at the synagogue or in our home. Jewish law and the *mohel* stated no preference. My husband expressed a preference to do it at the synagogue, and I initially wanted it in our home. We weighed the advantages and disadvantages of each choice. Stephen convinced me that a synagogue ceremony would be less work for my already fatigued body so I came around to my husband's way of thinking and agreed to do it in the synagogue with a breakfast catered afterward. Immediate family came back to the house later.

Strategies for Minimizing Stress at Life-Cycle Events

You may be a couple who doesn't struggle with Jewish issues on a daily basis, so you are shocked when your son's bris brings up so much conflict. Or you may have known from the time you tried to plan your wedding that different approaches to Jewish life would likely require negotiation at every ensuing life-cycle event. Whatever the case, here are some strategies to help you successfully negotiate your issues.

HONOR THE MOST BASIC RELIGIOUS NEEDS OF YOUR SPOUSE

If a Jewish practice is central to your spouse's religious beliefs, don't ask him or her to sacrifice it for your convenience. Friends of mine had a very difficult dilemma to resolve. The husband was a Jew by choice and had never been circumcised. He had strong feelings against circumcision and so when his wife got pregnant, the question of the bris came up. She was raised as an observant Conservative Jew. Not circumcising her son was unimaginable to her. They argued all throughout her pregnancy about how to handle it, perhaps secretly hoping that the first child would be a girl so they wouldn't have to confront the issue. They finally agreed to flip a coin after delivery if a boy was born.

Of course, their firstborn was a boy, and the coin toss landed in the father's favor. No bris, no circumcision. He had won the argument, but he realized very quickly he was in danger of losing something else. His wife couldn't live with the decision. She was willing to be flexible on some issues, but the bris and circumcision of her son was not really negotiable. She eventually convinced her husband to allow her this absolute need.

Whenever you and your spouse are arguing about a Jewish practice, isolate what the basic religious need is that would be violated if one of you didn't get your way. Look for a creative solution that will appease that need. Sometimes, like in the case of a bris, it's not possible to reach a solution that will please each of you—you can't do a circumcision halfway. In that case, try to honor the one of you who has the strongest needs for a particular practice, and the other of you can ask for concessions in other areas of conflict.

STEP OUTSIDE OF THE SYNAGOGUE IF NECESSARY

When Stephen and I met, we were each active in separate and very different kinds of synagogues. I participated in a midsize, funky Reform synagogue, and he davened regularly at a huge Conservative synagogue to which his family had belonged for five generations. In which of our synagogues should we marry? And, accordingly, which rabbi would marry us?

Stephen and I resolved the controversy by getting married in the living room of his parents' home, by an unaffiliated friend and teacher of mine, Rabbi Alan Ullman. We could have wasted a lot of time arguing over which of our previous synagogues was better, but neither of us was comfortable in the other's synagogue, nor were we close to those rabbis. Instead, we found a third alternative that appealed to both of us.

Sometimes, rather than trying to decide which synagogue to hold a life-cycle event in, you are better off finding a neutral location.

DON'T NAG

Rick Popowitz of Potomac, Maryland, is frank about how he expects to lose the bat mitzvah battle with his wife Sandy:

> I want to have our daughter's bat mitzvah celebration in Israel, with a simple reading of the Torah and lunch after-

ward, but my wife wants to have a $20,000 party here, which is modest in this area. I see it as superficial to spend that kind of money on one day. I know my wife will wear me down and we'll have the big party. She nags and nags and I don't want to hear it anymore, so I'll finally give in.

Rick is not the only husband in America who finally gives up the fight just to end the nagging. Here's the problem with this approach: If Rick isn't really okay with what Sandy is asking for, his resentment may be expressed in a passive-aggressive manner outside this context. She'll be shocked when they are fighting five years later and Rick says, "Yeah, well if you hadn't insisted on that $20,000 bat mitzvah . . ." Getting your spouse to surrender to a plan that he or she despises is a setup for marital conflict.

Instead, remember the discussion about negotiable and non-negotiable needs and preferences, and the recommendation that you identify where, on a scale of one to 10, your preference is. Rick and Sandy need to determine the real issues and how strong their feelings are.

Maybe Sandy has a *non-negotiable need* to keep her standing in a community of friends who are all throwing $20,000 bat mitz-vah celebrations. Perhaps it's only a *preference* of Rick's for him to not spend the money in the way Sandy wants. Or perhaps Sandy desires to create the kind of bat mitzvah party she never had, and then the kind of bat mitzvah celebration becomes nego-tiable. She has learned to nag Rick because the strategy works, but on this one, if Rick's needs are stronger than Sandy's prefer-ence, coercing him to give up his need may backfire on her. Then of course, the needs and wants of the child should factor in as well—not last in consideration, either.

Nagging is only a short-term solution. Keep brainstorming alternatives until you arrive at a workable solution that you both feel okay about, even if one or both of you is giving something up. Remember, a win/lose approach makes you both losers.

KNOW WHEN TO COMPROMISE AND WHEN TO SAY NO

Family life-cycle events, which are theoretically joyful gatherings, can bring out the worst in people. The spirit of the event is lost in battles for "my way." When you bring together families of different customs and backgrounds, you'll inevitably encounter differences of opinion. At worst, you'll get stuck mediating between your spouse and parents, wondering how you can possibly honor your parents and your partner at the same time. Sometimes you can't, and someone will be unhappy. Ideally, that person shouldn't be your spouse, but it doesn't always work that way.

Make accommodations for extended family, but also be willing to draw the line to protect what you and your spouse really want. For example, at your wedding, you may decide to hire a kosher caterer in order to feed kosher family members, but when your brother's family requests no mixed dancing between men and women, you might politely decline. Or if an observant cousin wants to read Torah at your son's bat mitzvah and insists that the service be done with no microphone, you might offer to turn the microphone off for his *layning*, but leave it on for the rest of the ceremony. One Jewish woman planning her son's bar mitzvah ceremony ran into difficulty when her Orthodox mother insisted that she not invite anyone to the service who would have to drive to the synagogue on Shabbos—thus encouraging a sin in the mother's eyes.

What if these solutions work for one of you but make the other uncomfortable? Perhaps one of you is more concerned than the other about accommodating the requests of extended family. It is easy in life-cycle events to get pulled away from being united as a couple, torn between pleasing each other and making extended family feel comfortable. You must discuss when a compromise is acceptable and when it asks too much of one of you. For example, if one of you would find separate dancing acceptable, but it breaks the heart of the other, you've got a problem. Return to the strategy we discussed earlier—determine on a scale of 1 to ten how strongly each of you feels about it. Maybe mixed dancing is a ten for one of you, but only a 6 for the other. The one with the strongest feelings should, when possible, be able to veto a compromise that requests giving up something too important.

Also be careful of creating triangles, allowing complaints to come to you through a third person, or using your spouse as a messenger for another family member. Avoid a scenario like this:

Your brother calls to tell you that Mom has a problem with your decision to keep the bris small and not tell anyone beyond immediate family. He suggests that you reconsider because he's tired of hearing Mom complain about it. In this case, you've got to deal directly with Mom to see if a compromise can be worked out. Maybe her real issue is that her sister, Aunt Susan, isn't being invited, but she can let go of the cousins in New York. You'd never find out what her real complaints are—and how they could be satisfied—if you don't move beyond family gossiping.

FOCUS ON THE SPIRITUAL

Too often, Jewish life-cycle events with the potential to be spiritually significant milestones turn into expensive and extravagant social affairs, with far more attention paid to the color of napkins and tablecloths than to the religious significance of the celebration. This woman laments:

> On my son's bar mitzvah sign-in board, one of his friends wrote, "Lucky you—you're bar mitzvah. That means no more Hebrew school!" My son was planning on expanding his Jewishness, not eliminating it! He saw his bar mitzvah as the beginning of taking on new obligations.

Many families agree to make the child and the Torah the focus of the bar or bat mitzvah, not the party. However, in the midst of bar and bat mitzvah planning, sometimes the family loses track of that commitment.

Life-cycle events are both spiritually significant, as well as financially and emotionally draining. Families feel the pressure to put on an affair of the same caliber as friends and the synagogue community and to orchestrate and control hundreds of small details. We use the expression "holy matrimony," but how many of us take the time to infuse holiness into our wedding ceremony—the start of our married life? Add to that the stress of accommodating a multitude of family demands and it's enough to make you count the days until the event is over, instead of greeting it with joy. I remember thinking when planning for Elijah's bris, "This is preposterous, to expect all of this from a woman who just gave birth a few days ago!"

It may not be easy to approach these events with the spirituality component foremost in your mind, but if you don't try, you won't get as much out of the event as you could. Whenever possible, study the religious and spiritual meaning behind the rituals and ritual objects you purchase. For example, if you are shopping for wedding rings, and you learn that Jewish wedding bands are usually solid gold with no stones, find out why the Jewish tradition advises this, so you know the religious meaning behind the ritual. When you and your fiance purchase a *ketubah*, don't just select a pretty one from the store display. Learn together what it says, and discuss any changes you'd like to make to it to reflect your unique beliefs.

Ask your spouse to pull you back to what matters when you get off track, and vice versa. Each of you will probably stress out about different issues at different times so the one of you who is more detached can remind the other to remain spiritually centered and calm.

Do You Agree on What to Do for Your Daughters?

The question arises about whether to create a baby-naming ceremony for a girl instead of the bris, and whether to enroll her in Hebrew school and encourage her to celebrate becoming a bat mitzvah with a ceremony. While boys are named at the *brit milah*, girls are traditionally named in synagogue on the Sabbath after their birth. In some synagogues, the father is called to the Torah and receives a blessing in which the child is named. Another blessing prays for the healing of the mother. The baby and mother may not be present, although in modern times, the baby-naming ceremony for a girl is often turned into a family celebration, much like the bris. In some Orthodox communities, any length of time from a week to a year or so after the girl's birth, the mother and daughter may come up to the *bema* after the father's *aliyah*. (In other Orthodox communities, women are not allowed to come up to the bema in front of the male congregation, for any reason).

Most Conservative, Reform, and Reconstructionist synagogues now hold a bat mitzvah ceremony for girls. In some Conservative synagogues, the service for a girl is held on Friday night, when the Torah is not chanted. In Orthodox synagogues, girls may read from the *Haftorah* or give a *drasha* at the age of twelve. Depending on the custom of the synagogue, the girl may or may not be permitted to read or chant in front of the entire congregation in the main sanctuary. In some communities she celebrates with a small party for her girlfriends, away from the main sanctuary.

How will you and your spouse decide about Jewish life-cycle events for your daughters when you might not agree? Here are some ideas:

Respond to strong feelings in either one of you. Some women feel passionate about their daughters participating in these rituals, especially if they were deprived of them as children. For the bat mitzvah celebration, your daughter can have a vote. That vote will be biased by whether you have included her in Hebrew school education at an early age. If so, she will likely want a bat mitzvah party, just like all of her friends, although some girls and boys do choose not to go to Hebrew school or to celebrate becoming a bar or bat mitzvah for any number of reasons.

Whenever possible, back up your feelings with an understanding of how your request fits in with Jewish tradition and practice. Rabbi David Wolpe remarked about his wife: "I could respect her coming to me with a developed Jewish opinion, but I didn't want to hear, 'I just don't feel like it.' Your developed opinion doesn't have to be rooted in Jewish tradition, but it's helpful to explain to your partner where your feelings are coming from, and to offer a Jewish context for your preference if there is one.

Working Out Differences About Handling Death

Jews who have been sporadic in Jewish practice sometimes feel a sudden and strong need for connection to Jewish tradition when they lose a loved one. In the chaos and grieving that follow a death, they want an authority—like a rabbi or Jewish law—to tell them what to do and how to get through the hardest part. They might also be concerned with honoring the final wishes of their loved one.

Let's say your husband believes he needs to say *Kaddish* twice a day in the year following his father's death. You find this practice demanding and unreasonable. Because of this he may not be home for dinner or he'll be unable to drop the kids off at day care for an entire year. This will be terribly inconvenient for you as a family and a hardship on you when you have to pick up the slack.

Remember, Kaddish is designed to help the living person mourn and strengthen his connection to God. Your husband might also believe that saying Kaddish is important for his father's departed soul. A few days after his father's death is not the time to argue about what a foolish religious practice you think it is, especially if fulfilling this religious obligation is sacred and healing process for your husband, or because he made a promise to his dying father. You might discuss these issues while your parents and in-laws are still alive so that you can determine how your spouse feels about Jewish mourning laws and what will be expected of each of you.

Shift to brainstorming solutions how to structure your family routines to allow for this commitment with the least amount of hardship. Don't worry about what it will be like to support his fulfilling this obligation for an entire year. Either he will relax the practice after a period of weeks or months, or you will learn to handle it.

Let's say that your husband never got along with his father. Ah, you think, ammunition for my cause. You point out to him how stupid it is to turn his life and yours upside down for the sake of honoring a father he didn't like very much when his father was alive. You are on tricky ground. Are you imposing your opinion for selfish purposes, to release you from this major inconvenience, or are you being a friend, helping your spouse determine whether daily Kaddish makes sense for him? Leave your religious opinions out of the room and help him, mostly by listening, to figure out what will make him feel right with himself and God, or suggest that he speak with a rabbi about it.

Death can also have the opposite effect, causing an individual, in anger, to turn away from God and his or her faith. Death and dying can exacerbate any marital differences in values and religious beliefs. It is a hard time for a marriage, since the death has made each of you hurt, angry, or depressed.

Discussing death and dying issues with your spouse, before anyone you love has died, can ease this painful period. Here are some questions to clarify, before you need the answers:

Where will each of you, your children, and parents be buried? Some families run into complex issues because of second marriages, intermarriage, and divorce. Maybe you've purchased a burial plot, but it's next to your ex-wife's!

What about organ donation, cremation, or an autopsy? These practices are not observed by many Jews, but you may be married to a Jew who desires on of these alternatives. How will you handle this difference of opinion? If you die, how do you want your spouse to respond to the custom for Jews to be buried within twenty-four hours? What if, depending on circumstances, family members might not be able to get there fast enough? If you have a sister living in Israel, do you place greater value on following the halakhah, which demands a quick burial, or on having close family present? How do you feel about the Orthodox commitment to a *tahara* (ritual purification) performed on the body?

What kind of funeral do you want? Do you want a eulogy? Which rabbi do you want to officiate? If you are in a mixed marriage, have relationships with more than one rabbi, or are still close to the rabbi you grew up with, you may want more than one rabbi involved in the service.

What shivah traditions do you wish observed for your death or the death of a child? Have you asked your parents what each of them wants in the event of their death? Traditionally, during the seven days of sitting shivah, the family doesn't go out of the house and they stop all the usual amenities, like bathing, shaving, sex, or small talk. At least ten men must be there, morning and evening, for a regular religious service, so that the mourners can say the mourners' Kaddish. A memorial candle burns for seven days. Friends and family come to visit throughout the shivah week. Less observant Jews might observe only the first three days of shivah or might not require ten men for a religious service.

Will you engage in a full year of mourning if you lose a parent? What will that entail for you? It could include refraining from entertainment and buying new clothes, in addition to going to synagogue to say Kaddish every day for eleven months, and on every year on the anniversary of the parent's death. Would you do the same for 30 days if you lose a spouse or child, as Jewish tradition instructs? Some people can imagine observing these laws for a full year for their spouse and children, but would have trouble with even thirty days for a parent who has been removed from their lives. Will you follow the Jewish tradition precisely, or modify it according to your heart? What do you want if you die, and what are you willing to do for your spouse if he or she dies?

Do you want extraordinary means used to save your life? Judaism argues against euthanasia, but you can ask not to be resuscitated and to allow nature to take its course without life support. Do you want to assign power of attorney to your spouse if you are incapacitated?

If someone close to you dies, and you are disagreeing with your spouse over how to proceed, seek the counsel of a trusted rabbi and give up as much as you are able to satisfy your spouse's needs for religious observance and mourning rituals. Traditional mourning rituals are recommended for a reason—to assist the bereft Jew through predictably painful stages of grief. The practices available to a mourning Jew can provide stability and emotional healing to your partner and yourself.

Remember that in the shock and grief following a death, each of you may not be at your best and many strategies for conflict resolution are temporarily forgotten. Rely on the help of your rabbi, community, and other extended family members to give you the support and guidance you need, and forgive less than optimal communication.

How many times have we been a part of, or witnessed this phenomenon: A lifecycle event designed to be a celebration turns into a fiasco and an affair so stressful that everyone involved wishes only for it to be over. You have a choice about how you approach these affairs. Despite your best intentions, you *will* get pulled off track and stressed by the number of decisions you need to make. Hundreds of opportunities for resolving conflict will present themselves. Chances are good that you and your spouse will not agree over all of the details—and maybe even some of the big ones.

Refer back to the basic principles we have discussed in this book for enhancing positive communication. There is no time you'll need it more than when preparing for a major family life-cycle event.

11

In The Kitchen

When we began dating, the first meal my wife Yael ever cooked for me was quiche—with ham in it. I didn't want to offend her, so I ate it. She's Jewish, but she didn't have a clue about kosher laws. It never even occurred to her that I kept kosher, or what that meant.

—Marty Cohn, Needham, Massachusetts

Kosher Practices in Modern Times

WHATEVER OTHER JEWISH PRACTICES you choose to observe or not observe, you've got to eat. You may daven alone, but eating is a shared experience with your family, and therefore one that necessitates working out disagreements in the kitchen.

Traditional Jewish foods have symbolic power; every Jewish festival and holiday has special foods associated with it. Can you imagine Pesach without matzoh or Rosh Hashana without apples and honey? There is even a term for Jews who observe no Jewish practices other than consuming Jewish foods at designated times of the year—"bagels-and-lox Jews."

In this chapter we will focus primarily on conflicts that center around kashrut—keeping kosher. Even if neither you or your spouse has any intention of keeping kosher, you'll still learn plenty about conflict resolution from reading this chapter, as many of the techniques apply to other emotionally charged decisions as well. What could be so complicated? Why an entire chapter devoted to kashrut? As you'll see, nothing is simple when you are dealing with people's food.

RESISTANCE TO KASHRUT

People restrict their diets from certain foods for any number of reasons: to lose weight (a low-fat diet), out of respect for animals (vegetarian), food allergies (avoid all soy products), health concerns (organic food), or personal taste. Yet the restrictions of a kosher diet meet with resistance or lack of interest in 90 percent of Jewish homes. Ironically, even as Jewish observance of kashrut has declined, the word "kosher" has become a part of mainstream American vocabulary. (Did you know that only 20 percent of all kosher food sold is bought by Jews?) Now that mass-produced kosher food is available in many supermarkets, we can no longer blame the decline of kosher observance on the scarcity of kosher food.

So why do most Jews prefer not to observe the laws of kashrut? Consider these reasons:

- The majority of Jews don't believe that keeping kosher serves any meaningful purpose in the modern day.

- The majority of non-Orthodox Jews do not believe that we are commanded by God to keep kosher.

- Kosher meat is hard to find if you don't live near a kosher butcher and is more expensive.

- Keeping kosher can restrict your social life, depending on how you choose to eat outside of the home. Most modern Jews prefer assimilation to separation from gentiles.

- Keeping kosher when your extended family does not creates tension, because its difficult for you to eat in their home.

- Your spouse must participate in the commitment to a kosher kitchen and many spouses are reluctant to do so.

- Adults don't want to be told what to eat and when to eat it.

- Keeping kosher isn't fashionable in the Jewish community anymore.
- Kitchen preparations and shopping for a kosher kitchen is more work.
- Kosher rules appear too complicated and cumbersome.

ATTRACTION TO KASHRUT

For the 10 percent or so of Jews who continue to keep kosher, here are some of their motivations:

- God commanded it. It doesn't matter whether it makes sense or not.
- It makes the home comfortable for family members and synagogue friends who keep kosher.
- A child requested a kosher kitchen after attending Jewish summer camp or Jewish day school.
- Kosher ritual slaughter of animals is more humane.
- It sanctifies eating and provides a way to bring God into daily meals.
- It makes Judaism a regular part of daily life and connects the individual to the Jewish tradition and community.
- It reminds us that human beings are not animals and that we are able to exercise self-control.
- Some of our ancestors were killed for refusing to eat pork. If we keep kosher, they haven't died in vain.

STYLES OF KASHRUT

Once you commit as an individual or family to keeping kosher, there are hundreds of variations, ranging from full acceptance of the biblical and rabbinic regulations to simply avoiding pork. Even individuals within Orthodox communities disagree about what is considered "kosher enough."

Clearly some of the kosher alternatives described below would not meet the test of the spirit or law, but most rabbis agree on one thing: A little bit of kosher is better than none at all, even if the practices would not meet the rabbinic test of true kosher. Here are what some present-day couples do to infuse Jewish ritual into their kitchen and eating experiences:

- Some Jews eat only those packaged foods marked with certain types of rabbinical certification, while others read labels to verify that the ingredients are not nonkosher.

- Some Jews limit kashrut to abstaining from pork and shellfish, but they still mix meat and milk and eat nonkosher meat.

- Some Jews are willing to eat nonkosher foods in restaurants and other people's homes but stay away from blatant treyf like pork and shellfish. Others "pig out" (literally,) when they are away from home but keep the strictest standards of kashrut in their house.

- Some Jews are willing to eat fish and vegetables outside of the house, while still others do not eat any cooked foods away from home.

- Some Jews separate milk and meat, both in and out of the house. The separation ranges from not eating milk and meat together at the same meal (but ice cream may still follow a meat meal for dessert) to waiting one to six hours after a meat meal to eat dairy.

- Some Jews use separate dishes and utensils for milk and meat meals, others have three sets of dishes—one for treyf foods as well. Some households have six sets of dishes—both milk and meat for regular meals, for Shabbat, and for Passover.

- Some Jews eat only kosher meat at home but nonkosher meat when eating out. One couple has an unusual strategy for kosher meat at home: "We couldn't keep spending $300 a month on kosher meat to feed our large family, and vegetarian didn't appeal to anyone. My husband told me, 'If you are going to start buying nonkosher meat, just don't tell me about it. I haven't committed a sin if I assume the hostess is following the laws and I won't insult you by asking whether the meat is kosher or not.'"

- Some Jews run their empty dishwasher at its highest temperature between milk and meat uses. Others use the machine for only one category of utensils, have two dishwashers, or wash one set of dishes by hand.

- Some Jews don't keep kosher during the year, but only on Passover. Others don't keep kosher during the week, but serve only kosher food on the Sabbath. This gentleman remembers, "My parents' version of keeping kosher: Friday nights, we didn't have a glass of milk with our meat meal, we had grape juice instead. That was about it. On Sunday night, some kosher Jews in the neighborhood would come to our house for Chinese food, since they wouldn't eat treyf in their homes but they would eat it in ours."

- Some Jews make individual choices to eat only kosher, but have not been able to convince their family to kosher the home. In the home, they may eat separately, store and cook their food separately, or make small kosher choices like keeping the cheese off of the hamburger or eggs with no bacon for breakfast.

- Some Jews drink only kosher wine, while others believe that kashrut does not apply to alcohol.

DEVELOPING A KOSHER SYSTEM THAT WORKS FOR YOU

Given all the kosher choices you have, what will work for you and your family? Here are four ground rules for choosing a kosher system when you both agree to set up some version of a kosher home, but you still need to work out the details:

Determine your primary reasons for kashrut. If your reason for keeping a kosher home is to make it comfortable for your kosher in-laws to eat in your home, you have a measuring stick for "how kosher" you need to be. If you weren't clear about your primary motivation, you might defeat the whole purpose by not checking in with your in-laws to determine what standard of kashrut is acceptable to them.

Choose the highest standard that one of you needs and the other can tolerate. Define your nonnegotiable needs (no pork in the house), what is a negotiable want (separate dishes for milk and meat), and what is take it or leave it (separating milk and meat in the dishwasher). Whenever possible, shift your nonnegotiable needs to wants, so that your spouse experiences your flexibility rather than your rigidity. Ask for what you *want*, but be willing to compromise. Ask for what you *need* and insist on it. Don't confuse the two.

Share the work if your help is wanted. Don't put the lion's share of work (kashering the kitchen, shopping and preparing the food) on the shoulders of just one of you, unless that person agrees to it. This is especially true if the person doing most of the kitchen preparation (usually the woman) is also the one most resistant to keeping kosher. On the other hand, some women like to have control over their kitchen and may express a preference for you to keep your nose out of her soup. The key is to ask what your partner wants—help or to be left alone. If you are the kosher cop and always snooping in her kitchen to be sure she's "doing it right," it will drive her crazy in a period of short time.

Go easy on mistakes. If your less observant spouse agrees to try keeping kosher, and then makes a mistake in the kitchen, be extraordinarily patient. If you can take over most of the cooking and preparation, terrific. If not, then give your spouse plenty of time to adjust and praise him or her profusely in the learning process. Nothing will turn your spouse off from kashrut faster than getting yelled at because he or she used the wrong fork.

When You Want a Kosher Home and Your Spouse Refuses

Move slowly and on your own, if necessary. If your spouse refuses to consider kashering the kitchen and you don't want to separate yourself from your family by eating your meals separately, don't give up entirely. Your spouse may come around slowly if you don't push too hard. Start with small steps that won't rock the boat. Perhaps it's substituting fake bacon bits for real ones on the salad, or buying foods with a kosher symbol on it when you have a choice. One gentleman purchased two jars of mustard, one for meat and one for milk meals, as a small but symbolic gesture of his movement toward greater kosher observance.

A kosher rabbi might not eat in your home, but you and your spouse can be creative in compromises on both sides. Here are two examples:

> We made our kitchen dairy. When we have meat we use glass dishes which we can instantly kosher before using them. My wife keeps her Oscar Meyer bologna in the fridge in a plastic bag so it doesn't come into contact with anything else.

> My wife won't agree to a kosher kitchen, but she agreed to serve kosher style for Friday night dinner, out of respect for the Sabbath. She serves a kosher chicken, we don't put milk on the table, and we get a challah.

Join your nonkosher spouse in eating outside of the house to whatever extent you can tolerate it. When a spouse decides to fully observe kashrut and his or her mate won't join in, socializing together outside of the home can be tricky. If the observant spouse chooses not to dine in any nonkosher restaurant and kosher restaurants aren't plentiful, or they are invited to a function that isn't serving kosher food, this can create a serious rift. The nonobservant spouse blames the laws of kashrut and the perceived rigidity of his or her partner for destroying their social life. Instead of opening that spouse up to greater observance, the door often slams shut, as he or she becomes disgusted with the outcome of being married to someone who has, in his or her opinion, taken Jewish observance too far.

Richard and Phoebe McBee are a New York City couple struggling with how to accommodate Richard's decision to become an observant Orthodox Jew after several years of marriage. Phoebe feels cheated because prior to Richard's decision to become Orthodox, they traveled all over the world together and dined out frequently. Now, Richard prioritizes his need to keep shomer Shabbos and to eat only kosher foods, so now they eat out and travel very little. Richard offers to go with Phoebe to a restaurant and order a salad, but to her it's not the same as when they dined together compatibly. Richard has gained the depth and richness that observant Judaism brings to his life, but Phoebe views kashrut, the laws of Shabbos, and many other Orthodox rituals as the opponents who have taken away her husband and companion.

Each individual must make his or her own choices about where to draw the line with kashrut. If you can find a way to join your spouse at social functions, by eating vegetarian or fish, for example, it will go a long way toward easing the tension.

Don't let your family rile you. Don't be surprised if your spouse and family test your commitment to kashrut, hoping you will quickly get over your temporary insanity. Lee Hendler demanded few changes at home from her family when she announced that she had decided to stop eating shellfish. This was a big deal in a family that regularly enjoyed cooking up a pot of crabs together. On the first Mother's Day after her new commitment, her husband Nelson took her to their favorite crabhouse for a Mother's Day celebration with the kids. When she protested the choice of restaurant, he teased, "Oh, come on. Stop being such a stick-in-the-mud. It'll be fun. You can start tomorrow. It's Mother's Day. Loosen up!" Lee's husband was probably hoping that one good meal at the crabhouse would convince her to change her mind, but she stuck with her commitment.

Look at these moments as opportunities to reaffirm your commitment to kashrut and keep your sense of humor. When your family is acting childishly and selfishly, remember how frightened they are that you will demand something extraordinary from them. They need time to adjust. They will eventually stop testing you, and if you don't turn this into a fight, they may even join you.

Eat separately if you must. Sometimes you and your spouse will really be at loggerheads. One of you finds eating nonkosher food nauseating and disgusting and the other refuses to consider creating a kosher home. This kind of rift is unusual because these kinds of strong preferences are usually worked out before marriage, and the less observant one agrees to a kosher kitchen in deference to the strong feelings of the more observant. However, occasionally the one pushing for a kosher kitchen comes to that desire later in the marriage. If there isn't a lot of goodwill in the marriage or the less observant spouse is resentful of overall changes in his or her partner, the kitchen becomes a battleground. It becomes a line that he or she draws in the sand: "You can ask for all these other changes in our marriage, but don't mess with my kitchen and my food!"

In this situation, you are often wise to leave the issue alone until you can communicate about it calmly and the resentment toward your new observancy has eased. The kitchen may be the last place you demand change rather than the first. In extreme cases, the more observant spouse will separate him- or herself from the rest of the family, choosing to cook and eat his or her own food on kosher dinnerware. Make this decision cautiously. Separating yourself at meals is often experienced by your family as rejection.

Never give up hope. A wise Rabbinic principle says, *mitoch sheloh lishmah bah lishma:* one should perform the proper action even if it is done without proper intention, because the intention will follow. At first, your spouse may adamantly refuse to even consider keeping kosher. Then, when he or she realizes that you aren't going to just "get over it," your reluctant spouse may agree to keeping kosher to some extent. At first your spouse may seem more like an angry hostage than an enthusiastic partner. Over time—and it can take years—your spouse may become enamored with kashrut for his or her own reasons, and even thank you for opening the door. There is always hope, as long as you walk the line between not giving up and not pushing so hard that you only spark rebellion.

EXPERIMENT BEFORE YOU DECIDE

Marjorie Freiman, an involved Jew in Wellesley, Massachusetts, personifies the approach that many rabbis recommend these days.

If you are unsure about whether keeping kosher makes sense, or one of you wants to and the other does not, try kashrut for a period of time as an experiment. It doesn't have to be forever if it doesn't work. Even though Marjorie's family didn't feel the need to try kashrut as she did, they generously went along with her wishes. She shares their experience:

> My husband Lenny was very supportive when I said I wanted to try kashering our kitchen when our boys were ages 12 and nine. We spent over $1,200 for new pots, silverware, dishes, dish towels, sponges, etc. We emptied the cabinets of everything and restocked them with kosher alternatives. We gave it a good try but keeping kosher didn't work for us. Our food bill went up 25 percent. It was inconvenient—I couldn't run to the grocery store and pick up a pound of chicken nuggets when I needed to. Entertaining and going out was difficult since no one we know keeps kosher. Mealtime became an aggravation which defeated the whole purpose. After a year and half and a lot of discussion, we gave it up.

If Lenny had blocked Marjorie's need to try a kosher home, a divisive power struggle would have ensued. Marjorie would have believed that if only Lenny would get out of her way, she could have what she needed to further her Jewish exploration. Instead, she reached the same conclusion about kashrut that Lenny already held. And because Lenny was willing to experiment, they reached that conclusion together, harmoniously.

Jack Paskoff, a Reform rabbi, offers helpful guidelines for members of his congregation who are debating whether to try keeping kosher or to observe any Jewish ritual. He explains:

> Keeping kosher isn't antithetical to Reform Judaism. If the family says, we think this might be meaningful, do it. Here's a guide to healthy Reform decision making: What does the tradition and Halakhah say? Is there some moral or ethical problem with keeping the tradition? If yes, then as a Reform Jew, you can throw it out. If no, then try it for a period of several months. Is there some positive value for me person-

ally in observing the ritual? After trying it, was there anything negative about it? Is there a positive value in performing the act as an affirmation of *K'let Yisrael*?

As Rabbi Paskoff advises, an experimental period with thoughtful consideration will help confirm or reject your commitment to
kashrut. You may find after this experimental period that one of
you decided that keeping a kosher kitchen works, and the other
wishes you would return to making Chicken a la King. These
decisions require ongoing thoughtful conversation about what
each of you wants and how to achieve it. A decision as significant
as keeping a kosher kitchen or not, should not be made in haste
or in the middle of an argument. Avoid turning this into a power
struggle. Instead, determine how to meet the religious needs of
the most observant of you, without causing the less observant too
much stress.

Kosher Kid

If you are an Orthodox family keeping strictly kosher in and out
of the house or if you are a couple with no children, you haven't
faced one of the most difficult challenges for families who are
observing kosher laws, but not to their fullest. Introducing your
children to what it means to keep kosher when they haven't been
raised with it since birth, and imposing limits on their eating
habits when most of their friends aren't keeping kosher, will force
you and your spouse to deal with issues like these:

- When do we enforce milk and meat separation for young children who don't yet understand the meaning behind it?

- Do we allow our children to eat nonkosher food outside of the
  home in restaurants or at their friends' houses? If so, are there
  any limits? (that is, no pork or no pepperoni on the pizza, but
  a nonkosher hot dog is okay.)

- How do we explain to our children why we keep kosher and
  why other Jews, including Grandma and some of her Jewish
  friends, do not?

- What do we expect of our children if one parent keeps kosher and the other does not?

- Do we insist that the children pack their own lunch and snacks if they will be in a day care or school setting that does not serve kosher food?

- If we decide to start keeping kosher when the children are older, how do we deal with their rebellion and frustration when we take away a favorite food?

- How do we make keeping kosher a positive experience for our children?

Stephen and I have been keeping a kosher home since before our children were born. One of our most heated debates centered around how old the children should be before we enforced kosher rules for them. Stephen was repulsed by the thought of his children eating nonkosher food—he wanted them to follow kosher rules from the beginning of their life. I saw no reason to insist that a two year old "keep kosher" if he or she had no sense of what it meant. This became a problem when our children attended a day care center where, as the only Jews, they were regularly fed nonkosher snacks, including ham sandwiches, for lunch.

Stephen would have preferred we pack a lunch and snacks for our children. But at their young age, they didn't understand the difference between Jews and Christians and what keeping kosher meant. I knew that it would be impossible for the teachers to enforce the "no day care food" rule, and I didn't want the children to resent keeping kosher because it deprived them of eating what all of their classmates were eating. I believed that it would make them hate keeping kosher, so I agreed to a strictly kosher home, but I wanted them to eat what they wanted outside of the home. Ideally we could have found child care in a kosher setting, but where we live there is no such place for children under age four.

We compromised by asking the day care staff not to serve our kids nonkosher meat for lunch. It didn't always work because the staff frequently forgot about the restriction. Stephen wouldn't read the daily reports that came home with "ham sandwich" circled on the lunch menu. I agreed to insist on the separation of milk and meat in the home, even when they were too young to understand why. If the children asked for ice cream after a meat meal, we explained that they couldn't have it because it wasn't kosher, believing that eventually they would understand what that meant. It would have been much easier to give in to an insistent child who was upset when she felt deprived, but Stephen was right: as they grew older, they naturally accepted the concept of milk and meat separation and stopped complaining about it.

At the age of four, we saw a marked change in our daughter Sarah's Jewish identity, and allowing her to eat ham sandwiches became unacceptable, even to me. We enrolled Sarah in a small private Jewish day school, which created logistical challenges for us, but it was really the only workable solution if we stayed in Lancaster. There, everyone packs a kosher lunch, and before long, she was learning how to bensch after meals. Now, at the age of five, when Sarah accompanies me to the supermarket and sees something she wants, she asks: "Mommy, is this kosher?" Even I am delighted to hear that, despite my earlier ambivalence about kashrut. Keeping kosher has strengthened her identity as a Jew.

IS IT OKAY TO LIE TO YOUR KIDS ABOUT KOSHER FOOD?

If one of you is more committed to keeping kosher than the other, you have conflicts similar to one we encountered in our household. When we attend social functions in nonkosher homes and restaurants, Stephen eats vegetarian and I will eat nonkosher meat, but not pork or shellfish. For the most part, Stephen respects my right to make my own choices although I find it difficult to eat nonkosher meat in front of him.

One weekend, we visited nonkosher Jewish friends for Sunday lunch. Our friends served nonkosher chicken and a vegetarian dish so that my husband would have something to eat. The vegetarian dish was of no appeal to my children, and I served Sarah a plate of chicken as she requested. Just as she was about to dive in, she asked me: "Mommy, is this kosher?" Perhaps that was a teaching moment, and I should have told her the truth. Instead, I chose to lie. "Yes, sweetie, it is." She smiled and dug in with great delight.

Stephen does not approve of my decision. Why did I lie? Because I didn't want to offend the hostess. Because I didn't want to deal with an unhappy toddler who couldn't eat the meal she wanted. Because I didn't really believe that it mattered if she ate nonkosher chicken or not. Because I didn't know how to explain to a toddler the concept of kosher chickens and nonkosher chickens. Because I planned to eat the chicken and how would Sarah feel if she watched her mommy eating nonkosher food? It seemed that telling the truth would only confuse her.

Stephen prefers to teach our children not to eat nonkosher meat outside of the house. This is one freedom I have been reluctant to give up. If my children are restricted from eating nonkosher meat outside of the house, surely I will do the same.

Defining what I should tell my daughter when she asks, "Is this kosher?" has everything to do with understanding how "kosher" I wish to be, and what Stephen and I agree on for our children. Notice I said, *agree*. We are still working this one out.

WHEN YOU AND YOUR SPOUSE DON'T AGREE ABOUT KOSHER RULES FOR THE KIDS

In many kosher homes, members of the family vary in their kosher observance. Kids are raised seeing one parent eating treyf and the other not. Is this a problem? It depends on the age of the children and how the parents handle the differences. If one of you has expressed a preference for the children to keep kosher, explain to them once they have enough education to make their own decisions, that keeping kosher is a choice adults make. Here are a few recommendations for discussing issues of kashrut with your children:

Do's

- Discuss kashrut openly with your kids from the earliest age possible.

- Present a united position. Hash out the issues with your spouse in private so that you won't be battling it out in front of the children.

- Be consistent. Whatever level of kashrut you select for your family, enforce it consistently so that your children don't get confused or stop taking it seriously.

- Be flexible. As the children grow up and circumstances change, continue to evaluate what the kosher rules should be in your family. You may find yourself loosening or tightening the rules as the children age and start socializing with non-Jewish friends

Don'ts

- Don't make one of you the "kosher cop" by saying things like, "You can't go to the party; Daddy doesn't like them serving nonkosher food," or, "Mommy says you can't have ice cream because you just had a meat meal." Even if you don't really think this level of kashrut observance is necessary, if you and your spouse have agreed on kosher rules, enforce them together. All you need to say is, "That's not kosher," even if a part of you resents the fact that kashrut exists at all.

- Don't teach your children it's okay to sneak around. ("Shhh, don't tell your Daddy we're eating fried clams, okay?") You destroy any respect for kashrut, and turn it into a masquerade. If you agree that the children can eat nonkosher outside of the home, allow them to do so consistently, not just when "Daddy isn't around." Never tell the children to lie about what they eat to their kosher-observant parent.

- Don't despair if your children rebel once in a while against eating only kosher food. That's normal. If you react with disgust or anger ("How dare you say you want a cheeseburger! What kind of Jew are you"), you will only spark their desire to rebel even more, or discourage them from being open with you. Instead, empathize with the longing they express. One morning my toddlers started whining for a bagel after five days of eating Passover food. I was feeling the same way. I empathized with them, told them that I wanted a bagel badly too, and asked them to describe to me in detail the kind of bagel that they wished they could eat. Doing so did not make them want a bagel even more, it diffused the tension.

Adolescents may experiment with nonkosher food as a form of rebellion. It's better that they are telling you how they feel rather than keeping it private and sneaking around. Don't overreact or you will give the child exactly what he or she is looking for—a means to upset you and to take an independent stand.

Dealing With Your Extended Family

My mother-in-law makes matzoh balls that are repulsive to me.

—(Anonymous, in the interest of saving a marriage)

One of the trickiest issues to negotiate is when there is a significant difference in kosher observance between you and your parents, in-laws, or other extended family. It creates strife either way—if your mate won't eat in your parents' home, for example, or if your home is not acceptable for parents or other extended family. Family squabbles like the following can tear a family apart:

My brother married someone much less observant than he is. It is a constant struggle. On Thanksgiving, his wife got very insulted because my parents wouldn't eat her turkey. They will only eat from an oven that is used only for meat.

Each situation is unique, but here are recommendations that apply to every family situation:

Deal with it in a straightforward way. Rabbi Reuven P. Bulka recommends:

The biggest difficulty is anticipatory anxiety, thinking "I can't say anything," so you skirt around it. Let's say that your in-laws are uncomfortable with your level of kashrut. They might be afraid to say anything about it for fear of offending you. Treat them with respect: "We love you, we want to be able to enjoy being with you, we have this problem and we hope we can come to resolution. How about if we don't serve meat or anything hot? Or you can bring your own dishes and food and cook it here?" Approach them with menschlicheit.

Keep your judgments to yourself. Remember that one person's level of kashrut is as legitimate as another's. If you feel disdain for either someone's level or lack of observance, nothing is gained by expressing those feelings. An individual's or family's kashrut choices are up to them to determine. Keep your nose out of their kitchen.

Don't put your spouse in the middle. Don't ask your spouse to choose between honoring his or her parents or honoring you. It's a miserable place to be and a setup for trouble. Search with your spouse for a solution that will honor everyone's needs and be willing to compromise. Also, remember that one's parents and in-laws are not around forever. You may make certain choices now that you will not stick to once the older generation has passed away.

Don't let kashrut be a scapegoat. If you have relationship issues to work out with your daughter-in-law, mother, or whomever, be careful of setting up kashrut as the bad guy. If you don't want to spend time with your family, it's cowardly to blame kashrut disagreements as the sole reason for your separation. It can be a convenient excuse not to confront more significant difficulties in your relationship.

Stick together. If you both agree to keep a kosher home, but one of your parents is sabotaging your efforts by offering nonkosher food to grandchildren, speak to that person together and ask him or her to honor your requests. Present a united position, even though the person creating difficulty is related to only one of you by birth.

Don't compare your wife's cooking to your mother's. Hannah Turner's greatest fear about marrying her fiance Alexander Kukurudz is that he will expect her to perform as well in the kitchen as his mother does. Hannah was raised by parents who went out for dinner every night; they ate hot dogs and beans once in a while at home. She never learned how to cook, and she has a demanding career that keeps her out of the kitchen most evenings. Alexander's mother serves meals each weeknight with a table set like a fancy restaurant.

Hannah has made it clear to Alexander that she will never be the cook his mother is, nor does she want to be. Alexander has to fight the temptation to think, "Maybe she'll change once we are married." Maybe she will, and maybe she won't.

Be careful not to make your spouse feel as if he or she has to live up to the kitchen standard that you were raised with. As a couple, you must develop your own kitchen style, and if you were raised by a gourmet mother or a strident kosher frum woman, you may not match that in the kitchen of your adulthood.

Donna Brosbe is a Jew by choice, who was introduced to kashrut by her husband Bob. She started out keeping a kosher kitchen "the way Bob's mother always did it." Over time, Donna felt the need to create her own kosher practices unique from Bob's mother.

Create your own traditions in the kitchen so that you come to view kashrut practices as your own rather than just as the conventions you inherited from your mother-in-law.

Blessing Your Food

Even if you and your spouse disagree about kashering your kitchen, you can still bring Judaism into your meal times with a simple prayer before meals, such as the ha motzi. Although it will feel awkward at first if you are unaccustomed to saying a prayer before meals, once you put it into regular practice, it will become so natural that it will feel strange if you skip it.

Our daughters, Sarah and Elana, have memorized the mealtime prayer and fight over who gets to say it before anyone at the table can eat. (Of course saying it together is a natural solution, unless you have toddlers, who "want to do it by myself!") If your family is unresponsive or resistant, you can still say a blessing silently to yourself before eating your meal.

Some observant Jews also chant *Birkat Ha-Mazon* (grace after meals) which is found in many traditional books and booklets. If some family members are reluctant to try the grace after meals because of its length, consider an abbreviated version.

Fasting

Ironically, we end this chapter about Judaism in the kitchen with the question of how fasting is observed in your home. It is not unusual to see variations on fasting practices. For example, one of you may fast on Yom Kippur and the other might not. One of you might fast on other fast days, such as *Tisha b'Av*, and the other may only fast on Yom Kippur. One of you may fast with strict observance—a 25 hour fast from all forms of bodily pleasure (eating, drinking, sex, washing, anointing, or wearing leather). The other might drink liquids throughout the day. Regardless of what practice you choose, remember these three pieces of advice:

Never judge your spouse's fasting practices. Fasting behavior is between your spouse and God to work out. If your spouse is less observant than you, keep your judgments to yourself—or better yet, don't get judgmental at all. Your spouse's fasting behavior is none of your business.

Make it easier for your fasting spouse. If you, the husband, are not fasting, respect your wife by not eating in front of her. Or if you, the wife, aren't fasting but your husband is, don't pull out the sexy lingerie on a night he is trying to abstain from sexual relations. Remember, the duration won't be longer than 25 hours. Surely you can accommodate your spouse's wishes for one day.

You don't have to fast at home. If it's too hard for you to be around nonobservant family when you are fasting and they are not, spend the time in synagogue with other observant Jews.

12

In The Bedroom

True intimacy in marriage—fiery love—is created by constant withdrawal and reunion. If a husband and wife are never separate, their love begins to sour because they are not creating an environment appropriate to that love. The environment of constant togetherness is not conducive to man-woman love; it's the environment for brother-sister love or parent-child love. That's why the ideal blessing for a married couple is: "Your honeymoon should never end."

—Rabbi Manis Friedman, *Doesn't Anyone Ever Blush Anymore?*

The Laws of Mikvah

The Hebrew word *kodesh*, most often translated as "holy," actually means "that which is separated." The separation in marriage described above by Rabbi Friedman is created for Jews by observing a collection of laws described in Leviticus as "the laws of family purity"(*taharat ha-mishpachah*). We will refer to them as "mikvah." The word "mikvah" refers to the ritual bath in which traditional Jewish women immerse themselves and recite a special blessing following their monthly menstrual period and a seven-day waiting period before reconnecting sexually with their husbands.

According to these laws, during the time that a Jewish woman is menstruating, and for one week afterward, the couple abstain from any physical and sexual contact. This period of approximately twelve days is called *nidah*.

172

If you think asking a less observant spouse to keep kosher brings up resistance, it pales in comparison to how some men and women feel about curtailing their sexual freedom. On the surface, mikvah looks like punishment—removing that which is most enjoyable for nearly half of the month. The laws of family purity appear archaic, irrelevant for modern times, and decidedly unpleasant to some Jews. However, when a couple engages in the monthly ritual of mikvah and experiences the benefits, many women and men change their minds. I speak from personal experience on this one.

My husband and I have practiced the laws of mikvah since our wedding. When he first broached the subject during our courtship, I had never even heard of the mikvah and it all sounded strange to me. Stephen presented it as a strong request but not a demand, so I was free to make up my own mind. It was clear, however, that the man I was marrying needed us to observe mikvah for him to have a sense of well-being and comfort in our marriage, so I didn't give much thought to refusing his request. Rather, I searched for a way to make it right with me. In the beginning, I went to mikvah strictly as a gift for my husband. Over the last several years, however, it has become a gift to me as well.

Men's Resistance To Mikvah

This is easy to explain. Quite simply, some men don't appreciate being prohibited from making love to their wives for half the month, especially if they think the laws of family purity are nonsense. If a man sees no spiritual or emotional value in the process, he'll only see mikvah as control and restriction. If he is already feeling some distance from his wife, he may interpret mikvah as her weapon to keep him away—an excuse to reject him. No man wants to be sexually pushed away, so if that's how he views the mikvah, he'll put up a great deal of resistance.

Sometimes, it takes a while before a reluctant or angry husband will come around to seeing the benefits of mikvah. Also, if the man is worried that his wife is becoming too observant, he'll fight the mikvah and declare it the "last straw." Of course, she can still practice the laws of family purity by herself, since he'd have to rape her to force her to have sex against her will. But doing mikvah when your husband isn't agreeable is a very painful process.

Women's Resistance to Mikvah

Much of the resistance to mikvah comes from Jewish women, not men, for several reasons:

"HOW DARE YOU CALL ME UNCLEAN!"

Since the laws of mikvah designate a woman as "clean" or "unclean" during certain times in her cycle, many women, especially feminists, interpret the rules of nidah as denigrating to women. The mikvah is an ancient institution, dating back thousands of years. In the days of our ancestors, anyone who contracted various kinds of "impurity" or had come in contact with death was forbidden to enter the Temple without first immersing in mikvah waters to restore themselves to the state of purity. These ancient terms—pure, impure, clean, unclean—refer to spiritual states, not physical ones. When a women menstruates, there is a death, the loss of the egg and potential for life. *Taharah*, or purification brings the woman out of the impure spiritual state that results from being in contact with death. It has nothing to do with her body being dirty, but the language can instigate enormous defiance.

"I DON'T WANT TO GO IF WE ARE DONE HAVING CHILDREN"

A woman is usually at the most fertile point in her cycle in the days immediately following her immersion in the ritual bath. Meanwhile, her husband is carrying around 12 days worth of sperm production. Because of these two biological facts, mikvah is an effective fertility ritual that appeals to women who wish to conceive.

When a woman desires more children but her husband announces firmly that he is done, tension can develop around the mikvah. Every time she returns home from the mikvah, ready and wanting to conceive and he insists on birth control, she might question why she bothers doing mikvah anymore.

This Jewish woman shared her recent refusal to continue the practice of going to the mikvah after doing so for several years:

> We had two children and I desperately wanted another. My husband refused. The whole structure of mikvah is designed to help you conceive, but we were doing it with no intent to have a child. The mikvah stopped being a pleasant experience for me and I decided that I wouldn't do it anymore. My husband said, "This is not negotiable," but I replied: "I understand how important this is to you, but I'm too bitter and angry to go." He's not happy about it, and we abstain from having sex during my 12 days of nidah.

I asked her if she was worried about losing her marriage over this, since her Orthodox husband feels quite strongly about mikvah. She replied: "If I compromised myself at an essential level, so much resentment and anger would build up I couldn't keep on. It was better to take a stand, even though I knew it would precipitate a crisis, because I did it cleanly and lovingly."

"I Don't Want to Get Pregnant"

According to Jewish law, Jews are obligated to have at least two children, a girl and a boy. Unless it is medically or emotionally not possible, a Jewish woman is supposed to continue to have babies until she has met this obligation. Most modern Jews, other than Orthodox, do not make family planning decisions according to this law. Mikvah-observant Jewish couples will tend to produce a sizeable brood unless they tackle the birth control issue.

The mikvah's power to time sexual relations with a woman's most fertile period for conception is fabulous when you want another baby, but problematic when you don't want to become pregnant again. Having conceived three times in just over four years, I'm here to tell you—mikvah works! When you want to stop having babies, but continue going to the mikvah, you are faced with a myriad of birth control choices, many of them unpleasant, unreliable, and against Jewish law.

Jewish law allows only birth control methods that interfere minimally with sexual relations. The pill ranks number one, but it can be a health hazard, especially for women in their late 30s or older with medical conditions. A vasectomy is against Jewish law because a man is commanded to have children and avoid self-mutilation. Jewish men are supposed to avoid using a condom, since it wastes his sperm. As you can see, few appealing birth control options are recommended by Jewish law, so modern couples have adjusted by making their own decisions. Many Jewish couples elect a vasectomy or a tubal ligation, even though both are not in accordance with Jewish law. In fact, most Jews today use forms of contraception that are forbidden by rabbinic law.

Most birth control options are less than 100 percent guaranteed, some significantly less. For many Jewish women, the mikvah rituals present too great a risk for another pregnancy, and they choose to stop going for a period of time, until they work out these issues with their spouse or move into a less fertile phase in their life.

> One Orthodox rabbi advised, "If you want to practice mikvah, but you don't want to make love during your most fertile time of the month, delay going to the mikvah until a few days past the most fertile period of the month rather than skip the mikvah entirely."

"ABSTAINING FROM SEX MAKES MY HUSBAND GRUMPY"

Some men, deprived of sex for 12 days, get downright ornery. A wife can easily come to resent mikvah when she isn't being treated affectionately by her husband. She may start grumbling to herself, "Why should I schlep all the way to the mikvah tonight in the cold and dark when he treats me like this? I don't even want to have sex with him anyway." Since the couple is expected to make love when the woman returns from the mikvah, if she doesn't want to have sex with her husband she'll feel trapped and resistant to going to the mikvah. Technically, she can refuse her husband on mikvah night, but it goes against the entire spirit of going to the mikvah.

If a husband doesn't handle sexual abstinence well, the woman will likely want to abandon mikvah practices.

"I ABHOR THE INSPECTION"

Before a woman immerses in the mikvah, a female attendant known as a *shomeret* glances at her naked body to be sure that she has removed all items, including makeup, loose strands of hair, and even nail polish that might prevent the water from covering her entirely. It is uncomfortable to have one's naked body inspected by a stranger. When the immersion is complete, this attendant will pronounce "kosher" if the immersion is done according to halakhic standards, the whole body being entirely submerged. If not, the woman will be asked to immerse again. On one occasion, the shomeret asked me to immerse myself three additional times to meet her strident standards. I was tempted to nickname her "Sergeant."

A woman entering the mikvah must either become grateful for this assistant's help, or detach from the inspection process so that it does not feel degrading. Otherwise, she will dread the mikvah process and make excuses not to go. Also, some shomerets are more lenient than others in the inspection process, so it may not be uncomfortable, depending on your attendant.

Motivations for Doing Mikvah

Despite the present-day resistance from many men and women to the practice, thousands of Jewish couples are following the laws of mikvah every month. Those who do find great reward in the practice. Here are some of the positive results a couple can achieve from mikvah:

A rebirth and spiritual renewal. When a woman participates in the mikvah ritual, she gives herself the time and space to experience a spiritual renewal and a ritualized way of honoring the natural cycles of life and death that accompany her menstrual cycle.

When I am soaking in the tub and preparing my body for my ritual immersion, it is often the only hour of that month when I am totally alone, without children or husband, and able to give myself over to prayer and relaxation. Being silent for even 15 minutes allows me to get in touch with the spiritual part of me that is often shut down in my crowded, chaotic life. I know I should take time for spiritual reflection more often, but I don't. The mikvah ritual forces this opportunity on me even when I think that I've got too much to do. It's also the one time when I can tell my husband, "You handle the kids. I'll be back in a few hours" and I don't feel guilty about it.

Increased fertility. If you want to get pregnant, there is no better way! Stories abound of women with histories of infertility and miscarriages who find the mikvah ritual to be healing both spiritually and physically.

The mikvah is no guarantee if infertility is a medical issue in your marriage. But if fertility is at all possible, it brings you together at your most fertile time after a period of abstinence (increased sperm count and a ripe egg!), sets the stage for a romantic, and perhaps more relaxed union, and some women believe, brings hashem into the process through more fervent prayer and whatever power the waters of mikvah may have.

A spicier sex life. In long marriages, sex becomes routinized. It doesn't take long before the mystery you reveled in during your early courtship is replaced with a familiarity that dulls your sexual desire for your partner. The mikvah helps protect couples against one of the enemies of married life—sexual boredom. The drama of reconnection is experienced by many couples as a romantic renewal of sexual interest in their partner—and it happens every month. The mandatory monthly separation instills feelings of longing and desire that often disappear after several years of marriage. Men who start out resistant to mikvah often come around when they realize that the sex they have after mikvah is much more satisfying for both of them.

Rabbi Reuven P. Bulka comments on the perception that the *Taharat Hamishpachah* laws deprive the marriage of sensual opportunity and spontaneity:

> This is true, at least to some extent. First, what is lost in spontaneity on the night of immersion is more than compensated for by the heightened sense of anticipation.
>
> Second, the argument for spontaneity can sometimes be a facade masking a desire to indulge when one wants, without assuring the eagerness of the other. More important than spontaneity is sensitivity to one's spouse.
>
> Finally, there is still ample room for mutual spontaneity during the more than two weeks when conjugal union can take place. Potential conflict arising from uncoordinated desires, in which one is in the mood but the partner is not, is minimized. Almost two weeks apart is an effective way to establish correlated moods.

Furthermore, when a couple can't make love, they find new ways to relate to one another. They often talk more and communicate in nonphysical ways. It is especially beneficial for a man to find new ways to relate intimately other than through sex.

An alternative to fighting. Couples pick fights with each other when one or both individuals need space. When tempers flare and harsh words are spoken, it may be an unconscious need to push away one's mate rather than have a valid disagreement. The mikvah ritual allows the couple to plan a separation that is beneficial rather than waiting for the need for separation to build up, precipitating a fight.

Connection to previous generations. Some men and women relish knowing that they are part of a long chain of Jewish ancestors who have observed the laws of family purity since the earliest days of our people. During generations of persecution, Jews built mikvahs in hiding—in underground tunnels, in cellars, under tables, and even in closets. If your grandmother and great grandmother observed these laws, it is a powerful way to feel connected to them once they have passed on. Some women even visualize these women from generations past when they are immersing themselves in the mikvah.

Recommendations for Working Out Mikvah Conflicts

If you are negotiating mikvah in your marriage, here are some suggestions to keep in mind:

FOR THE HUSBAND

You can't force your wife to comply. It's her body, and if she does not want to go to mikvah, you endanger your marriage if you give her an ultimatum. Ask her to try it, and give her the exit option after six months if she doesn't like it. Educate her about mikvah and help her to see the benefits, not just the constraints. If she agrees, express your gratitude for her willingness to give you this gift.

    The last thing you want to do is lecture her about the theological and historical reasons for why she *should* do mikvah. Make mikvah inviting through your behavior. When you treat her like a queen and she sees how it benefits your relationship, she may be motivated for that reason alone. A woman is often driven by the desire to connect more intimately with her husband. If she says "No, not ever," don't react by pushing too hard—she'll just dig her heels in deeper. Revisit the issue when you are cuddling together in bed, and her heart is open to you. Always respect that it is her decision, and that she is responsible for her body and sexuality.

    You may encourage using mikvah to assist with fertility, but *never* blame a woman's miscarriage on her lack of attendance at the mikvah. Do not refer to the counting of the postmenstrual days as the "clean" days if that triggers a defensive response from your wife.

FOR THE WIFE

Don't focus on how the laws of mikvah will take away sex from your husband. Unless he is motivated by the feeling of obligation for observing this mitzvot, he will likely view mikvah as a very bad idea. Help him understand how the quality of the sex between you will likely be enhanced, and encourage him to experiment for six months. To help reframe the rejection, tell him that you want to do mikvah in order to connect more deeply and have even better sex, not to have an excuse to not have relations with your husband for half the month. Then, show him through your behavior how mikvah gives him a better sexual experience, not a lessened one.

He has little choice but to accept your wishes, but do everything you can to help him feel that this is his choice too—that it's not just something you've done to him.

Create a mikvah date and make it special. With the exception of medical emergencies and very few religious obligations (such as Yom Kippur), nothing should keep you from making love when your nidah period has ended. This is one night you are entitled to put your relationship before all other needs, including those of your children. Hire a babysitter, go out for dinner, or light some candles and put on some soft music at home. Men, she just spent over an hour making herself as clean and attractive to you as possible. Prepare for her as you did when you were dating her, trying to convince her to marry you!

Here's a tip that Stephen and I have learned from experience. It's much harder to create a romantic mikvah date when you have children, especially young ones. When I leave for the mikvah, Stephen is responsible for our three little ones. Sometimes, that task zaps all of his energy so that by the time I come home from the mikvah, ready to reconnect, all Stephen wants to do is sleep. Ideally, when I go to mikvah, he starts getting the children ready for bed early in the evening, shortly after I leave. On a good night, he has them asleep in their beds with enough time to get himself ready, put out some flowers, and light some candles. When I come home, we are able to sustain that newlywed atmosphere for at least a few hours.

WHEN A SPOUSE REFUSES TO DO MIKVAH

If your spouse refuses to consider mikvah for now, let it go and focus on increasing observance in other areas of your life that you can do alone, like davening or studying. One woman shared this thought with me: "No matter how beautiful the picture of spirituality I painted and how it would enhance our sex life, my husband saw it as giving up half of a good thing. He wasn't willing to try it. We stalemated."

When you reach an impasse, your reaction may be to close yourself off from your spouse in anger. Just the opposite is advisable. When you gain your spouse's affection and appreciation, he or she is more likely to consider giving you the gift you are asking for. When you are demanding and hostile, you destroy any lingering hope that your spouse will change his or her mind.

Like all issues we discuss in this book, don't despair if, for the time being, this difference is irreconcilable. You may eventually be able to work it out. Even if you never reach an agreement both of you feel good about, according to many of the Jewish couples I spoke with, you will learn to live with it.

13

Expanding Observance in Nonthreatening Ways

The more Jewish you do, the more Jewish you feel.

—Rabbi Laibel Lam, Monsey, New York

WE OFTEN THINK THAT Jewish practice and tradition come down to what we have concentrated on thus far in this book—going to synagogue, observing significant Jewish holidays and the Sabbath, studying Jewish texts, keeping kosher, observing the laws of family purity, and of course, celebrating the occasional wedding, bris, or bar mitzvah. Certainly, these practices are the cornerstones of our tradition, which is why I have focused on them. However, to end the book there would be shortsighted. If you did none of these things, you'd still be a Jew.

Many Jews value their Jewish identity and want to create a life with their spouse that celebrates it, but they aren't drawn to traditional observance. Judaism doesn't need to be found in the synagogue. Judaism can infuse all aspects of your being—the way that you think and relate to others, the music you listen to, the art you appreciate, the ethics that guide your decision-making, your thoughts about God, and your purpose for being on this planet—even your philosophy about marriage and parenting.

If you take away nothing else from this book but this one thought, it will be enough to save your marriage from despair: *If you want to reconcile the Jewish differences in your marriage, stop focusing on the issues that are the most divisive and emphasize*

183

the Jewish observances you can and do share with your mate. Gil Mann states in his book, *How to Get More Out of Being Jewish*:

> Judaism is a way of life consisting of these three separate sacred components: E.S.P.—ethics, spirituality, and people-hood. You can choose to enter the Jewish way of life through any of these circles. And from each circle you can access the other two circles. You can choose to emphasize or de-emphasize any or all of the three and still be considered a Jew.

Too often Jewish couples in conflict spend all of their emotional energy trying to find a way to coexist in the spirituality circle, even though they hold radically different notions of God and preferences for practicing their Jewish faith. Don't give up reconciling those differences, but in the meantime, you can share many other meaningful Jewish traditions.

22 Ways to Expand Your Jewish Identity

Here are several ideas you might not have considered for celebrating Judaism together. Many of these ideas and activities are less emotionally charged and contentious than some of the hotter issues we've discussed so far:

1. Take classes in or read about the Jewish code of ethical behavior. For example, how Jews are supposed to treat a disadvantaged person, the Jewish viewpoint on medical ethics, or how a Jew might handle a tricky work situation that borders on the unethical. Engage in conversation with your family about these matters and teach your children. Debate the grey areas and how each of you might handle a difficult situation. When you have the opportunity to turn a disciplinary session with your children into a teaching about Jewish ethics, do so. Traditional text from *Pirke Avot*, for example, offers timeless wisdom on these issues.

2. Do acts of chesed in the community, and involve your children. Visit a neighbor who is sick and bring some homemade goodies. Bring the kids to a nursing home or involve them in reg-

ular volunteer work. Serve the homeless at a shelter on Christmas Day. Get involved with synagogue social action projects. Teach your children about mitzvahs and help them find ways, every week, to do one or two. It will make them feel proud and help them develop their identity as Jews. Soon they will start asking for opportunities to do a mitzvah. When you praise them for a job well done, thank them for doing a mitzvah, and explain to them the mitzvah they have done.

3. Attend Jewish music festivals, concerts, and cantorial performances. Instead of listening to the radio in the car, play Jewish CDs and tapes. The kids will start singing along—and so will you. You can also play Jewish music in the house, especially during Shabbat preparation.

4. Read Jewish fiction and nonfiction.

5. Exhibit Jewish and Israeli art in your home. Put your ketubah in a prominent place. Put ritual objects of beauty and meaning, such as menorahs and Sabbath candlesticks out for viewing all the time, instead of just pulling them out for holiday use. Shop together for special ritual objects that you would be proud to display.

6. Celebrate special events, like the holiday of Tu'b'Shvat, by planting a tree in Israel.

7. Take a family trip to Israel, or go on your own to study at one of the many yeshivas available. Or take a vacation to Jewish sightseeing places in the United States, such as the Holocaust Museum in Washington, D.C.

8. Hang a Jewish calendar on the wall and use it as your primary family calendar.

9. Get involved in Jewish community organizations other than synagogue, such as *Hadassah*, the Jewish Federation, Jewish family services, social action groups devoted to Middle East peace, and so on.

10. Volunteer on synagogue committees.

11. Affix a mezuzah on each outside door, and if desired, on every doorway in your home.

12. Write an Ethical Will for your spouse, children, and grandchildren. It is a Jewish custom to put in writing your beliefs,

values, and the personal messages you wish to pass along to loved ones upon your death.

13. Keep a tzedakah box prominently displayed in the kitchen and develop a ritual with the children of placing coins in it every week. Once in awhile, roll up all the coins and let the kids give it to the charity of their choice.

14. Subscribe to Jewish magazines and newspapers and read the Jewish magazines that often accompany synagogue membership.

15. Frame photographs of family Jewish life-cycle events and family descendants from the "old country," and display them on your walls and bookcases.

16. Wear Jewish jewelry, like a Star of David, or a mezuzah on a chain. On special occasions, like birthdays and Hanukkah, purchase such items for family members.

17. If you have artistic ability, create Jewish art and ritual objects yourself, or take a class to learn how.

18. Tithe a percentage of your income for local and national fundraising efforts to support Israel and Jews around the world.

19. Take a Jewish adult education class together with your spouse or with a group of couples with whom you regularly socialize.

20. Learn Jewish blessings and prayers you can say throughout the day—such as when you rise, before you eat, after washing, and so on—so that you can pray throughout the day, not just in synagogue.

21. Sing the shema with your kids every night before they go to sleep.

22. Celebrate the so-called "minor" Jewish holidays that you don't normally celebrate as a family. Read Jewish holiday books to give you creative ideas for how to create family fun and meaning. Celebrate Sukkot, Shavuot, Simchas Torah, Purim, and Tu B'Shvat. For example:

• Dance with the Torah at synagogue on *Simchas Torah*.

• Make hamantashen cookies on Purim and deliver baskets of Purim goodies to your neighbors.

- Build and decorate a sukkah and invite neighbors and friends for a meal.
- Stay up all night on Shavuot studying Torah at your synagogue.

Although you may have purchased this book because you are concerned with working out your Jewish differences, don't miss out on the myriad opportunities to celebrate your shared Jewish identity. Take your eyes off of the conflict and place it on your mutual love and commitment to being Jewish and passing along a Jewish identity to your children. You will quickly rediscover what you believed when you first got married—that as fellow Jews, you have much in common, indeed.

Conclusion: *Beshert*

The one Torah concept that will make the most practical difference to the emotional quality of your life is the awareness
that everything the Almighty does is for your benefit.

—Rabbi Chaim Zaichyk

This, Too, Is for the Best

IS BEING IN A MIXED Jewish marriage a curse or a blessing? On a
bad day, you might be thinking that your life would have turned
out so much better if you had only found a Jewish partner who
wasn't so . . . different! But guess what? Every married person
says those same words at difficult moments—mixed Jewish marriage or not. Don't fool yourself into thinking that the Jewish differences are the only reason that you are sometimes stressed in
your marriage, and that if only these differences would disappear,
everything would be wonderful.

Jewish practice and observance issues are simply one of many
challenges you will work out in your lifetime together. Unresolved,
they can lead to misery or divorce. But being in a mixed Jewish
marriage may be the *best* thing that ever happened for you, even
if you didn't ask for it.

The Talmud teaches a vital Jewish lesson about believing that
whatever is, is for the best—even the struggles of your marriage:

There was a man nicknamed Nahum of Gamzu, because
no matter what happened to him, he would always say,

"This too is for the best," which in Hebrew is *Gam zu letovah*.

One time, the Jews of the land of Israel wanted to send a gift to the emperor. After much discussion, they decided that Nahum should carry the gift because he had experienced many miracles. They sent him with a saddlebag filled with precious stones and pearls.

On the way he stopped at an inn overnight. While he slept, the people at the inn emptied his bag of its precious stones and filled it with earth. Next morning when Nahum discovered what had happened, he said, "This too is for the best!" When Nahum arrived at his destination and his gift was opened, it was found to be filled with earth. "The Jews are mocking me," the emperor cried, and ordered Nahum put to death. Once again, Nahum exclaimed, "This too is for the best!"

At that moment Elijah the prophet appeared disguised as one of the emperor's ministers and said, "Perhaps this is some of the earth of their patriarch Abraham. When he threw earth against his enemies it turned into swords, and when he threw stubble, it changed into arrows."

There was one province that the emperor had not been able to conquer. Now his men took some of the earth and threw it at the warriors in this province, and quickly defeated them. The joyous emperor had Nahum taken to the royal treasury. There his bags were filled with precious stones and pearls and he was sent home with great honor.

When he arrived at the inn where he had stayed before, the people asked him: "What did you take to the emperor that you have been treated with such honor?"

"I brought only what I had taken from here," answered Nahum. The innkeepers took some earth to the emperor and said to him, "The earth that was brought to you before belonged to us."

The emperor had the earth tested but it had no power. And the innkeepers were put to death.

—Babylonian Talmud, tractate Ta'anit, pages 21a-b,
Voices of Wisdom

Believe in your heart that your marriage, exactly as it is, is for the best, and you will start finding more good in it. From there, you will create more good in it. Embrace the learning and personal growth, and even the struggle, if you believe that your mate is your beshert, and your union was designed by Hashem. If that is true, then the Jewish differences between you are also beshert.

Finding the Perfect Mate Is a Miracle

Lest you start wondering if it wouldn't be much easier to just find a mate who is more like you are, remember this story:

> A Roman matron asked Rabbi Yose ben Halafta, "How many days did it take God to create the world?" "It took him six days," was the answer. "And from then until now, how does He spend His time?" she asked. "The Holy One, blessed be He," answered Rabbi Yose, "sits and pairs off couples—this one's daughter with this one's son."
> "That's his work?" she asked incredulously. "I can easily do the same thing. I have a number of male and female slaves, and in a single hour I can pair them all off." "It may appear easy to you," said the rabbi, "yet every marriage is as difficult for God as was the parting of the Red Sea."
> Rabbi Yose went on his way. And what did the matron do? She gathered a thousand slaves, male and female, arranged them in rows and said, "This one will marry this one, and this one will marry this one," until she had paired them off in a single night.
> The next morning they came to her—this one's arm was cut, this one's eye blackened, this one's leg broken. "What's happened?" she asked. One said, "I don't want her." And the other cried, "I don't want him."
> The matron immediately sent for the rabbi and said to him, "Rabbi, your Torah is true and exalted, and everything you spoke well."

—Francine Klagsbrun, *Voices Of Wisdom*

You Can Be Happy—Despite,
Even Because of, Your Differences

Many of us have been brainwashed into a fairy tale image of falling in love and marriage. We believe that happiness is an entitlement and if we aren't always delighted, it's because we have married the wrong person. If only he was less religious, she was more observant, and so on, becomes our excuse for our unhappiness. When the "if only's" have invaded our mind, we have lost touch with the blessings of our marriage and the responsibility that we each have for our own spiritual growth. These differences are a big deal, and they will complicate your life and greatly challenge your marriage. However, they pale in comparison to some challenges married couples deal with—disability, poverty, lack of love and respect, the tragic loss of a loved one, and so on.

Shalom bayit is present in the homes of couples with far greater differences, and far more tragedy, than any you have known. Happy couples have the same problems as couples who are miserable. The difference is that happy couples learn how to resolve the problems in their marriage with love, respect, and infinite patience. You can learn to be a happy couple, regardless of your Jewish differences. Such joy and contentment may not come to you on a silver platter—you will have to work for it—but it can happen regardless of your Jewish differences, or maybe even because of them.

RIDING ON THE SAME TRAIN

Judy Lederman, an Orthodox Jewish woman who is far more observant than her husband, shared an insightful metaphor that gives her ongoing hope and encouragement, despite the significant conflicts in her marriage:

> I like to think of my husband and me as being on two different trains, heading in the same direction. I'm on the express train, and he's on the local train, so we are moving at different speeds and making different stops along the way.

Hopefully though, we continue to head in the same direction. When a married couple are on different trains, headed in opposite directions, the marriage is in real trouble.

Taking this metaphor a step further, I hope you and your spouse will eventually come together in the same train, headed in one direction. That train may go slower than one of you would like, and faster than the other prefers. It might stop at a place that one of you finds irrelevant and speed by a location one of you wishes to hang out in for awhile. That train might serve only kosher food, kosher food in one section and treyf in another, or nonkosher food entirely. It might have a place to pray where the men and women sit together or separately, or different cars with a choice of prayer environment in each. Available Jewish reading material could range from Hebrew commentaries to English biographies of Jewish leaders. It might have a mezzuzah posted on the doorway of each car and Jewish artwork all over the walls, or it may be unadorned.

Your commitment to be together, traveling on the same train, will make each of you willing to sacrifice as needed. It may not be the perfect train for each of you, and the journey at times will be frustrating and difficult. But at least it's a Jewish train, and with God's help, you are together on it, working toward your destination of shalom bayit. Over time, you will come to love the ride, even when you end up in places you didn't expect. Always, you will remember that you love one another and that this is the train you are supposed to be on, guided by your conductor, Hashem.

Peace in your home and in your heart is God's wish for you, and mine, too.

Shalom.

Recommended Resources

BOOKS

A total list of the books used as research for *"Two Jews Can Still Be a Mixed Marriage"* appears in the bibliography. Here are my top ten recommendations on this topic:

Fighting for Your Marriage: Active Steps for Preventing Divorce and Preserving a Lasting Love, by Susan L. Blumberg, Howard Markman, and Scott Stanley (Jossey-Bass, 1994).

God Was Not in the Fire: The Search For A Spiritual Judaism, by Daniel Gordis (Simon and Schuster, 1995).

The Heart of Commitment: Compelling Research That Reveals the Secrets of a Lifelong, Intimate Marriage, by Scott Stanley, Ph.D. (Thomas Nelson, 1998).

How to Stay Lovers for Life: Discover a Marriage Counselor's Tricks of the Trade, by Sharyn Wolf, C.S.W. (Plume, 1997).

The Lord Will Gather Me In: My Journey to Jewish Orthodoxy, by David Klinghoffer (Free Press, 1999).

Marriage: A Wise and Sensitive Guide to Making Any Marriage Even Better, by Rabbi Zelig Pliskin (Mesorah Publications, Ltd., 1998).

The Eight Essential Traits of Couples Who Thrive, by Susan Page (Little, Brown, 1994).

Our Love Is Too Good to Feel So Bad: A Step-by-Step Guide to Identifying and Eliminating the Love Killers in Your Relationship, by Mira Kirschenbaum (Avon Books, 1998).

Stalking Elijah: Adventures With Today's Jewish Mystical Masters, by Rodger Kamenetz (HarperCollins, 1997).

The Ten Commandments: The Significance of God's Laws in Everyday Life, by Dr. Laura Schlessinger (Cliff Street Books, 1998).

Total Immersion: A Mikvah Anthology, edited by Rivkah Slonim (Jason Aronson, 1995).

The Year Mom Got Religion: One Woman's Midlife Journey Into Judaism, by Lee Meyerhoff Hendler (Jewish Lights Publishing, 1998).

JEWISH EDUCATION AND COUNSELING

Making Marriage Work. A 10 week course for engaged or newly married couples that discusses both interreligious concerns and general marriage issues. General issues include marital communications, handling two careers, money and time management, sexuality, and decisions about child rearing. Religious issues include problems of parents and in-laws and religious identification of children. In interactive seminars, groups of 10 couples meet with a licensed tharapist, a rabbi, and a certified financial planner. The course is now offered in Washington, D.C., Philadelphia, Houston, Denver, Kansas City, East coast of Florida, and in the San Francisco, East Bay, and San Jose areas in California. Contact:

University of Judaism
Making Marriage Work
15600 Mulholland Drive
Bel Air, California, 90077
(310) 440-1233
e-mail: mmw@uj.edu

Marriage Encounter. The movement exists to help basically healthy couples strengthen their relationship. It also has a religious message: by fully experiencing your unity as a couple, you experience a oneness with God. Marriage Encounter began as a Catholic concept and now is offered in Jewish and Protestant forms as well. Its centerpiece is the intensive encounter weekend. There is no national office to contact, so look in your phone book under "Marriage Encounter/Jewish."

National Jewish Outreach Program. Learn to read Hebrew or the basics of traditional Judaism. Courses available throughout the country.

NJOP
485 5th Ave, Suite 701
New York, NY 10017
1-800-44HEBREW
e-mail: njop@worldplaza.com

Florence Melton Schools. Two-year school in which adults can gain foundation in Jewish knowledge. Set up in synagogues around the country.

Sometimes set up in a federation, bureau of Jewish education, a JCC, or a college. Contact:

Betsy Katz, North American Director
Florence Melton School
255 Revere Drive, Suite 112,
Northbrook, IL 60062,
714-9843 ext 301.
e-mail: bracha@ix.netcom.com

Me'ah Program. An intenstive Jewish Adult Study program offered as a joint project of Combined Jewish Philanthropies, Union of American Hebrew Congregations, United Synagogue of Conservative Judaism, the Council of Orthodox Synagogues, and the Synagogue Council of Massachusetts. Contact:

Carolyn Keller, Director
The Commission on Jewish Continuity
126 High Street
Boston, MA 02110
(617) 457-8542

School for Jewish Studies. Rabbi Alan Ullman offers Torah study for adults as a path for spiritual growth and learning. Contact him at:

288 Newtonville Ave,
Newtonville, MA, 02460
(617) 641-2089

Foundations for Jewish Learning. National outreach organization offering adult Jewish study and Shabbaton headed by:

Rabbi Laibel Lamm
10 Wallenberg Circle
Monsey, NY 10952
(914) 352-0111

Pairs International Inc. Couples counseling workshops available throughout the country, offered by local PAIRS leaders. Contact:

National Office
Rabbi Morris Gordon and Lori Gordon
1152 N. University Drive, Suite 202
Pembroke Pines, FL 33024-5031
(954) 431-4540
e-mail: info@pairs.org

Makom Shalom, A Mid-Atlantic Jewish Retreat Center. Recreational and educational conference space and kosher retreat center located in Northeast Maryland. Contact:

Ken Firestone, Director and Coordinator
2626 Pinewood Road
Lancaster, PA 17601
(717) 569-5717
e-mail: firek@makomshalom.org
Web site: www.makomshalom.org

Elat Chayyim: A Center for Healing and Renewal

Rabbi Jeff Roth and Rabbi Joanna Katz
99 Mill Hook Road
Accord, NY 12404
(800) 398-2630
e-mail: elatchayyi@aol.com

The Center for Jewish Spiritual Practice of The Academy for Jewish Religion. The Academy for Jewish Religion offers evening courses called Jewish Spiritual Intimacy for Couples and also offers Jewish spiritual guidance in private sessions for individuals and couples.

Rabbi Goldie Milgram, Director
15 W. 8th Street
New York, NY 10024
(212) 875-0540
www.ajrsem.org
e-mail: eminary@erols.com

Jewish Resources

Judaica Book Guide. A catalog of Jewish books and mailorder.

Jonathan David Co, Inc.
68-22 Eliot Avenue
Middle Village, NY, 11379
(718) 456-8611

The Torah Tapes of Rabbi Yissocher Frand. Tapes for Jewish learning; a catalog of hundreds of tapes available.

Yad Yechiel Institute
PO Box 511
Owings Mills, MD 21117-0511
(410) 358-0416

Internet Web sites for Jewish Life

www.JewishFamily.com/
www.marketnet.com/mktnet/kosher/recipes
www.aish.edu/
www.jewhoo.com

The Jewish Video Catalog from Ergo Media, Inc.

Ergo Media, Inc.
668 American Legion Drive
P.O. Box 2037
Teaneck, NJ 07666-1437
1-800-695-3746
Fax: (201) 692-0663
e-mail: ergo@intac.com
Web site: www.businessview.com/ergo/

SYNAGOGUE OFFICES

Jewish Renewal

Aleph: Alliance for Jewish Renewal
7318 Germantown Road
Philadelphia, PA 19119-1793
(215) 247-9700
e-mail: Alephajr@aol.com

Conservative Judaism Headquarters

United Synagogue of America
155 Fifth Avenue
New York, NY 10010
(212) 533-7800

National Havurah Committee. The central address for chavurahs all over the country.

7318 Germantown Avenue
Philadelphia, PA 19119-1720
(215) 248-9760
e-mail: 73073.601@compuserve.com

P'nai Or Headquarters

P'nai Or House
6723 Emlen Street
Philadelphia, PA 19119
(215) 849-5385

Reconstructionist Judaism Headquarters

Federation of Reconstructionist Congregations and Havurot
Church Road and Greenwood Avenue
Wyncote, PA 19095
(215) 887-1988
e-mail: jrfnatl@aol.com

Reform Judaism Headquarters

Union of American Hebrew Congregations,
838 Fifth Avenue
New York, NY, 10021
(212) 249-0100

Secular Jewish Groups

Congress of Secular Jewish Organizations
19657 Vukka Drive North
Southfield, MI 48076
Web site: www.netaxs.com~csjo

Society for Humanistic Judaism
28611 west Twelve Mile Road
Farmington Hills, MI 48334
Webs site: www.shj.org

List of Interviewees

RABBIS AND CANTORS

Rabbi Chaim Adelman and Yocheved Adelman, Hasidic, Chabad House at Amherst, Amherst, Massachusetts

Rabbi Dan Alexander, Reform, Congregation Beth Israel, Charlottesville, Virginia

Rabbi Reuven P. Bulka, Orthodox, Congregation Machzikei Hadas, Ottawa, Canada

Rabbi Carl Choper, Reconstructionist, Temple Beth Shalom, Mechanicsberg, Pennsylvania

Rabbi Andrea Cohen-Kiener, Renewal, West Hartford, Connecticut

Cantor Renee Coleson, North Shore Synagogue, Syosset, New York

Rabbi Darryl Crystal, Reform, North Shore Synagogue, Syosset, New York

Rabbi James Gibson, Reform, Temple Sinai, Pittsburgh, Pennsylvania

Rabbi Jonathon Girard, Reform, Covenant of Peace, Easton, Pennsylvania

Rabbi Elyse Goldstein, Reform, Kolel Center, Toronto, Canada

Rabbi Leonard Gordon, Conservative, Jewish Centre, Mt. Airy, Pennsylvania

Rabbi Morris Gordon, Ph.D, Conservative, PAIRS Foundation, Pembroke Pines, Florida

Rabbi Graubart, Conversative, Congregation B'nai Israel, Northhampton, Massachusetts

Rabbi Richard Hirsch, Reconstructionist Rabbinical Association, Philadelphia, Pennsylvania

Rabbi Daniel Karapkin, Orthodox, Sons of Israel, Allentown, Pennsylvania

Rabbi Michael Klayman, Conservative, Temple Israel, Great Neck, New York

Rabbi Kornfeld, Hasidic, Chabad Labovitch, Seattle, Washington

Rabbi Laibel Lam, Director of Foundations for Jewish Learning, Monsey, New York

Rabbi Levi Meier, Cedars-Sinai Medical Center, Los Angeles, California

Rabbi Goldie Milgram, Dean at Academy for Jewish Religion, New York, New York

Rabbi Kerry Olitzky, Reform, Wexner Heritage Foundation, New York, New York

Rabbi Jack Paskoff, Reform, Temple Shaarai Shomayim, Lancaster, Pennsylvania

Rabbi Stephen Carr Ruben, Reconstructionist, Pacific Palisades Synagogue, California

Rabbi Shaya Sackett, Orthodox, Congregation Degel Israel, Lancaster, Pennsylvania

Rabbi Sandy Sasso, Reconstructionist, Beth El Zedeck, Indianapolis, Indiana

Rabbi Ian Silverman, Conservative, Temple Beth El, Lancaster, Pennsylvania

Rabbi Rifat Sonsino, Reform, Temple Beth Shalom, Newton, Massachusetts

Rabbi Ira Stone, Conservative, Beth Zion/Beth Israel, Philadelphia, Pennsylvania

Rabbi Alan Ullman, Founder, School for Jewish Studies, Newton, Massachusetts

Rabbi Emmanuel Vinas, Jewish Community Center on the Hudson, Tarrytown, New York

Rabbi Arthur Waskow, Renewal, Sholom Center, Accord, New York

Rabbi Sheila Weinberg, Reconstructionist, Jewish Community of Amherst, Amherst, Massachusetts

Rabbi Simkha Weintraub, Conservative, New York Jewish Healing Center, New York, New York

Rabbi David Wolpe, Conservative, Sinai Temple, Los Angeles, California

Cantor Laurel Zar-Kessler, Reform, Beth El, Sudbury, Massachusetts

Rabbi Elaine Zecher, Reform, Temple Israel, Boston, Massachusetts

JEWISH INDIVIDUALS, COUPLES,
AND EXPERTS INTERVIEWED

Kurt and Jane Ackerman
Leslie and Joel Ackerman
Robert Adler and Billy Berkowitz-
   Adler
Chava Alexander
Christa and Stephen Alperin
Julie Applebaum
Amira Bahat
Susan L. Blumberg, Ph.D.
Claire Boskin and Stand Selib
Deborah Brodie
Donna and Bob Brosbe
Elliot and Beatty Cohan
Yael and Marty Cohn
Carole Dickert
Doris and Sam Engelman
Edith Feist
Leonard Felson and Julia
   Rosenblaum
Ken Firestone
Rona and Dennis Fischman
Marjorie Freiman
Dan Garfield and Amy Mager
Anne Goergen
Les Goldberg
Robert Gordon
Roberta and George Gordon
Amy and Norman Gorin
Lisa Grant and Billy Weitzer
Sheila and Joel Grossman
Kathy and Paul Hart
Andrew R. Heinze
Shel Horowitz and Dina Friedman
Lee Meyerhoff Hendler
Robert Jaffe, Ph.D.

Stephen Jaffe
Betsy Katz
Marc and Jackie Kramer
Phyllis R. Koch-Sheras, Ph.D.
Jill and Joey Korn
Jeff Klunk
Cheryl Krasner
Judy Lederman
Carol and Marc Levin
Leslie and Jon Levine
Richard and Phoebe McBee
Judy Meltzer
Janice and Warren Morganstein,
   Ph.D.
Quincy and Rae Ohaire
Rick and Sandy Popowitz
Ira and Ruth Rifkin
Michael Robbins
Shari and Shep Rosenman
Joanne Rouza
Martin Rutte
Laura Marshall Sapon
Renee and Vince Schlesinger
Peter L. Sheras, Ph.D.
Robin and Steve Silverman
Scott Stanley
Michael Stern, Ph.D.
Ralph and Lori Taber
Leslie and Baron Taylor
Hannah Turner and Alexander
   Kukurudz
Glenn and Marlene Usdin
Sylvia Weishaus
Ron Wolfson, Ph.D.
Ilene Zeff
Hillil Zeitlan
Elana Zimmerman

Bibliography

Artson, Bradley Shavit. *It's a Mitzvah: Step-by-Step to Jewish Living.* West Orange, NJ: Behrman House, 1995.

Berkowitz, Rabbi Allan L., and Moskovitz, Pattie. *Embracing the Covenant: Converts to Judaism Talk About Why and How.* Woodstock, VT: Jewish Lights Publishing, 1996.

Blumberg, Susan L., Markman, Howard, and Stanley, Scott. *Fighting for Your Marriage: Active Steps for Preventing Divorce and Preserving a Lasting Love.* San Francisco: Jossey-Bass, 1994.

Boteach, Shmuley. *Kosher Sex.* New York: Doubleday, 1999.

Cowan, Paul, with Cowan, Rachel. *Mixed Blessings: Overcoming the Stumbling Blocks in an Interfaith Marriage.* New York: Penguin Books, 1987.

Friedman, Manis. *Doesn't Anyone Blush Anymore? Reclaiming Intimacy, Modesty, and Sexuality.* San Francisco: HarperCollins, 1990.

Gordis, Daniel. *God Was Not in the Fire: The Search for a Spiritual Judaism.* New York: Simon and Schuster, 1995.

Gordon, Lori H., Ph.D. *Passage to Intimacy.* New York: Simon and Schuster, 1993.

Hendler, Lee Meyerhoff. *The Year Mom Got Religion: One Woman's Midlife Journey Into Judaism.* Woodstock, VT: Jewish Lights Publishing, 1998.

Hyman, Meryl. *Who Is a Jew? Conversations, Not Conclusions.* Woodstock, VT: Jewish Lights Publishing, 1998.

Kamenetz, Rodger. *Stalking Elijah: Adventures With Today's Jewish Mystical Masters.* San Francisco: HarperCollins, 1997.

Kaplan, Mordecai. *Judaism as a Civilization: Toward a Reconstruction of American-Jewish Life.* New York: Jewish Publishing Society, 1994.

Kertzer, Rabbi Morris N. *What Is a Jew? A Guide to the Beliefs, Traditions, and Practices of Judaism That Answers Questions for Both Jew and Non-Jew.* New York: Touchstone, 1996.

Kirshenbaum, Mira. *Our Love Is Too Good to Feel so Bad: A Step-By Step Guide to Indentifying and Eliminating the Love Killers in Your Relationship.* New York: Avon Books, 1998

Klagsbrun, Francine. *Voices of Wisdom: Jewish Ideals and Ethics for Everyday Living.* Middle Village, NY: Jonathan David, 1980.

Klinghoffer, David. *The Lord Will Gather Me In: My Journey to Jewish Orthodoxy.* New York: Free Press, 1999.

Koch-Sheras, Phyllis R., Ph. D., and Sheras, Peter L., Ph.D. *The Dream-Sharing Sourcebook: A Practical Guide to Enhancing Your Personal Relationships.* Los Angeles: Lowell House, 1998.

Lamm, Maurice. *The Jewish Way in Love and Marriage.* Middle Village, NY: Jonathan David, 1991.

Mann, Gil. *How to Get More Out of Being Jewish.* Minneapolis: Leo and Sons Publishing, 1997.

Meier, Rabbi Levi, Ph.D. *Moses, the Prince, the Prophet: His Life, Legend, and Message for Our Lives.* Woodstock, VT: Jewish Lights Publishing, 1998.

Orenstein, Rabbi Debra. *Lifecycles: Jewish Women on Life Passages and Personal Milestones.* Woodstock, VT: Jewish Lights Publishing, 1994.

Page, Susan. *The Eight Essential Traits of Couples Who Thrive.* Boston: Little, Brown, 1994.

Petsonk, Judy, and Remson, Jim. *The Intermarriage Handbook: A Guide for Jews and Christians.* New York: Quill, William Morrow, 1988.

Pliskin, Rabbi Zelig. *Marriage: A Wise and Sensitive Guide to Making Any Marriage Even Better.* Brooklyn, NY: Mesorah Publications, Ltd., 1998.

Pliskin, Zelig. *The Power of Words.* Brooklyn, NY: Benei Yakov Publications, 1988.

Rosenthal, Gilbert S. *The Many Faces of Judaism.* West Orange, NJ: Behrman House, 1978.

Schlessinger, Dr. Laura. *The Ten Commandments: The Significance of God's Laws in Everyday Life.* New York: Cliff Street Books, 1998.

Schwebel, Dr. Robert. *Who's On Top, Who's On Bottom: How Couples Can Learn to Share Power.* New York: Newmarket Press, 1994.

Slonim, Rivkah, Editor. *Total Immersion: A Mikvah Anthology.* Northvale, NJ: Jason Aronson, Inc., 1995.

Stanley, Scott, Ph.D. *The Heart of Commitment: Compelling Research That Reveals the Secrets of a Lifelong, Intimate Marriage.* Nashville, TN: Thomas Nelson Publishers, 1998.

Waskow, Arthur. *Godwrestling, Round 2: Ancient Wisdom, Future Paths.* Woodstock, VT: Jewish Lights Publishing, 1996.

Wolf, Sharon, C.S.W. *How to Stay Lovers for Life: Discover a Marriage Counselor's Tricks of the Trade.* New York: Penguin Books, 1998.

Wolpe, David J. *Teaching Your Children About God: A Modern Jewish Approach*. New York: HarperPerennials, HarperCollins, 1997.

Wolpe, David J. *The Healer of Shattered Hearts: A Jewish View of God*. New York: Penguin Books, 1990.

Wolpe, David J. *Why Be Jewish?* New York: Henry Holt, Inc, 1995.

About the Author

Azriela Jaffe is the author of:

Honey, I Want to Start my Own Business: A Planning Guide for Couples

Let's Go Into Business Together: Eight Secrets to Successful Business Partnering

Starting from No: Ten Strategies to Overcome Your Fear of Rejection and Succeed in Business

Heartwarmers, Award-winning stories of love, strength, encourgement and hope from the Heartwarmers4U Internet community

Create Your Own Luck. 9 principles for attracting good fortune into your life and work

She also writes the nationally syndicated business column, "Advice from A–Z" and several free online biweekly newsletters for entrepreneurs and entrepreneurial families.

To subscribe to her newsletters, ask about her other resources, or to contact her with your questions or comments about *Two Jews Can Still Be a Mixed Marriage*, e-mail az@azriela.com or write P.O. Box 209, Bausman, PA 17504.

Visit the website for Anchored Dreams at:
www.isquare.com/crlink.htm.

To discuss potential speaking engagements, e-mail or call (717) 872-1890.

Azriela Jaffe lives in Lancaster, Pennsylvania with her husband, Stephen, and their three children.

Index

Jealousy in marriage, 101
Jewish identities
    expanding your, 184-187
    shaping your, 1-73
Jewish Renewal/New Age, 14
    distinct features, 24
    misconceptions, 23
    realities, 23-24
*Jewish Way in Love and Marriage,
    The,* 125
Journeys, spiritual, 8
    merging, 32-39
Judaism as a Civilization, 22

Kabbalistic traditions, 24
Kaplan, Mordecai, 22
Kirshenbaum, Mira, 37, 64
Klagsbrun, Francine, 190
Kosher, keeping, 3, 18-20, 42, 65-66,
    68, 153-171
    forming a working system, 157-158
    extended family and, 168-170
    resistance to, 154-155, 158-163
    variations on, 155-157
    with kids, 163-168
Kushner, Rabbi Harold, 91
Kushner, Rabbi Larry, 86

Labels, limitations of
    denominational, 14-16
Lamm, Rabbi Maurice, 125
Life-cycle events, 5, 140-152

Marriage
    counseling, 52
    handling fear in, 9-11

jealousy in, 101
religious conflict in, 40-54
renegotiating "rules" of, 101
three stages of, 51-53
Marriage, 39, 55, 69
Membership dues, for synagogue, 79
Memories
    positive, 29-31
    unhappy, 31-32
Mikvah, 18, 43, 95
    laws of, 172-173
    men's resistance to, 173-174,
        181-182
    motivations for practicing,
        177-182
    women's resistance to, 174-177,
        181-182
Modern Reform, 20

New Age/Jewish Renewal, 14
    distinct features, 24
    misconceptions, 23
    realities, 23-24
Nurturing your relationship, 71-72

Observance,
    expanding, 183-187
    returning to, 20
Orthodox Judaism, 14-16
    distinct features, 17-18
    misconceptions about, 16-17
    realities, 17

Page, Susan, 50
Paskoff, Rabbi Jack, 20
Passover/Pesach, 113-119